RePurposables

and other stories

(the New Genesis series)

by H.M. Friendly

Also by H.M. Friendly:

"Quality, Protein-Rich Meat Products"
and other stories
(Science Fiction/Horror)

Available on Amazon and Kindle:
http://bit.ly/HMFriendly-ProteinRich

This book is dedicated to the following people:

~ **Ann Beck**, my editor and mentor, without whose frank honesty and lack of sugar-coated bullshit, this book would be just doggamn awful.

~ **Alex Laughlin,** illustrator of the totally badass cover art.

~ **Andy from Cavity Curiosities,** who keeps me stocked with awesome sci-fi story collections from last century.

~ **Amber Overall & Al Lindskoog**, and other friends who graciously endure me foisting story drafts upon them.

~ **Leslie & Maurice Maynard,** my family, who patiently listen to me ramble on... and on... about new plot ideas.

~ **Ivy & Alaya,** my girls, who make my life something I want to be a part of. ♥

Author's Foreword:

After seven and a half consecutive years in university, my exhaustion and disillusionment culminated in total burnout during which I missed class for two weeks, because I was too depressed to get out of bed.

With the guidance of my former English instructor, who is now my unofficial editor and writing mentor, I had an epiphany: I was chasing a prestigious degree in neuroscience because of a fundamental insecurity in my position in the world, in both a societal and monetary sense. I often joked that I was working towards a "Social Validation Certificate". I strove to maintain straight A+ grades, and it was slowly killing me.

"What I find interesting about this situation," said Ann, as I slouched lugubriously in her office, "is that most people never discover what they *really* want to devote their lives to, and still more lack the freedom, opportunity, or ability to pursue it. You have *all* of this, and yet you have spent nearly the last decade *not doing it,* because you're too busy being miserable doing something you hate."

I could not argue this. How much more of my life can I afford to squander on self-imposed misery and disillusionment?

It is not an easy position to find oneself. I was beset with convictions of failure and inadequacy. I felt like a quitter. Yet, suppose I decided to take up basketball and gave everything I had for three quarters of a decade; if I ultimately found that I really didn't enjoy it and didn't see a future in it, after such a diligent effort, would I be considered a quitter? Of course not. Yet our career-focused culture would have us believe that if we start a degree and don't finish it, we are filthy dropouts and unfit for society. This is evident in the fact that it is, by design, an all-or-nothing achievement. You cannot have ¾ of a degree. You either have the degree, or you are unqualified for life. But the unassailable truth is that the many benefits to education are gained as a constant data flow, not an instantaneous download.

I decided to take the plunge. With less than five courses remaining, I made the decision to walk away from the degree for which I had slaved so long, in order to pursue writing science fiction full time. It is my desire to continuously improve my skill at crafting stories which sweep users into another world and encourage them to question pervasive aspects of life and the human condition.

This particular collection encapsulated exactly 1,000 days of my life. I hope you enjoy it. ☺

Sincerely,

~H.M. Friendly

Contents

RePurposables 1

New Genesis RePurposing Enforcement Bureau 34

The Omega Faction 49

The Lamb 72

"Quality Protein-Rich Meat Products" 103

// One-Self // 124

Dark City 148

Choice & Consequence 161

New Genesis Timeline

Historical Event:
WWIII: 9/11; USA vs Taliban, al-Quaeda, ISIS, N.Korea, Syria

2001 - 2108

2022 — **Historical Event:** United Continents of America (UCA) Forms

Historical Event:
WWIV: UCA launches nuclear offensive vs Eurasia; incites global retaliation. Civilization collapses.

2112

2151 — **The Lamb** (Story #4)

Dark City — **2968**
(Story #7)

2982 — **Historical Event:** First RePurposing Factory Opens

The Omega Faction — **3009**
(Story #3)

3014 — **RePurposables** (Story #1)

"Quality, Protein-Rich Meat Products" — **3015**
(Story #5)

3016 — **NG-RPEB** (Story #2)

//One-Self// — **3017**
(Story #6)

3023 — **Choice & Consequence** (Story #8)

RePurposables

(3014 A.D.)

Abruptly, Nathan jolted awake. Apparently, he had been dozing at his post. Something had woken him. Something didn't feel right. *What was it??*

He looked at his watch. *2:17 AM.* Damn. Still another three and a half hours until his shift ended. For the remaining time, he had to listen to the incoherent mumblings, wailings, and jabberings of the Sub-F's as they slowly conveyed past his station. Beneath that noise was the pervasive rumble of machinery and a strange growl which invaded his dreams.

Nathan sat in a small chair in a small booth in *Station RP_Sub-F Shaft 06*, a dimly lit, sloping tunnel 12m squared, and 200m long. His prison was a tiny cubicle made of steel, glass, and iron, perched halfway down a grade steep enough it couldn't be climbed without steps, even if it weren't for the smooth, polished metal surface. Both the top and bottom faded into darkness.

Down the slope ran three parallel tracks, the sort that used to be found in roller coasters and certain types of trolley car from the 19th and 20th centuries – back when civilization was free and chaotic and uncontrolled, and utterly vulgar.

Down each of these tracks descended an unending procession of seats. Each of the three columns of seats ran along a belt, a single, thick chain of steel. The seats were, in fact, styled after the old carnival rides, with metal bars that swung down, pinning the occupants into place. In this case, they were Sub-F's, a standard subsection of RPs, (RePurposables) characterized by an inability to work due to severe mental or physical retardation, or very low IQ.

Nathan listened morosely to the noises of the creatures trundling past him. He made a point of not looking at them, or listening to them, if he could help it. It always creeped him out to stare into their peculiar eyes, to see their awful faces, some moon-shaped, others unnaturally elongated. Some of them had gnarled, twisted bodies, and they jerked their heads and limbs in a stiff, grotesque fashion. All of them drooled hideously. For many, it came naturally, but there were quite a few who did so because they were heavily sedated. The vast majority of them had been weeded out of the Old Society which still persisted in the ghettos.

There were several categories of RPs, all of which shared a single trait: they were unable to work or contribute to society in a way considered productive or useful. Sub-As were senior citizens who suffered from dementia; Sub-Bs were the ill or physically infirmed elderly; Sub-Cs were violent or psychopathic criminals; Sub-Ds were the schizophrenic, clinically

1

depressed, anxious, bipolar, or otherwise psychologically unstable; Sub-Es were anyone who contracted an incurable disease; Sub-Fs as mentioned above; Sub-Gs were children whose standardized test scores had consistently shown to be below the acceptable level; Sub-Hs had sustained severe body or brain injuries... the list went on and on. This lethal conveyer belt, transported them slowly downwards, into the deepening darkness, where they would contribute to society in a great and final way.

The ones who had been sedated had all recently had a birthday. Sub-F males were kept until they were 29, and females until they were 22. These were their respective ages of neurological maturity, after which time they were considered no longer useful for research, and therefore, a burden on the food system as a whole.

For the advancement of society, infants who were born with some noticeable deformity, or who carried the genetic markers of certain conditions, were promptly segmented and donated to the *R. Janus Neurodevelopment Foundation*, which aimed to study the brains of these mutants, to determine the causes of these diseases and conditions, and advance the field of human genetic modification. Such was necessary, if the human race ever hoped to once again thrive as the dominant species on Earth, after the global devastation for which they alone were responsible.

The history is long, but necessary, because it is only by becoming intimate with the problems of the past that we can hope to avoid them in the future.

World War III (2001-2108) was handcrafted by the USA to be invisible by virtue of emotional burnout. It began with the careful orchestration of a "false flag" terror attack wrongly attributed to Islamic Afghanistan, which left the world in shock, allowing the USA to declare unfettered war in the unassailable name of *Liberty*. This war burned slowly for decades, long after people had become so desensitized that the idea of military crime could easily be buried under Facebook feeds and Reddit memes. Every week, citizens heard news of isolated acts of terror and senseless mass-murder of innocent men, women, and children, in faraway lands, until it became something to momentarily frown at before changing the station or turning to YouTube videos of farting cats and celebrity scandals. They were so perfectly primed to ignore human suffering, that they reached the point where they were barely fazed by dozens of school shootings in their own backyard. It was just too much pain to hold in conscious mind for long. The psyche necessarily tuned it out. Finally, the United States of America was ready to act.

In 2022, The USA initiated a systematic takeover of the entire Western Hemisphere. They expanded upwards into Canada, and downwards into

Mexico, before moving on to absorb Central and South America. The United Continents of America (UCA) had become the self-appointed leaders of the free-trade world, and a skilled purveyor of the fallacy that is America's unique brand of democracy: a single party masquerading as multiple, giving the illusion of choice.

At first, it seemed like humanity had been incensed into humanitarian response. The air was electric with protests and outrage. Social media, internet, television and radio buzzed incessantly, making ugly parallels to long-forgotten wars and conquests. The privileged world was alive with protests by "social justice warriors" and millions of "Likes" of anti-war posts on Facebook.

However, despite repeated sanctions from the United Nations, it was apparent there was no force on Earth that could take on the UCA, who had controlled the nuclear landscape for the last 70 years through intimidation and double standards. As weeks became months and years, people gradually went back to their lives. War had once again become normalized. Nothing more than background noise for your latte.

Centuries ago, on July 16th, 1945, nuclear physicist Kenneth Bainbridge stood in the sweltering *Jornada del Muerto* desert in New Mexico. The air was rippling with heat, and he looked anxiously into the distance at the Trinity nuclear bomb developed by the Manhattan Project. Detonation was imminent. Bainbridge desperately hoped all would go well; otherwise, as head of the project, he would have to drive the long miles to the bomb to try to determine why it hadn't detonated.

He needn't have worried. Countdown elapsed, and in the distance, he and the rest of the team saw a fantastic flash of light, followed what appeared to be a dome of glass rapidly expanding outwards from the blast, an effect created by the compression of the air molecules by the blast wave, changing its refractive properties. There was no sound. A moment later, the ground shuddered laterally, then shivered vertically, like ripples in a pond. Still there was silence. The team saw a wall of sand being pushed by a furious wind, then heard a terrific concussion. The shock wave hit them like a freight train, knocking them to the ground.

They climbed to their feet and stared in awe at the billowing mushroom cloud ascending high into the atmosphere. History had been made that day. Bainbridge turned and looked at his friend and fellow physicist J. Robert Oppenheimer, and said quietly,

"Now we're all sons of bitches."

He had no idea his legacy would be the devastation of the planet Earth and its soft, arrogant inhabitants.

Every sentient soul on the planet breathed a collective sigh of relief in 2108, when the UCA announced an end to the fighting in the Middle East, due to unprecedented diplomatic negotiations. The world lowered its weary arms and climbed into bed for four years of blissful peace and hope for the future.

In 2112, without warning or provocation the UCA launched hundreds of thousands of nuclear warheads at Eurasia, particularly their old rivals in Afghanistan, Iraq, Syria, and Pakistan. Although UCA had the element of surprise, standardized early-warning technology alerted their victims immediately, and Eurasia had no choice but to launch a counterattack, despite being significantly outmatched.

However, unknown to the UCA, North Korea had been harbouring a Megaton nuclear missile, biding their time, and now that America had blown their load onto the belly of a different mistress, Korea could launch an offensive without fear of reprisal. The UCA was inflicted with a crater so huge the Earth wobbled on its axis. They were crippled. However, there was no time for celebration. Due to the sheer volume of nuclear detonation around the globe, a vicious nuclear winter of death, misery, and horror ensued.

This had been World War IV, and it was over barely seven days after the first warhead was launched. As quickly as the world had been created, so it was destroyed.

The global ecosystem staggered from fallout effects. Rain forests, both tropical and temperate, were completely wiped out. The few plants that did survive were met with the futility of their victory: radiation had killed even the most fundamental of fungi, without which mycorrhizal symbiosis could not occur: they could not obtain Nitrogen. During centuries of unending winter, they also could not adequately photosynthesize, and much of Earth was reduced to a barren wasteland.

However, Australia and certain areas of Northern Eurasia missed most of the nuclear action and still retained a living, albeit tremendously crippled, ecosystem. It was out of Australia in particular that humanity re-established itself. Around seven centuries later, humanity had once again built itself into a sizeable, semi-stable civilization.

This time around, however, it had to be done right.

The nuclear radiation on that continent was not fatal, but the soil was unsuitable for large-scale food growth, and prolonged exposure to radioactive isotopes caused horrifying birth defects in humans and animals alike. Humanity established an interlocking system of polymerized-glass domes, each 5 kilometers in diameter, laid out in a grid system interconnected by massive tunnels which accommodated migratory ground/air traffic. The entire setup looked from space very much like a patch of bubble wrap.

At least half of these bubbles were devoted to food production with controlled greenhouse climates, growing many of the most cultivatable fruits and vegetables from intelligently placed underground seed reserves from millennia prior. Each bubble had a collectively controlled hydrologic cycle and air exchange system. However, the poor soil quality was an imminently lethal threat, and aggressive, irresponsible agricultural practices further stripped the soil of its nutrients, forcing boom-and-bust cycles where entire bubbles had to be left alone for four or five seasons to recuperate. It was entirely unsustainable. By the beginning of the 21st century, this problem had become gravely serious, but addressing it would have meant lost productivity and wasted capital with negative return, so the issue was openly denied for centuries, until agricultural yields dramatically plummeted, and it could no longer be ignored. By this point, however, the synthetic environment and weather system, and a complete lack of species diversity, greatly impeded the progress of soil recovery.

Food became scarce, population sharply declined, and in 2982, a decision was made to ensure the survival of humankind: they would create their own fertilizer. More aptly stated, their composted soil treatment would be composed of their expendable citizens. Any humans deemed no longer useful to the interests of society were to be proudly "RePurposed" via immediate shipment to the mulching factories where they would be crushed, diced, and fermented in a massive compost heap.

Nathan was in the employment of RePurposing Facility #18, which, like all of the factories, was a direct subsidiary of the New Genesis RePurposing Enforcement Bureau (NG-RPEB) which controlled the police force, the military, the major news networks, and the government of New Genesis.

The creatures trundling down the gradient beside Nathan were confined into chairs which functioned essentially like ski lifts, except they traveled downwards, into the belly of the earth. At the bottom of the gradient, the chairs would loop back under and would travel upside down and shrouded in darkness, back up to the top of the grade to receive new passengers. The instant the chairs dipped over the edge of the loop, the restraining bars released, and the chair's contents were tossed downwards into a massive pit 500m in diameter, constructed of the same smooth metal, with sloping sides like a massive funnel. The bottom was 60m below, and sharply funnelled inwards to the central mechanism. The RPs would fall into the mulching machinery and soon be working harder than they ever had while living.

5

Around the circumference of the pit, dozens of these conveyer belts were oriented radially, and operated without pause. It was always possible to find RPs. Sometimes, however, new classifications of Subs had to be created, or the criteria defining existing ones relaxed a little. Such was the price to pay to benefit humanity. The year was now 3014.

And Nathan was bored. He had just turned 17. Why did he have to work in this dungeon, with these Subs yawning ghoulishly at him? He would rather be with his friends, the online personas he engaged with in chat rooms and video game feeds, through *GenNet*. He looked over to the line of chairs slowly descending into the darkness with a hypnotic chattering of metal on metal. The sight appeared to him to resemble a memory from when he was a child, on a field trip to this very same mulching factory, when he was 10 years old. He had been allowed to see the Heap – the mountainous pile of decomposing human remains.

He stood in a group with two dozen other kids, all clothed in disposable transparent polyethylene ponchos, gloves, shoe coverings, and hair caps. The smell was terrible at first, but they were given an invigorating salve to rub under their noses, and after that it was okay. The heat was brutal, the humidity revolting, and the air swarmed with flying insects which crawled all over Nathan's hygiene suit.

The guide appeared to be enthusiastically entrenched in a speech about the future of humanity, and how becoming RePurposed was a great honour which they should eagerly anticipate.

"Remember, kids, everyone is RePurposed eventually! It's not something to be frightened of! It is for the glory of mankind, and the future of New Genesis!"

Nathan didn't care. He surreptitiously stole away from the group. They were standing in a fenced-off area at the edge of the Heap, most of which was composed of a homogenous mixture of a dark reddish-brown substance, which he understood to be crushed, ground-up RPs. However, something caught his eye, just beyond the fence. Something was not like the rest.

He quickly looked around; nobody had noticed him, so he climbed through the railing of the fence, and jumped down into the Heap. When he landed, his impact produced a profoundly wet noise, and his feet sank into the muck halfway up to his knees. He grimaced. He hadn't anticipated that.

With great effort, he lifted his right leg. There was an obscene sucking sound as he pulled his foot out of the sludge... and he discovered with some chagrin that his foot was now bare. He considered trying to retrieve his shoe and sock, but the steaming biological material gently settled into the hole where they had been, and the footwear was forever lost.

He looked back to the fence and considered abandoning his mission... but he was already knee-deep in the dead. Might as well keep going. Gingerly, he began to move toward the unusual object. The mush felt warm and bizarrely soft between his toes. He lost his other shoe and sock, and continued. The puree of human meat made erotic-sounding wet noises with every step.

Presently, he came up upon the strange object. It was an odd, cylindrically-shaped lump of a consistent size all the way down except for the very end. He reached out with his gloved hand and rolled it over. The partially decomposed face of a woman turned and stared vacuously up at him. Her eye was white – the other one was missing – and her jaw was not there. She had only a few bits of stringy, matted hair, that looked like it used to be blonde, clinging to what was otherwise merely a wet skull. He could see the ragged lines which segregated the bone, like tectonic plates. The odd cylindrical shape was her torso, sans arms and legs, torn off just above the hip. Intestines spilled out. He observed, in an oddly detached manner, that, opposite a gaping hole framed by several shattered, jagged white ribs, her only remaining breast was visible. It was the first boob he had ever seen. He didn't know how to feel about it.

Yet, what really fascinated him was what he saw when he peered into the hole in the chest cavity. Millions of tiny white maggots coated the insides. They reached upwards towards him with their unseeing anterior encephalized mounds, twitching and flicking in spastic, jerky motions... as if beckoning to him.

As he stared at the slowly moving sea of Sub-F's which passed before him, Nathan saw the parallels. Millions of faceless, writhing creatures serving no purpose other than to progress the decomposition cycle. He shuddered a little, and turned away again.

Nathan's job, if it really could be considered work, was to monitor the progression of the belts to make sure that nothing unusual happened on the long, slow downwards journey. Monitoring stations were installed in all of the shafts, manned by people such as Nathan. A radio was installed on the wall. If anything out of the ordinary happened, he was instructed to push the only other piece of hardware in the booth, which was a big red button which halted the belts and set off an alarm. Someone would radio him, he would tell them what was going on, and they would take care of it. He was expressly forbidden to do anything else.

And in the two years, three months, and eleven days Nathan had worked there, nothing had *ever* happened. He had heard that only five years previously, two Subs had broken free from the belts, and had escaped. Why couldn't that happen *now?!* Nathan dearly wished he had a gun, and another one of the Subs would break free, so he could act like a daring huntsman, shoot them with a powerful rifle, be hailed a hero, and maybe receive a shiny medal, and a hefty promotion! But **no**. He was mind-numbingly bored, slouching there every night, watching his fingernails grow.

Abruptly, his attention was caught by a bizarre noise. It was a tense, urgent vocalization, different from the usual moans and groans and almost-merry hoots and insane laughter of the Sub-F's. He spun towards the sound, and saw, two columns away, a terribly deformed creature. One arm had such a low range of movement that it appeared bound to its chest. The other was hideously bent, but undeniably reaching towards Nathan, its gaunt, knobby fingers outstretched. The Sub's mouth was twisted open, and its eyes were terrifying – they were sharp, keenly aware... *intelligent!* Despite the vocal distortion from between lips coated in froth and glistening drool, Nathan distinctly heard the word "help". He gaped, paralyzed, as the chair slowly passed by him, on its way to the mulching pit. The Sub appeared to become more frantic and agitated, twisting in its seat to keep Nathan in its sight, actually yelling hoarsely,

"Help... Help me! Please help!"

Before long, it faded into the darkness, its beastly noise drowned within the constant rumble and murmur of the environment. Nathan wiped the sweat from his brow. He was shaken up; he was honestly *creeped out.* He had never seen the Subs act like *people* before. In fact, while the term "Sub" was officially the abbreviation for "Sub*section*," it was derisively joked among the factory workers that they were Sub*human*.

They were merely fuel for a better tomorrow.

After his shift, Nathan walked quietly down the streets of New Genesis, the last known city on Earth. The moniker was meant to instil hope and optimism in its citizens, but for many, it was a farce. These tended to be the people from the Old Society, the ones who had refused the highly regimented, sanitary conditions of the new world, stubbornly sticking to their obsolete technologies and outdated cultures. They called the city "Blister Pack", and joked that it should one day be popped.

The walk home passed without incident, as Nathan stared at his feet and daydreamed. A swipe of his subdermal wrist ID chip granted him access to his apartment building, or *beehive,* as they were mockingly called. The units were small and cramped, like densely packed compartments in a honeycomb, each containing a single, solitary drone. This was the sort of lodging his status as a young New Society bachelor afforded him. It was the price he paid for the rampant overpopulation of New Genesis. Still, it was better than the slums and ghettos of Old Society.

His apartment was a tiny cuboid two meters squared. His cot lined one wall, opposite a toilet, shower, and sink (with a small puck of greasy soap that refused to lather, no matter how vigorously he abused it). The intermediate space contained the door on one side, and a small shelf on the other, which held a hot plate, a saucepan, one bowl, one spork, one knife, and a plastic cup. Beneath this was a mini-fridge which kept food only a couple of degrees colder than room temperature. Nathan hung his clothes from a rod over his bed extending the length of the cot. If he sat up in bed, his head was lost within a jungle of shirts and pants, but if he stayed lying down, it was okay. There were no windows, only a couple of buzzing fluorescent tubes overhead, which cast the space in a sickly greenish-blue hue, as they flickered spastically.

He stood for a moment in the exact center of the room. On one side, the toilet bowl pressed against his leg; on the other side, a shirt sleeve aggressively tangled with him. He sighed. As always, there was nothing here for him. Might as well go for a walk.

The sterile metal structures of the New Society buildings encroached claustrophobically upon him from all sides. None of the buildings had windows, not in this district. Sure, New Society was awarded a higher standard of living than Old Society, but the extent of this was set on a bell curve according to usefulness in society. Nathan was abominably low on that distribution.

It didn't take long for Nathan to get bored. He was surrounded by the usual New Society district architecture which consisted of perfectly rectangular buildings of metal and glass, with no distinguishing features beyond a small letter and number indicating the address. A few other pedestrians walked the streets, all dressed in the same grey coveralls of the New Society working class. All were shuffling along with their heads bowed, their hands in their pockets, as faceless and featureless as the buildings themselves.

A gravcar silently floated past, and a few seconds later, a maintenance robot hummed by, sweeping the street with its rotating broom, devoted to keeping its small section of the district spotlessly clean. Nathan sighed. It all just felt so fake, and *dead*. He yearned for something asymmetrical, something interesting and unusual.

I'll go to Old Society, he thought. He used to venture into the OS district closest to his home as a child, to go to the cinema and watch action comic book movies from centuries ago, like *Sin City* and *Deadpool*.

He approached one of the many checkpoints along the OS/NS border. As usual, the guard barely looked at him before pressing the button to open the gate. As he had before, Nathan wondered why it was so easy to get through a patrolled border crossing. *I guess they're here to stop the Old Society miscreants from getting out, not to stop me from getting in.*

As soon as he stepped into OS, the architecture drastically changed. On his left, a tall building towered over him.   It was constructed of red brick, filthy, corroded and falling apart. What impacted him the most was the presence of dozens of yawning black windows, the glass smashed and jagged, or missing altogether. It was creepy. He looked down at the sidewalk. The cement was scarred, pitted, and cracked. It was very dirty. Abruptly, a brown glass bottle whizzed past his nose, smashing upon the brick façade. He whirled in the direction from which it had come. A *car*, a real electric car, not an airjet [anti]gravcar, was slowly *rolling* along the street. Out of the window protruded a spectacularly ugly male.

"Get the fuck outta my streets, ya little NS faggot!" He spat at Nathan, and the car sped off, its tires screaming.

Across the street, a theater blinked its fluorescent lights, advertising some holofilm. No, wait. They still used old screen-projection technology, not the immersive 3D hologram tech common in New Society. And the outside of this building was fantastically *weird.* It pointed outwards in a triangular shape, upon which the titles of films were displayed, and there were dozens of spherical yellow light bulbs, many more than were necessary, marching in an endless line, for some obscure function. Nathan smiled. He had never seen such impractical architecture. All the New Society buildings were perfectly symmetrical rectangles which often extended into the sky beyond the artificially generated clouds. The lights were low-wattage, high-output fluorescent strips or magnified LEDs, and only existed in a concentration necessary to minimally light an environment to a level which accommodated functional efficiency in the workplace or living area.

He continued walking further into Old Society. The deeper he dove, the more strongly the streets began to throb and pulsate with life. Men were *drunk* on the streets! (Spirits were manufactured by synthesizing glucose from the cellulose present in the discarded stalks and leaves of food crops, then fermented.) He knew that cheap liquor was available from vending machines installed in every New Society apartment building, but public intoxication was strictly illegal. Nathan was aghast.

Why isn't anybody stopping them??

Nathan's deep contemplation was drastically interrupted as he felt someone's hand fondle his genitals through his trousers. He gasped and jumped back. The clutching hand belonged to a ghastly painted and garishly dressed woman who appeared to be much older than his mother, but it was hard to tell – New Society women were mandated regular liposuction and facelifts, so their appearance never revealed their true age.

"Hey, little darlin', you lookin' for a good time?" she crooned. Her half-closed eyes were heavily raccooned by absurdly blue eye shadow, and the wrinkles extending outwards from the atrociously bright red lips, which sucked luridly upon an ersatz cigarette, were deeply furrowed... *like a sphincter!* Nathan blinked, agape.

"No – no thank you!" he stammered. The woman smirked and exhaled a billowing cloud of blue smoke into his face. (Ersatz cigarettes were not made of tobacco; rather, synthesized nicotine, ammonia, benzene, and acetaldehyde were added to the same byproduct leaves used for alcohol production. These two vices were thereby cheaply manufactured with no added burden to the agriculture system, and provided a simple means of population control.)

Nathan coughed and gagged, then literally ran away. He heard raucous laughter chasing after him. *Maybe this wasn't such a good idea!* he thought. Terrified, he ducked into the nearest innocuous-looking shop. A very old wooden sign hung above the door. In fading paint, it proclaimed its name, *Asimov's Den,* in bold calligraphic font.

A bell tinkled as Nathan burst through the door. A young man dressed all in black, with long, straight, dark hair, looked up with mild bemusement at his explosive entrance.

"Hey man, how's it goin'?" he said good-naturedly. Nathan merely stood there, looking anxious. "Well... let me know if I can help you find anything," the man offered, peering at this strange boy as quizzically as possible without being noticeably rude. "My name's Andy." He smiled.

Nathan stammered something inarticulate before diving into the depths of wall-to-wall shelves of books extending at least 3m high, separated by isles so narrow he had to strafe like a crab to fit between them. He gawked, overwhelmed, encroached upon on all sides by stacks of hundreds of used paperbacks. He felt slightly dizzy. *What is this place?! What are these things?!* He timidly asked the man, who looked at him as if he had just asked after the function of his own teeth.

"Books. Reading material. Literature." Andy intoned, raising an eyebrow. The boy nodded dazedly, and turned away, embarrassed, but not really knowing why. He reached out and plucked at random a book from a shelf. He flipped the pages. A luxurious, woody smell fanned up into his nostrils. It made him heady. These rectangular objects appeared to be manufactured of pulpy material pressed into thin, dry sheets, upon which were printed words. It was *weird.*

Centuries ago, books had been phased out, and production was outlawed, enforced by a crippling fine, and threat of a full commercial shutdown and jail time. There just weren't enough resources to be wasting trees on *recreational drivel.* Any such media could be viewed through eBooks, or, for the wealthy, ocular corneal lenses which allowed a person to read anywhere, the text scrolling across their field of view without the need for any mechanical apparatus. The printed page was reserved for legal documentation and New Genesis' ubiquitous *Solidarity!* flyers, containing inspiring political phrases, which arrived in the mail at regular intervals.

"Great choice!" exclaimed a feminine voice in Nathan's right ear. "That's a book about a precocious young boy sent off to a cold, heartless, violent battle school, where he must train to one day save the world!"

He started at the voice and looked over, his eyes wide. A girl stood beside him. She appeared to be about his age, perhaps a couple of years younger. She had blindingly white skin, and wore some sort of head covering the colour of simulated-lemon-flavoured candies. She wasn't beautiful, and even looked a little sickly, but her intensely hazel eyes caught Nathan off guard, and he just stared.

"Y'okay?" Her eyebrows were drawn on with what looked like pastel pencil, and they wriggled with her perplexity like two little dancing worms.

"Uh, yes! Yup. You bet! Just fine!" Nathan bobbed his chin animatedly, like a hyperactive bobble-head doll on someone's gravcar dashboard.

The girl looked at him strangely for a moment. He thought she would turn away. He *hoped* she would; he wanted her to just leave him alone. He was not used to talking with people, especially *girls.* He felt exceedingly uncomfortable. However, she abruptly extended her small hand towards his abdomen. He startled and jumped back a little in alarm.

"My name is Madelaine; what's yours?" She smiled disarmingly.

"Uh...!!" *Her eyes are so deep!*

"Forgot your own name, huh? Hard life." joked the girl, but when Nathan just stared at her, she shrank a little, withdrew her hand, and abruptly averted her gaze, as if eye contact had suddenly become painful.

"Well... I... I guess I'll let you get back to it..." she faltered, then quickly turned and walked away. Nathan thought he could see her cheeks flush, though with skin *that* pale he didn't know if it was even possible.

He stared, dumbfounded, at the book in his hand. *Ender's Game,* the cover proclaimed. Without really knowing why, he stomped, wooden-legged, back to the front desk, and wordlessly thrust the book at the proprietor.

"Four dollars," said Andy.

Dollars?? He must mean credits, Nathan thought, and jabbed his right hand forward sharply. Andy raised his eyebrows at Nathan's palm, which was held forward in a "stop" gesture, then a flash of understanding washed over his features. He smiled sympathetically.

"I don't accept subdermal credit chip payment, unfortunately. Cash only."

Nathan withdrew his hand and stared at it as if he had just developed raging leprosy upon his palm. Andy eyed his New Society outfit. "Um, look, since you're... not from around here... and you're unfamiliar with the protocol, that one is on me. Enjoy it! I hope to see you back soon!" He smiled politely.

Nathan hastily grabbed the book, mumbled his thanks, and bulldozed out of the building. A few meters down the road he stopped and gawked at this unusual prize. After a moment, he tucked it deep within his coveralls. It seemed *taboo,* illicit!

He smuggled the book back into New Society, anxiously nodding at the NG-RPEB foot soldier casually patrolling the border. He was a *criminal!* It felt kind of exciting, despite the slight feeling of nausea which turned his stomach, and the clammy, cold sweat coating his palms.

For the first time ever, Nathan actually could not wait for his shift at the factory to begin! He spent the entire time absorbed in the curled, yellow pages of *his book* (it felt weird saying it). He found himself actually *within* the battles, flashing the enemy; their gate was *down!* Bernard and Bonzo withered under his ferocity!

Nathan had never felt *not-himself* before. Not like this. Sure, video games were fun, but they were only a vicarious extension of himself, and in chat rooms, he could pretend to be anybody, but beneath it all, he was still *Nathan,* small and insignificant, like he'd always been.

Yet, with this book, Nathan felt himself *ceasing to exist.* He began to crave it. Yet, each morning, the buzzer blared in his ear from out of the speaker in the upper corner of his booth, shattering his reverie and ripping him back, and he again found himself trapped deep underground, in a dank, dark, stinking mulching factory smelling of rotting human flesh, with these wretched, drooling animals ceaselessly conveying past him.

Nathan was a slow reader. Weeks later, he was still working on the book, but far from dragging on, he felt like it had almost totally replaced his life!

Within these textured pages, Nathan was an admired, respected *hero.* In real life, he shuffled, his head downturned, through the dim corridors of the factory, crushed within the crowds of coworkers to whom he was nameless, and faceless. He had no friends there; most everyone was older and taller than he was, they passed him by, speaking over his head to one another. He was carelessly jostled into the rough, unfinished concrete walls; his things were knocked to the floor and trampled on.

It wasn't that Nathan was being intentionally abused; he simply went unnoticed. He thought it probably would have been better if this maltreatment was in malice; at least then he would have felt acknowledged in some demeaning sense.

No, Nathan was not even important enough to be mistreated.

Yet within these curled, yellow pages with their intoxicating smell of wood pulp and aged ink, Nathan was leading the human race to victory. The Buggers were closing in. As the toon leader of Dragon Army, Ender had been undefeated in victory; now, he had been promoted and was undergoing gruelling training from the legendary Mazer Rackham. Everyone was counting on him, and (at least at first) he did it all for the love of his gentle sister Valentine, and to spite his cruel brother Peter.

For Nathan, the factory was the personification of Peter: cold, unfeeling, and vicious, crushing him relentlessly. Valentine... well... Nathan had no Valentine. But he loved her, as dearly as Ender did.

Yet, all too soon, it ended. The last word on the last page slapped him in the face harder than his mother ever had. He stared down it, bereft, unwilling to believe that these characters who had breathed life into him were suddenly *dead,* as if, in that moment when his brain decoded those four simple letters and that crushing period, he had personally *murdered* them! He actually felt the sting of tears coming to his eyes, and swallowed them down quickly, grimacing.

That morning, he wandered home in a daze. It was *over.* It was *done.* He slept fitfully. Upon awakening, however, he was gripped with an insanely logical thought. He would go back to the bookstore! Maybe he could find another book which was just as amazing!

The next morning, he was waiting at the door of *Asimov's Den* even before Andy strolled up the street. "You're back!" he said, with a smile, unlocking the door. "Did you like the book?"

"YES!" Nathan exclaimed without hesitation, surprised by his own exuberance.

"Well then, you'll probably like this one, too..." The man wandered over to a shelf and, sliding his finger across the many creased spines, stopped and extracted a thick paperback, which he presented to Nathan.

The cover prominently displayed the words *Speaker for the Dead.* Nathan merely gawked, overwhelmed.

"It's the next one in the main series, which is huge." With a broad gesture, Andy indicated 18 other books. "Only the first four are any good though."

He offered the book to Nathan, and the boy grabbed it with both hands, almost disbelieving. He had simply thought he was going to get a whole different book. Now the characters would live on! He hadn't killed them, after all! His eyes shone.

He produced the first book from his pocket. "Can I – can I trade? I... I still don't have any cash..." His voice quavered slightly; he felt his cheeks burning.

"Yeah, man, totally. But here's the deal: you're gonna go over there and dig through that box of books, and segregate them into genre and alphabetical order, and we'll call it even. Ten, maybe fifteen minutes, easy."

It took Nathan close to an hour. He had no idea what a "genre" even was, let alone which was what. He also kept getting distracted by the absurd titles and fantastic cover art. A man, transformed into an omnipotent god with glowing eyes, reaching out and crushing a whole planet with a single hand... Soldiers on a desolate planet, armed with ray guns, facing off against giant crablike aliens... it was all very interesting!

By the time he was finally finished, he had learned a great deal, and had found *even more* books to add to his to-read list. On his way out, looking raptly down at the precious book in his hands, he ran headlong into that girl, actually knocking her over. Abashed, he helped her up, apologizing profusely. Madelaine laughed.

"It's okay," she said softly, smiling up at him. Her chestnut eyes sparkled brightly. Nathan was speechless.

She was 16. Her head was covered by a closefitting, sun-yellow knitted shawl. She looked exhausted: the dark, weary circles under her eyes starkly contrasted her pale skin. Yet, although she wasn't exactly beautiful, Nathan certainly wouldn't object to seeing that face every damned day. Her clothes were characteristically worn, while his were characteristically uniform. Nathan told her he envied her diversity of style. Madelaine remained silent.

The two children wandered aimlessly around Old Society, chatting about storylines and authors for almost two hours. More accurately, she mostly talked and he mostly listened, simply soaking it all in, enthralled. His heart was beating out of his chest. At first he thought it was because he was talking to a Real, Live *Girl*, but there was a moment when he told her a joke he had read online, and she threw back her head and laughed heartily, a robust *HA-HYUK-HUK!* and Nathan felt like he could swagger down those factory corridors and tower over everyone. He was once again *not-himself* with this girl, and it was a dizzyingly gratifying feeling.

They continued chattering, oblivious to the world, until they reached an unmanned border between Old and New Society. Madelaine stopped short. Lost in a thought, Nathan kept walking and talking for a few strides, before he discovered he was alone. He turned around with a questioning expression.

"I can't." she said. "I shouldn't even be talking to you. I... I have to go."

After a moment's hesitation, Madelaine turned and walked away, her quick, sharp footsteps echoing off the pavement. Nathan stared after her, speechless.

For the next week, Nathan hurried to the bookstore every day after shift, and stayed there for hours, half reading and nodding off, but mostly waiting nervously for Madelaine. Although she had rejected him; he still wanted to at least *see* her again, even from a distance. There was just something about her, like a lantern in an abandoned warehouse, illuminating the dark, dingy corners of his existence with her vivaciousness.

Eventually, the shop door opened, and there she was, soaked from head to toe by torrential rainfall. Even with a synthetic hydrologic system, it still rained – even more so than it might have otherwise, considering the climate was kept in a semi-tropical greenhouse state.

Nathan put down the book he had been flipping through, and watched anxiously as she bantered with Andy, laughing and wringing out her shawl. When she looked up and saw him there, Nathan's heart leaped into his throat, then plummeted into his gut. *Did her eyes light up when she saw me, or was I just imagining it??* His breath arrested as she made her way through the shelves and stacks of books toward him.

"Fancy meeting you here, stranger." she drawled, winking. "Anything good today?"

"Uh!" he stammered, "D'jyou wanna go for a walk to a, um, a place I like to go for a walk to??" His intestines curdled and knotted. *That sounded so stupid!* he cursed himself.

"Right now?" Madelaine looked down at her soaking clothes. "It's really pouring out. Look, how about you relax for a bit, since you, ah... well you look like you're about to shit a candlestick sideways... and I'll read you some of this book of stupendous stories by Neal Asher. This one is called *Softly Spoke the Gabbleduck.* Sound good?"

Nathan nodded wordlessly.

The sun was just awakening from beneath its quilt of clouds when they ventured outside, squinting in the bright light.

"This way," Nathan said, and, without thinking, grabbed Madelaine's hand. At the moment of contact, an electric shock traveled from his fingertips to the pit of his stomach. *Her hands are so small and soft...!! So... girly!* He swallowed hard, tightened his grip, and strode forward, hoping that she had not noticed his momentary stutter.

She had. She wordlessly squeezed his fingertips, just a little.

"What?! No, I can't!" Madelaine pulled away and took a step backwards.
They were half a block from the patrolled border crossing.
"But it's okay! I *live* here!" the boy replied.
"Nathan, *look* at me!" Madelaine gestured to her ratty outfit made of a
colourful patchwork of many discarded fabrics. She fell silent, staring at her
toes.
Nathan looked down at his uniform grey coveralls. Surprising himself,
he held out his hand.
"Don't worry," he promised. "You're safe with me." He felt his neck
burning, his breath catching in his throat.
Madelaine chewed on her bottom lip and looked anguished. An eternity
passed, and Nathan lowered his hand, feeling stupid. But Madelaine
reached out to him.
"Okay..." she consented, as she slipped her small hand into his. "I'm
trusting you..."
Nathan suddenly felt much taller than he ever had before.
Yet, as they approached the border, he was keenly aware of the growing
knot in his stomach.

It was the same feeling he had gotten as a child, when he had made the
decision to steal a candy bar in an OS corner market, instead of paying 50
credits at the vending machine in his apartment.
After pocketing it, Nathan had made a show of poking around a bit
more, his hands buried in his pockets, then walked toward the door.
"I forgot my money at home," he had mumbled as he passed under the
burning eye of the shopkeeper. He couldn't breathe; he felt like his legs
were giving out under him. As he stepped onto the street, he braced himself
for the inevitable yell of alarm. *"Stop, thief!"* or something like that, and
knew he would be caught and put in jail, and his mother would disown him
and delete all the pictures of him from the photo album, in overwhelming
disappointment and shame. But nothing happened.
The only sound he heard was his own rapid footsteps as he ran home.
In his room, he devoured the candy in shame. He felt ill.

Now, he felt the same way; as if he were smuggling contraband. But
why? They were just two kids. It didn't make sense.
They walked up to the border gate. Inside a booth, a bored-looking
guard eyed them.
"She's with me," Nathan said, trying to keep his voice from trembling.
The guard raised his eyebrows and shrugged, punching the gate release

button. As they walked through, Nathan exhaled in relief. He hoped Madelaine had not noticed his terror, but a glance revealed she was trying to cope with her own. He squeezed her hand tighter, becoming more brave with every step away from the gate.

"It's okay," he reassured Madelaine. She looked up at him and flashed a thin, unconvincing smile.

"Oh my God, it's beautiful!" Madelaine breathed, gazing rapturously at clouds rimmed with gold, violet, cyan, and chartreuse. Nathan simply nodded, a soft smile playing on his lips. The sun was just setting, casting the world in hues of gold, orange, and violet.

They stood atop the tallest building in New Genesis. The apex of the underside of this dome could be seen mere meters above them.

Beneath them, artificial clouds swirled and rumbled: like smoke on a windy day, they cascaded and spiralled indecisively. Every so often, a flash of lightning could be seen illuminating the insides of the darkening mist, and a dry crack of thunder echoed a split second thereafter.

Madelaine's breathing was shallow and rapid. She had completely forgotten her fear. The story of her eyes told Nathan she was flying above those clouds, skimming the thinnest layer of oxygen off the top, within this surreal, giddy atmosphere. He couldn't help but watch her lips. They were a rich shade of fuchsia, especially striking in contrast with her pale skin. They quivered barely perceptibly, slightly open; tiny beads of moisture condensing upon those sculpted curves, betraying the heaviness of her breath. Her brilliant eyes were wide and enchanted. In the light of the sunset, Nathan could see traces of green, and flecks of gold, within those radiant hazel orbs.

He felt himself fighting an intensely carnal arousal, watching her standing there, so thoroughly and intensely gratified by the scene. She was so *sensual,* fully present within her body, not like his coworkers at the Factory who silently shuffled down the cafeteria line, with half closed eyes and slack lips.

She is so ALIVE!

After several moments of agonized hesitation, Nathan gently placed his hand on Madelaine's back, just below the curve of her shoulder blades. The moment his palm touched her warm body, she started: her eyes widened, her lips parted, and she gasped ever so slightly. Ashamed, he jerked his hand away, but to his infinite surprise, she turned and threw herself into his arms. She embraced him wholly and desperately, like a person who has never, ever before been touched tenderly by anyone.

Nathan was shocked; the warmth and voluptuous curves of her very, *very* womanly body pressed against his made him instantly, almost painfully hard, and he hoped she wouldn't notice. But, the very next moment, she was crying, sobbing into his shoulder, and he was confused about how to feel, and whether he was being vile and inappropriate? He was willing his body to *stop, just stop!* when her voice whispered, heavy and damp, into his ear:

"It's... It's just that... I'll never be able to..." but her words faded into silence, her tears hot on Nathan's cheek.

"...Be able to what?" he asked, but she suddenly pressed her lips to his, hard, and the question immediately abandoned him. Silhouetted by the long, golden rays of a sinking orange sun, above the boiling clouds, and against the shimmering honeycomb pattern of the dome, they clung to each other, children on the precipice of adulthood, frightened and never more alone than in that moment, as they unknowingly replaced their own desperation with that of the other.

Nathan walked Madelaine back to the outskirts of Old Society. He had offered to walk her all the way home, but she gently but adamantly refused.

"Thank you..." she whispered, the glistening reflection of the night moon upon her moist bottom lip quivering as she looked up at him.

Then she was gone, and, heady and confused, Nathan shivered despite the damp heat.

Four months later, he and Madelaine were wandering down a street in Old Society, hand in hand, chattering away as usual about books and stories. Garbage littered the cracked, weary pavement. Every surface was caked with grime. Even though he had become accustomed to it, it was still so different from the bright, hospital-like cleanliness of the streets whence he came.

Abruptly, their conversation was cut short. With a wailing of sirens and lights, a police airjet tore around a corner, stopping with a loud hiss as the air currents quickly reversed to counter the forward thrust. Four armoured soldiers piled out of the back. An official climbed from the front, wearing a trimmed black suit with the red and yellow insignia of the NG-RPEB.

"That's Commander Reichmann," Madelaine whispered, and shuddered.

"Is he bad?" asked Nathan.

"Let's just say that if Janus is the Hitler of New Genesis, then Reichmann is Himmler..."

"Who are Hitler and –"

"And you see *that* guy?" Madelaine pointed at a tall soldier who was carrying an explosive munitions case.

"Yeah that's Jackson; I know him from work."

"Well, he's Heydrich."

"Who??"

But their conversation was cut short by the sound of shattering glass, as Jackson threw a flashbang grenade through an upstairs window of a run-down house. Simultaneously, the other soldiers used a sticky concussion mine to shatter the wood of the front door, with an ear-splitting explosion and a spray of splinters, leaving a dusty black hole. All four soldiers filed inside. Soon, yelling and screaming could be plainly heard, then the buzz-crackle of electrical stun wands. More wailing, sobbing, and pleading.

Nathan and Madelaine watched in silence – Nathan stupefied, Madelaine sombre – as three of the soldiers exited the building, dragging a young boy of around seven or eight. He was heavyset, had a round face, a thick tongue, and was in hysterics. On the heels of the soldiers came a man and a woman. The woman was beseeching her captors, and reaching out for the child. A soldier restrained her. The man took a swing at one of his persecutors, and connected. The soldier reeled back, cursing, as blood streamed from his nose. The remaining marine extended his stun baton and jammed it into the man's throat. Blue sparks jumped from the wand to his flesh. He yelled, and instantly collapsed, seizing on the ground. The soldier gave him another shock for good measure, while his wife pleaded frantically.

Reichmann walked over to them and raised his hand. The soldiers stepped back. The point man, wearing a sergeant's patch on his uniform, addressed him.

"Sir, Sergeant Marxus Pollox reporting: we have recovered the illegal child Sub-F. We also found a Sub-A female and a Sub-B male, both unlisted. They are being monitored by Jackson."

"Very good, Sergeant Pollox. I will see you and your squad receive a small bonus on your next payday."

"Thank you, sir."

"Retrieve the Subs now."

"Yes, sir." He spoke into a radio: "Jackson, bring them down."

A couple of minutes later, Jackson exited the building, smirking and shoving an elderly woman, who was at least 80 and could barely walk. She stumbled and leaned heavily on an even older man. She seemed disoriented, repeatedly asking where her Mama and Papa were; they were supposed to take her and her big sister to the cinema that day, because it was her birthday. The old man continually tried to reassure her, but his eyes betrayed his horror.

All three Subs were restrained, and loaded into the back of the airjet. Upon seeing the older couple, the younger woman had begun protesting again, but she was quieter now, more broken. She fell to silent blubbering. The man was unsteadily rising to his feet, leaning on the wall, shaking his finger at Reichmann.

"You goddamned bastards!" he cried hoarsely. "None'a them ever hurt anyone! This is *sick!* You can't just take them away and just chuck them in a giant wood chipper to be turned into fertilizer for your goddamned gardens!" He stood, breathing heavily, bent over, his hands on his knees.

"If you don't appreciate our "gardens", you do not deserve the benefit of them." Reichmann said coolly. "As you know, the NG-RPEB controls the food production and distribution for all of New Genesis: New Society and Old Society alike. I will see to it your food stamp ration is reduced by half. This way you will not have to burden yourself too greatly with the nutritious sustenance made possible by these selfless members of your family."

He turned on his heel, climbed into the cab, and was gone. The man yelled hoarsely, then convulsed into a fit of coughing, before wearily dragging himself back into the building. His wife followed him, automatically groping for the missing door, before staring uncomprehendingly at the innumerable splinters embedded in the wall.

Madelaine and Nathan had retreated and were watching this event unfold from behind the wall of a nearby building. Madelaine hid her face in her palms and wept. When she pulled her hands away, her tear-streaked face was aflame with rage.

"He's going to fucking pay, I swear on my life!!" Her features were hard and ugly.

But the threat was empty, falling impotently from her lips. Her body sagged and she appeared suddenly overwhelmed by fatigue. She clung to Nathan, and they walked slowly away, leaving behind them a silent, empty street.

"Those Old Society worms, you know... they're perfect candidates for the Pit," NG-RPEB officer Jackson mused during lunch one day. "They're already dirt."

A few of his buddies snickered. He impaled a Brussels sprout upon his fork, and calmly watched it drip with its own internal fluids. "They're nothing but the shit that fertilizes my garden." The sprout splatted wetly as he flung it to the floor and ground it beneath his boot.

The entourage of soldiers sitting at the silver aluminum picnic-bench style table roared their approval, shouting vulgar epithets and jeers towards the nameless, faceless population of subhuman RePurposables.

Not far away, in the corner of the Factory lunchroom, Nathan watched this display among the soldiers. He had seen similar testosterone-fuelled performances, and he had always been complacent, not caring or even paying attention. Soldiers will be soldiers. But this time, he felt a nagging irritation goading him with every further syllable uttered by Jackson.

Why? Why, now, did everything feel different from how it always had?

Surprising even himself, he heard his own voice ringing out into the recycled oxygen of the enclosed steel atmosphere.

"RePurposables are derived from the eligible within ALL aspects of society!" he blurted. "Not just Old Society! R. Janus himself states that we, as privileged citizens of New Society, we have an *even greater* social obligation to submit for RePurposing, once we become eligible! The Old Society miscre— uh, citizens, they are less educated, and so they understand less about the necessities of the program, but WE, we need to be the driving force behind the RePurposing initiative! WE understand! We are passionate and willing to sacrifice ourselves for the greater good of New Genesis! I, uh, uh, I'm just as happy to contribute to this, this... uh, this piece of lettuce! – and even more so, probably, than most of the OS citizens!! Because I am *devoted!*"

Nathan had been speaking with intense, energetic conviction (to his astonishment), but as soon as he stopped, the air dropped dead around him. After a moment of agonizing silence, the atmosphere exploded with the raucous laughter of two dozen soldiers. Yet, in the midst of them, Jackson remained silent and solemn. Abruptly, he kneeled before his troops, who fell silent, curious.

"My friends," he said, quietly, his eyes downcast, his expression morose. "I have found myself to be... *impure.* I am eligible as a Subsection-D, and wish to be RePurposed *RIGHT AWAY,* for the good of our *GREAT NATION!*" At this point he dissolved into fits of laughter, along with all the others.

Nathan stormed out of the cafeteria, his fists clenched, knuckles white, fingernails biting into his soft palms.

Nathan was worried. He had not seen Madelaine in nearly a month. He went every day to *Asimov's Den*, but she was nowhere to be found. He did not know where she lived, probably because she had been careful to keep him from her neighbourhood. After three weeks of her absence, he was nearly panic-stricken. He could barely sleep. His days were spent dozing off in a dark corner of the *Den.*

One morning, he dragged his weary carcass into the store, and was immediately handed a handwritten note. It was from Madelaine.

I need to talk to you.
Meet me in the park at 08:30.

Nathan looked at his watch. It was 08:23. The park was at least a 20 minute walk away. He ran faster than he ever thought possible. At 8:32, he leapt breathlessly down an embankment to a synthetic creek crossed by a stone bridge. Madelaine was waiting beneath it.

She looks like death!! he thought, shocked. Her face was thin, even whiter than usual, and her eyes seemed to have gained a sunken quality. Her lips looked dry; they had lost much of their luscious colour and were mottled with cracks and peeling skin.

She said nothing, as she removed her bright yellow shawl. He gasped. She was almost completely bald, but not uniformly. Small patches of extremely short hair were scattered over her scalp like ragged pastures. Humiliated, she stared at the ground in abject silence, her hands wringing her shawl.

"What *happened?!*" Nathan exclaimed, stupefied.

Madelaine said something, very quietly. Nathan could not hear her; he asked her to repeat herself.

Without warning, the girl threw her arms around his neck. The full length of her body was pressed up against his. Her lips were by his throat; her breath hot and damp on his ear. He lost his breath, felt that same warm throbbing in his groin, as he had before, on the roof overlooking the sunset. She whispered in his ear:

"I'm a Sub-E."

"...Wait ...*What?!*" his voice felt hollow and far away, as if coming from someone else.

"I have Stage IV breast cancer." Madelaine said, her voice mechanical. "From what I understand, it started off in the inner lining of my milk ducts, and has since metastasized to my liver. I was diagnosed as Stage II two years ago. Now that it's in Stage IV I am not likely to survive another year. It's incredibly rare in someone my age... but I guess I'm just lucky."

She had pulled away, and was crying silently. Nathan grasped for a sense of reality and coherence.

"It looked like things were going well," Madelaine continued. "The cancer was in remission - until it showed up in my liver a few weeks back. Since then I've been aggressively undergoing chemotherapy, hence the hideous baldness." She pointed meekly at her scalp, and seemed to shrink a little. "We were hoping it would kill this new tumour, but results have been... minimal. To make matters worse, I... I won't be able to continue treatment." Her voice was barely a whisper, her eyes trained on the concrete beneath her feet.

"Why not?! You could just go see a specialist, they could probably cure you!"

A burst of anger flashed in Madelaine's eyes as she looked up at him.

"They could probably cure *YOU*. You or your rich NS family!" Her words were acidic. "And even if they couldn't, you would have a better chance of avoiding being forcefully RePurposed! Down here, anyone with any sort of terminal illness is immediately *eliminated!* The pills I am taking are from a friend of my dad, from NS – one of the few good ones – but he can't keep smuggling them to us. He says he's being watched. Besides, even if he could, we can't afford it anymore. It's not free, and we can't expect him to just give them to us. Our Old Society lives are not *that* valuable. Everything costs."

She looked up at him. "I don't have long. I'm gonna *die,* Nathan!" she said, her eyes alight with anguish. "I might as well be RePurposed."

"Don't say that! We'll think of something!" Nathan exclaimed, aware his words sounded empty and clichéd, but he *wanted* to believe it in his heart, even if he really didn't, in his mind.

"I... I love you!" he blurted incontinently. The words startled him. A long six seconds passed within which neither of them moved or spoke, and the short distance between them seemed to Nathan to become cavernous.

In an effort to bridge the divide, he attempted to pull Madelaine into an embrace, but she pushed him away. He stumbled back, splashing into the creek and nearly falling.

Madelaine balked and stepped back as if insulted. "How could you say that to me?!" she cried. Nathan's eyes were wide; he could only move his mouth like a fish. He reached out to touch her arm.

"Leave me alone!" she said, writhing away from him. "I don't want to see you ever again! Just go home to your privileged New Society District, and your job of *murdering* millions of *decent human beings* without even blinking an eye!! You're a hypocritical coward. You make me *sick!*"

Then she turned her back on him, and was gone.

Nathan sat at home browsing *GenNet.* He hadn't left the house in three weeks, other than to go to work. His place was filthy. Dirty instant-meal containers had accumulated around the small space.

He looked over to the small stack of books he had accumulated, all of which he had been excited to read. In some way, he still was, but whenever he tried, he couldn't concentrate on the words. He felt anxious and fidgety, and inevitably reached for his tablet to watch videos online and play games.

He was sitting up in his bed, and the clothes hanging down around him formed a little cocoon. Like he had done every day, he found himself flipping through pictures he had taken with Madelaine. There they were on top of the building where she had kissed him. The brilliant orange sun made them squint, but they were both grinning widely, embracing each other.

Nathan sighed, and tossed the tablet on the bed, choosing instead to curl up in a ball under his fetid blanket. No sooner had he done this, his tablet played a tone notifying him of a new email. He snaked one arm out of his cave and groped for the PDA, pulling it down into his dark hole. The bright screen illuminated his features. The email was from a bytehead friend who was involved with a small group of hackers.

```
from:      <haXXXor69@1337central.com>
to:        <nate-dogg80085@gen.net>
date:      Tue, Apr 3, 3014 at 11:20 PM
subject: (IMPORTANT!!!)


>hey m8 was lookin thru this weeks RP list n i saw
sumfin u mite wanna look at #482. thank me l8r.
```

Every person who was RePurposed was entered into a database which logged their name, photograph, age, height, weight, district, date of apprehension, and date of RePurposing. The database was updated once a week. Hackers had rigged a protocol to intercept all new entries which were then automatically compiled into 'RP lists'.

Nathan opened the attachment and hastily scrolled down the column of unknown persons to the 482nd entry, a feeling of panic arising in his throat. Sure enough, there was a picture of Madelaine looking haggard and frightened, along with her pertinent details. He was instantly alert, and noticed with anxious relief that her processing date was not for another four days, but also that she would be going down a different shaft than the one he worked in.

There were multiple shafts per subcategory, and they were organized according to the district the Sub originated in. He typed a quick reply to his hacker friend, asking for the shift schedule of *RP_Sub-E Shaft 18,* down which Maddy would descend. He then messaged the worker scheduled at the time she was scheduled to be RePurposed, and offered to relieve him for that day, in exchange for one of his night shifts. Switching shifts was not uncommon. There was no such thing as a "day off" in New Genesis, but day-shifters still needed a day every so often to get normal daytime chores done.

When Madelaine came down his shaft, he would jump out of the booth and hop onto the belts. She would be insensate – the sedative had been switched from an oral benzodiazepine to a shot of cheap synthetic heroin. The logic was that it would make the Subs quite pliable, and if one or two overdosed, who cares? They were headed for the mulcher, anyway.

Nathan would administer an injection of Naloxone, a direct opioid antagonist, which instantly blocks the heroin molecules from fitting into the lock-and-key receptors, conclusively preventing them from having any effect whatsoever. Recovery occurs within seconds. Naloxone was available over the counter at most drugstores (at least the ones in OS) so obtaining it shouldn't be a problem. New Society did not have a demand for it since no one had any use for an opioid antagonist: no one abused drugs. (At least, not *officially*.)

Nathan would somehow break her free from her containment bar and bring her to safety in his monitoring booth, while she recuperated. According to the records, she would have been mulched, and would officially not exist, so no one would be looking for her.

And then... what?? His brilliant, heroic plan hit a solid wall. Would he just guide his obviously Sub-E crush (who didn't want to see him anyway) casually through the factory halls, waltz out the front door, then magically make her cancer disappear??

Yeah, right.

But what else could he do? If it came down to it, he *had* to rescue her from the mulcher. What happens next was an afterthought.

On Saturday morning, Nathan began his double shift. He would have been exhausted, but he deliberately stayed up all the previous day, so he would have no trouble falling asleep in his regular shift previous to this one.

Two hours later, still hadn't seen her. He was beginning to panic. Maybe she had passed him and he didn't catch her amongst the dozens of other faces! He was looking for her yellow shawl – maybe it came off before she was put on the belts! He was frantic; the thought of her plummeting down into the mashers made him physically ill.

He had a strange epiphany while staring into this river of nameless creatures. Before he met her, Madelaine would have been just another one of them, and he wouldn't have thought twice as she went by, but now she was a *real person!!*

At this point it occurred to him, as a visceral shock, that every other one of these Subs was probably a "real person" to someone. Theoretically, every one of them was a Madelaine! He reeled as he thought of the thousands and millions of subs he had watched carried to their deaths without a second thought.

He waited... and waited.

Finally, three hours and sixteen minutes into his shift, he saw her. She was still wearing her shawl, and she was in the farthest of the three columns. She hadn't reached his booth yet.

He looked at the calculations he had written out earlier.

The belts move at 2.5 km/hr. The shaft is 200m. By the time she gets to me there will be only 100m left. This means that I have 2.4 minutes from the time she passes the station to get her out of her seat and off the belts, before we're dumped off the edge into the pit!

He swallowed hard, took a breath, and jumped onto the nearest seat.

He landed on a man of about 40 years old, with brown hair. His head was drooping on his chest, and when Nathan landed on him, it bobbed comically. Drool formed a long, glistening line from his lower lip to his hands in his lap. With a pang of sorrow, Nathan noticed his wedding band, meaningless now, about to be tossed into a giant compost heap.

He forced himself to move on. There was very little time. But he couldn't shake the realization that these were all *living humans* he was crawling over!

He stood on the lap of a Sub, braced his left foot against the confinement bar, and his right foot on their shoulder. Then he quickly stepped forward, put his left foot on the back of the chair, and hopped into the lap of the Sub directly behind. His first jump was disastrous. He landed on a woman in her fifties, and he impacted hard on her face, with his knees. Her head was slammed against the seat, then fell forward, oozing blood from her shattered nose. She did not react. Nathan automatically hesitated, but checked himself: *No time; must keep going!* They had drifted down the grade; Madelaine had just passed the booth. Nathan started the countdown timer on his watch.

2 minutes, 24 seconds.

Three upward jumps and a sideward scuttle later, Nathan found himself kneeling on the lap of the Sub directly beside Madelaine. He lifted her face toward him. She was effectively dead to the world, her eyes half open, her lips silently chanting some mantra deep within her muted consciousness.

Trembling, Nathan took his injection kit from his breast pocket, where he had already prepared the needle.

1 minute, 58 seconds.

He lifted her head and aimed for her right carotid artery; it seemed like the biggest, easiest target. (It also flows directly to the brain, therefore avoiding first-pass metabolism, but Nathan didn't know that.) The point of the needle slowly moved towards her skin. A drop of liquid beaded out, twinkled in the light of the lamps above, and fell into the darkness below.

Without warning, the woman on whom Nathan was kneeling made a terrible groaning noise like the undead and opened her eyes to show wild, rolling eyeballs. She convulsed spastically before subsiding and laying inert again. The syringe was knocked out of Nathan's hand. He watched it arc and spin gracefully through the air, before disappearing into the grinding chain below.   Fortunately, he had the foresight to prepare two needles, in case something went wrong.

1 minute, 16 seconds.

Working quickly, Nathan positioned the second syringe, slid the needle in almost parallel to the surface, at what he hoped was the correct depth, and depressed the plunger. The syringe emptied silently. He withdrew the needle. Madelaine did not respond.

Nathan let the drug spread through her blood as he set about trying to free her from her confinement bar. First, he attempted to hoist her up by her armpits, to slide out, but her hips were too wide to slip behind the bar. He retrieved the meter-long crowbar he had strapped across his back, wedged the point into the joint of the restriction bar, and pried against it with all his strength.

After a tense moment, there was a loud *snap*. The force of the bar giving way launched Nathan backwards. He landed down between two seats, desperately scrabbling to get up. He could see the gears and chain mere centimeters below. Each link was the size of his jaw.

With great strength, he sat up, grabbed the containment bar of the seat next to Madelaine, and hoisted himself up.

0 minutes, 31 seconds.

He looked over to see her body inert, still, and lifeless. *Have I killed her?!* He was beginning to hyperventilate, feeling rising panic. A wave of vertigo rushed over him, and he fought back the urge to vomit.

"Maddy!!" he shouted. She hated that name. "*Madelaine!* Come on, Maddy, wake up!" he yelled hoarsely into her face, shaking her. Groggily, she opened her eyes and looked up at him, totally out of it, and absolutely bewildered. Still, she did not move.

"GET UP! WE NEED TO MOVE *NOW!!*" Nathan screamed at her. The end of the shaft was fast approaching. He could see the gaping opening of the pit coming closer; he could smell the stench of millions of rotting human carcasses.

He slapped her hard across the face. It worked. She gasped. Her eyes flew open; she took a quick look around her and bolted upright in her seat, terrified.

0 minutes, 8 seconds.

They had reached the end of the belt.

"Like this!" Nathan showed her his Sub-hopping technique. She stood and turned around in her chair to copy him, only to realize that she didn't have a restriction bar to boost off of. She looked dumbly at Nathan, then down into the gaping pit behind her, as the third seat closest to her begun to curve over and under.

Nathan jumped off the seats, onto the smooth metal slope. Immediately, his feet slipped out from under him. He impacted hard, his chin bouncing off the steel. He saw a bright flash of light, then blacked out for a moment, before regaining his senses, struggling through the stars swimming in his visual field. A meter from the edge he somehow managed to jam his crowbar into the gears of one of the belts. There was a screaming of metal, a grating sound, and the belt stopped completely.

Nathan was hanging from the crowbar. Madelaine was dangling from the constriction bar of one of the chairs at the very edge, the back of the seat angled horizontally, on its way under. The chair was now empty, having ejected its cargo into the cavernous pit.

Madelaine looked down. She could see piles of living bodies being funnelled into the masher, 50m below. She felt immediately dizzy. One hand slipped from the bar. She screamed hysterically for help.

For a brief instant, the image of the palsied man flashed through Nathan's mind, the one reaching toward him with his crooked fingers, hysterically begging for his life…

Nathan was jolted back into reality as the crowbar he was holding suddenly shifted with a shriek of grinding metal.

He reached down with one arm and grabbed Madelaine's free hand, just as the other was about to slip off. He grunted as her full body weight pulled at his shoulder sockets.

He swung Madeline twice, like a pendulum. On the third time, with a yell, he hoisted her up, back onto the chairs. He then climbed back up. At that moment, with a loud, discordant *WHANG*, the crowbar was violently ejected from the mechanism, spinning like helicopter blades, arcing laterally downwards with a whining hum, disappearing far and deep into the pit. The belt began moving again.

This time, neither of them hesitated. They both scrambled upwards as fast as they could over the rows of people, until, panting and utterly exhausted, they launched themselves onto the platform upon which the monitoring station sat. They both lay there for several minutes, their breath ragged, groaning in pain and sobbing in exhausted relief.

"You know, you're heavier than you look," Nathan gasped. Madelaine managed a weak smile and a shrug.

The two teenagers sat inside the monitoring hut, on the floor, leaning against the wall. They had been resting for perhaps ten minutes. Nathan's head was back, his eyes closed. Madelaine spoke to him.

"So… what now?" she asked.

"Well, you're officially dead," he replied drily, without opening his eyes.

"And only slightly sooner than expected," was her response.

Nathan looked over at her. "I'm sorry about what I said to you the other day..." he ventured.

She sighed and shook her head.

"Look, I reacted the way I did because... I feel it too..." she said timorously, looking at the floor and fiddling with her shawl. "...but I never wanted it to be said, *ever,* because once it's acknowledged, it becomes formal, just another one of the many things I cherish, which I am going to lose." Her voice was hauntingly empty.

"I... I don't know about that..." Nathan said. He took her hand in his and squeezed it gently. It was very warm. "I never thought I would *ever* be able to connect with another person. Even if I had died today, it still would have been a better life than if I hadn't met you." His voice cracked, and he quickly looked away.

They both sat in silence for a bit, exhausted and overwhelmed. After a couple of long minutes, Nathan picked himself up off the floor.

"We should go."

"Where?" Madelaine looked up at him with renewed terror.

"Away from here." Nathan said, not wanting to admit he had never actually managed to come up with a further plan.

They began walking along the platform leading to the access hallway to the rest of the factory, passing through a heavy metal door into a narrow hallway of concrete and steel, lit from above by sodium lamps. The door closed with an echoing *bang*, and abruptly, silence fell upon their ears. They continued along the hallway, their footsteps echoing around them. The lamps above them buzzed, their aluminum cages throwing warped latticework shadows on the walls.

"This way," Nathan said, leading them down a short hallway which terminated at a hatch in the floor. He rotated the large, circular handle, and lifted the heavy steel door. He had just formed an idea: they would travel through the bowels of the factory, where nobody was likely to see them, and exit via one of the numerous maintenance shafts which tunnelled through the structure.

The ladder was dizzyingly high. It extended down a narrow chimney-like column for at least three stories. As they climbed lower, the air became hotter, more humid, more... *human.* The stench was becoming unbearable. Still, they pressed onwards.

They scurried down several branching corridors. Madelaine soon became hopelessly lost. She hoped Nathan wasn't. The roar of machinery was growing deafening. Abruptly, they emerged into a large open area, the same massive diameter as the pit, but only half the depth.

"What is this place?!" Madelaine yelled. Nathan did not respond. He simply pointed.

The ceiling of the monolithic room curved down and inwards to a central point, where there was a large hole. Through this flowed a river of living human bodies. Madelaine realized it was the underside of the funnel she had seen in the pit. The bodies were tumbling down into the mulching machine. Madelaine couldn't tear her eyes away from the cascade of bodies flowing from the funnel. A multi-coloured waterfall... of *live humans!*

Nathan led her onto a walkway which extended into the center of the room. As they slowly walked over the iron grating, Madelaine stared in horror at the human waterfall. As they grew closer to it, she was able to make out individual faces. *Grandparents, children, sisters, brothers...* For a moment, she could barely breathe. She became dizzy; her heart began beating in her chest, even louder than the mashing plates. She looked down, into the mechanism, and immediately wretched, the nausea coming easily, encouraged by the putrid stench and the aftereffects of the opioids.

The first stage of mulching was the mashing. Bodies fell down a deep shaft, within which, alternating in position, were parallel horizontal plates that extended on hydraulic pistons to become flush with each other, crushing whatever happened to fall between them. There were five massive plates which alternated perpendicular to each other down the shaft, compressing at different rates and intervals.

After this, the crushed biological material fell into another square vertical shaft which contained many thick cylinders, alternating perpendicularly, which were covered in hundreds of razor sharp blades. These spun extremely fast; anything that fell between the blades was instantly diced. Finally, the mashed and diced waste material fell into another large cavity below, where it splattered down to contribute to the homogenous, steaming, putrefying Heap.

Madeline was pale and sweating. She had not eaten that day, and vomited only bile. Her vision was blurred around the edges but clear at the center. She couldn't breathe. She was having chest pains. Frantically, she ran the rest of the way across the platform, once stumbling and falling, tearing open her jeans, but she scrambled to her feet and continued without even noticing. When she got to the far side of the pit, she collapsed with her back to the wall and hugged her knees, not bearing to look at the ghastly, clanging death-machine which still worked tirelessly, converting the good citizens of New Genesis into wholesome, Nitrogen-rich fertilizer.

"I... I'm sorry about all that," Nathan later mumbled abashedly.

These were the first words exchanged between them since the pit. They had spent the last hour silently navigating tunnels and shafts, searching for an exit. They had gotten lost several times. At long last, they turned a corner to see daylight, and ran towards a short vertical shaft which housed a ladder. Above, a hinged grille filtered beautiful sunlight which warmed their faces. They scrambled upwards and outwards, and exited the factory grounds via an unpatrolled employee exit, to which Nathan had a keycard.

They now sat in an alleyway in Old Society, leaning against the crumbling red brick wall of an abandoned warehouse. Green weeds sprouted stubbornly through the pavement; Nathan was surprised to see that some things still persisted, even after a nuclear apocalypse. He picked a yellow dandelion and tentatively stroked its soft petals with a fingertip.

Madelaine was silent for a moment.

"How could you..." she began, lapsing into silence. After a moment, she said quietly, "I never imagined it was so..."

Nathan said nothing.

"I want to hate you," continued Madelaine, "just for being a part of it..."

Nathan frowned. "But *why??* This is just *life!*"

"Why does that make it okay?!" Madelaine erupted, her eyes suddenly wide and intense.

Nathan shrank a little. "How else are we going to survive? We'll all starve otherwise."

Madelaine turned away and was silent for a moment, picking at the cracked asphalt with a shard of brick. "I'd rather starve," she said quietly.

"Sometimes humanity needs to make sacrifices to survive! It's a hard truth." said Nathan. "We don't have a choice." He recited the words mechanically.

"We *always* have a choice, Nathan," Madelaine said with irritation. She stood up, grimacing as she straightened her left leg; her jeans were dark with dried blood where she had gashed her knee on the walkway. "It's what makes us human. Even if we have *nothing*, we are free to choose! It is our ultimate freedom."

Nathan shuffled uncomfortably and shrugged. He didn't know how to respond.

"Can I walk you home?" He asked sheepishly, climbing to his feet.

Madelaine smiled gently. "Well, you *did* save my life. I'll have to find a way to repay you." She slipped her arms around him, then stretched up on her toes and kissed him.

Once again, Nathan felt dizzy with vertigo.

When Madelaine walked through the tarpaulin covering the decimated doorway of her home, her mother dropped the plate she was drying, and burst into tears. Her father rushed in from the living room, and when he saw his daughter, he ran over and lifted her into his arms, crushing her in a massive bear hug. He, too, began weeping.

Eventually, Madelaine's parents noticed Nathan, who had been standing awkwardly by. They were naturally bewildered at his presence; they had never heard of him before. When they heard that he had saved her, Madelaine's parents both embraced Nathan tightly, and insisted he stay for dinner. Often.

Several days later, Nathan was once again sitting restlessly within his job at the factory, and it was worse than usual. It wasn't just because it felt more pointless than usual: he discovered nobody had even noticed he skipped out on his shift that day.

No, it wasn't that. He simply could no longer bear sitting idly in that booth, watching as all these people were sent to their death. Each of them was a Madelaine to someone, and he felt that he was letting her die a thousand times over. Her caustic words haunted him.

We always have a choice, Nathan.

But he still needed a way to live! If he became homeless, he would be RePurposed for sure, and, contrary to what he had always thought, the idea did not fill him with anticipation, or pride. Dejected, he vented to Andy, who immediately offered him a job at *Asimov's Den.*

"Only thing is: I can't pay you. I'm barely managing my own rent. But I can give you room and board, as long as you're light on the fridge."

When Madelaine heard the news, she tackled him in excitement.

"I *knew* you could do it!" she exclaimed, kissing him on the cheek.

Nathan smiled and nodded, blushing.

Buried within the many stacks of books crowding her tiny bedroom, Maddy read him science fiction stories for hours, and, when she felt too tired or sick, she rested upon Nathan, and he read to her, as the moon rose, ice blue, over the shimmering domes of New Genesis.

[2015 – 2018]

New Genesis RePurposing Enforcement Bureau

[3016 A.D.]

Reichmann is dead. According to the official reports, he has taken an early retirement, but Marxus Pollox heard around the office that he was assassinated two days ago by insurgents of the *Omega Faction,* a terrorist organization whose base of operations is a small city in the deserts outside of the sealed domes of New Genesis.

Now Pollox, formerly Sergeant, has suddenly been promoted to *Commander*, and his new shoes feel too big. He can't for the life of him understand why they picked him over Jackson, who was probably better suited for the job, but, not one to turn down a pay raise, he certainly wasn't going to say anything.

He stands in the doorway of Reichmann's old office, carrying a small plastic crate. He scans the room in detail. Dark green carpeting. Faux-wood-paneled walls. Wide, faux-oak desk. Sconce lighting. Incandescent. But it doesn't smell right.

Pollox steps into the room and places the crate on the desk. He hangs his credentials, from New Genesis Military Academy, on the wall behind the desk. A centuries-old antique copy Sun Tzu's *The Art of War* on the bookshelf. His Order of Military Merit badge, in its velvet case, on the desk by the ink blotter. His favourite pen on the blotter, perpendicular to the edge.

Many of these things are useless; books, paper and ink haven't been used in centuries, but they are heirlooms, and Pollox finds them soothing and inspiring. He hangs an old replication of a Renaissance painting on the far wall. A small plaster bust of Julius Caesar on the desk. No, that's not right. On the shelf by the door. That's much better. Makes a striking impression upon entrance.

He walks over to the ornate mirror on the wall and examines himself. Fifty-four, noticeable creases in his cheeks and brow. Circles under his brown eyes. Balding, grey hair trimmed short. Clean fingernails. Clean shaven. He adjusts the tie of his new navy blue suit, takes a handkerchief out of his pocket and polishes the merit badges pinned to his left breast pocket. *Good.* He nods at himself and sits down at the desk. Looks at the clock.

09:34.

The room is silent except for the ticking of the clock. Then he leans forward, and his chair creaks, a long, plaintive shriek, like it's being slowly murdered. He feels a tinge of irritation. He'll have to oil it. Couldn't Reichmann take care of his things like any responsible person?

34

Evidently not.

He moves his pen from one side of the desk to the other, then stumbles upon the realization that he has no idea how to perform his role in this new job. *What is a Commander supposed to do?* He supposes he ought to find someone to command. He feels a twinge of what could only be described as homesickness for his old job, his old office, which was more of a home than his tiny, lonely bachelor's suite ever was.

At least it smelled right.

He used to be the New Genesis RePurposing Enforcement Bureau's chief boots-on-the-ground RP collector, personally tracking down people designated to be RePurposed into fertilizer, and enforcing the law. (So many ingrates ignoring the protocol. How else is a society supposed to function if people don't respect the rules?)

It is officially a great honour to be RePurposed, and everyone can expect to be processed at some point. Unofficially, however, public opinion of the mulching practice is less positive. The New Society Districts have embraced the benefits of new technology, upon certain terms and conditions, thereby accepting the restrictive regimens of a well-managed social system. These people are purportedly joyous and enthusiastic about RePurposing. The rhetorical dogma is that they recognize that they are serving their country and contributing to a greater good.

The Old Society Districts, however, absurdly prefer to live in archaic slums, still employing the same technology, architecture, and social customs of the 21st century. Rather than willingly submitting to RePurposing, these people have to be subjected to their patriotic obligation by any force necessary.

Reichmann preferred not to get his boots dirty, leaving the actual hands-on work to others. But Pollox doesn't follow the same path. His place is on the streets, with his men, like any officer.

The intercom on the desk buzzes. He presses the button.

"Yes?"

"Commander Pollox, sir, Senator Granger is here to see you.

Pollox raises the height of his seat to its maximum, and cinches his tie.

"Send him in."

Granger enters, without looking up from the tablet he is studying. He is a wiry man with short grey hair and a tidy moustache. He is outfitted in a grey plaid suit, white shirt, and charcoal tie.

"Commander, congratulations on your promotion," he says drily, still flipping through the files.

"Thank you, Senator. It is a great honour to be –"

"We have a problem in New Society districts 526-533." Granger offhandedly deposits the tablet onto Pollox's desk, knocking the pen from the blotter, causing Pollox to grimace.

Granger swipes through a few application windows and pulls up a report. "Population growth has exceeded carrying capacity for these two domes; residents are whinging. Last year's census shows the birth rate was more than double the mortality rate."

Pollox realigns the pen with the edge of the desk, then peers at the tablet. It displays a truncated map of the relevant domes, each containing four districts. Districts 1-599 belong to New Society, 600 and above to Old Society.

446	447	450	451	454	455	458	459
448	449	452	453	456	457	460	461
522	523	526	527	530	531	534	535
524	525	528	529	532	533	536	537
596	597	600	601	604	605	608	609
598	599	602	603	606	607	610	611

"Okay," Pollox says, then falls silent. He is accustomed to performing residential sweeps and collecting RPs, and once again has the humiliating realization he has no idea what he is doing in a management position. Yet Granger looks at him expectantly, raising his eyebrows.

"Okay," Pollox repeats, feeling his palms begin to sweat. "Well, how about we just diffuse the overload outwards into these 7 contiguous domes?" he says, pointing to the surrounding New Society bubbles.

"Impossible. Those districts are already at capacity. Any additional residency would merely shift the problem between domes." says Granger, checking his watch.

"Well, these are middle-class NS districts; from 200-599 inclusive we have up to, uh, 392 other districts over 100 domes; spreading the relocation between enough of them shouldn't cause a problem in any of them."

"Pollox, get out from under your rock. All the New Society districts are like this. These two domes are just the next escalation." says Granger.

Pollox frowns. "But I'm familiar with these districts; I've seen empty –"

"It's all in the figures, Pollox. Do your job, or we'll find someone else who will."

"Yes, sir," says Pollox quickly, his cold sweat increasing.

He taps some figures into the tablet for several minutes, while Granger sits restlessly. Presently, Pollox speaks.

"Dividing number of residents into number of districts shows that Old Society has less population density overall; the ratio of districts to residents is greater than it is in New Society. Therefore, they can stand to lose a couple of bubbles. Expand the affected NS districts downward, appropriating districts 600-607."

"Very well," murmurs Granger, tapping something into his PDA. "And the current residents?"

Pollox feels a surge of confidence with Granger's terse affirmation. His new role as Commander is beginning to grow on him! He speaks more authoritatively. "Give them a week's notice, with a warning that we'll seal off and sterilize those domes with gaseous Hydrogen Cyanide at that time, then begin restructuring!"

"We need to move on this *now,* Pollox. It's a pressure cooker in there." snapped Granger. Pollox falters again.

"Well, okay, organize a 48 – no, a 24 hour evacuation. Put a company of 200 men in each of the bubbles, divided into platoons of 50 men per district. Vehicle-mounted loudspeaker broadcast; nothing too intensive. Organize a 90 second news briefing broadcast every hour on the hour overriding all OS network channels." Pollox holds his breath.

"Fine. I'll have someone draw the order up and deliver it for your signature by the end of the day." Granger scoops up the file folder and walks curtly out of the room.

Pollox exhales heavily. He steps into the bathroom, rinses his face with cold water, and straightens his tie. He stares at his weary reflection for several seconds, before shuddering and walking back into the office.

He grimaces. The room still doesn't smell right.

By the time he gets home, it's nearly midnight. The door to his military-issue apartment creaks as he pushes it open. The cold fluorescent light from the barracks hallway reaches into the blackness of the unit; it crawls over the furniture and creates hard shadows which paint a grotesque mural on the far wall. The only light from within the apartment is the blinking green LED of the coffee pot. Pollox swallows the familiar empty feeling which descends upon him: the knowledge that, while other homes are teeming with life and interaction, and every door opening reveals a new, dynamic environment, in his living quarters, everything is dead and static, just as he left it. Not even dust motes dance within the unforgiving shard of light.

He heats up a TV dinner and assembles a folding tray table in front of the couch. He turns on the television. Abruptly, the walls are awash with colour and excitement, the murky corners reverberating with robust sound: he has happened upon a gravcar commercial. The sleek, silver vehicle cruises along pristine streets, hovering a short distance above the ground. The hexagonal pattern of the domes above catch the waning golden light, creating a prism of specular reflection upon the flawless, tinted windshield.

"*Introducing the 3017 Gravitron Raptor!*" says a luxuriously deep voice, as the car transforms into a fierce, screaming osprey which soars into the sky. "*Unleash your full potential!*"

Pollox flips the channel to his favourite political talk show and peels the plastic wrap off the segmented dinner tray, releasing a gushing cloud of steam.

"... and they can't be ignored forever. The people of New Genesis – specifically the Old Society districts – are getting tired of R. Janus and his perceived megalomania. He's going to have to find a way to retain their favour if he wants to stay in power." A heavyset older man with glasses and a dry face is sitting in the guest chair. The host is a middle-aged man who most would guess is much younger; he has impeccable blonde hair and impossibly white teeth.

"Well, I'm not sure I agree with you, Newt," he says, taking a sip of his coffee. "What are they going to do, knock on Janus' door and say '*Please sir, may I have some more?*'" He emits a high-pitched greasy laugh that sounds like a car refusing to start. "Like anyone, these people are going to have to deal with what comes their way."

"*Quis custodiet ipsos custodes?*" says the first man. "Who will guard the guardians? Who oversees the overseers? Complacency will only extend so far. Even the most flexible elastic has a breaking point." He shows his hands, palms up, his eyebrows raised, lips pursed.

Pollox's fork slips from his hand and clatters loudly upon the floor. He is slouched over and snoring, a thin line of drool creating a dark patch on his wrinkled uniform.

The central intelligence room of the NG-RPEB is filled with dozens of workers simultaneously chattering into radio headsets. They sit at rows of computer desks isolated on three sides; they interact only with the holofields in front of them, making swift movements with their hands, flipping and rotating objects and icons suspended in front of them.

In the center of the room is a gigantic table ten meters in diameter, a circular polygon upon which is a holographic representation of New

Genesis, divided into zones. This hologram can be resized as desired to any resolution, depicting a full-detail representation of the city at any scale.

An operative is currently manipulating the controls via a smaller holofield on the perimeter of the table. Pollox stands beside him. The models are rendered in real time, using data from millions of cameras. Pollox looks up at the bank of television screens which occupy nearly the entire wall behind them.

Hundreds of monitors form a floor-to-ceiling grid, and each screen is a tiny square of life in New Genesis. Every district is thoroughly monitored. Through camera relay, a person can be tracked from the moment they leave their house on one side of the metropolis, to the second they arrive at their friend's house at the opposite side. Cameras are installed every few meters on the sides of buildings, even moving on public transit, and squad cars. 360° eyes are installed in multiple positions on the undersides of the domes, in addition to inside every commercial building, and on utility poles.

Pollox turns back to the glowing, semi-translucent paintings of light which flicker on the table in front of him. The man highlights four sectors in red.

"The gas is prepped and ready... *Commander.*" he says. Pollox notices the title is delivered absently, as an afterthought. He opens his mouth to issue a reprimand, but the officer speaks again, and the moment grows stale.

"On your order, it will be released into the bubbles."

"Just a second," Pollox says. Something feels off. *What is it?* "Zoom in and activate soldier ID tags. I want to ensure that none of our boys are still in there when we pop this thing."

"Monitoring and tracking occurs only in the New Society Districts." the man answers flatly. "Old Society footage is only captured from the dome cameras, so the best I can give you is a bird's-eye-view, and no tags."

He stabs a command into a console. The nine screens directly in front of them consolidate to form one image approximating a satellite view of one of the OS districts. As predicted, the wide focal length and high viewing distance do not provide any discernable details other than dozens of roofs and the dark lines of roads.

"I'm not proceeding until I know all my men are safe," Marxus says firmly.

The man sighs, and activates his Bluetooth headset. "Dispatch, this is operative 13-1545, please confirm that sectors 600-607 are clear of operatives." He yawns. After a few seconds he nods impatiently at Pollox.

"Well, go on then. Release the gas." Pollox commands. The man taps a command into his PDA. On the screens, Pollox can see the bubbles gradually engulfed by a thick white cloud, until, after a few seconds, the buildings are no longer visible from above, and the entire space is obscured in a dense fog.

Well, that's it then.

Pollox checks his watch. Still plenty of time before lunch. Despite his personal convictions regarding hands-on involvement with his men, he hasn't been able to put enough time in on the streets, gathering RP deserters, like he used to. There's too much paperwork. But if he can't be there in person, he's going to make damn sure no straggler is missed. It's time to go through the records and make sure that no stone is left unturned. With Commander Pollox on the job, no one will succeed at abandoning their patriotic duty.

Pollox's desk is a mess. Reports are strewn everywhere. Scrap paper is scribbled with calculations. Pollox knows he can get in trouble for this sort of behaviour. Paper is a valuable commodity. New Genesis has long-since run out of trees; paper must be synthesized by processing raw cane sugar, which is a combination of glucose and fructose. The fructose is converted to glucose via multiple reactions, then the total glucose is hydrolyzed to form cellulose, which is processed into paper. Not a simple or cheap process. Consequently, paper is reserved for propaganda, important reports, and government correspondence, not scribbling. But Pollox isn't concerned about this.

His numbers look weird.

It's probably nothing, he thinks. Yet, he cannot put it out of his mind. He defines his life by order and predictability, and trying to ignore it is like trying to will himself not to scratch an itch – it becomes all he can think about, and sooner or later he will give into the compulsion.

He scowls. According to party doctrine, RePurposing is a utilitarian process required by all members of New Genesis, regardless of socioeconomic class. But the data just don't make sense! He reaches for his telephone and punches in the number to the NG-RPEB statistics department. He reads off a list of report titles sequentially. Are any missing? *No. Please confirm the following figures... Yes, they check out according to records. Nothing is unusual.*

He hangs up the phone and curses, then dials another number.

"Senator Granger, this is Commander Pollox."

"What do you want, Pollox?"

"Sir, there's a problem – with the reports."

"The *reports.*" Granger repeats peevishly . "Pollox, I'm eating my lunch; call back in an hour.".

"Yes, sir."

Marxus Pollox strides down A-Wing of NG-RPEB headquarters. The walls are covered in portraits of prominent military figures from over the years, as well as group photographs of memorable platoons. He vaguely wonders if he'll end up on that wall. The information he has is of vital importance to the future of New Genesis.

Granger didn't think so.

"Quit wasting my fucking time and get back to work." he had said, then abruptly disconnected the call.

So, now Pollox is on his way to meet with R. Janus, CEO of the New Genesis RePurposing Enforcement Bureau, and Chairman of the Board of Trustees.

After waiting for 20 minutes in the lobby, Pollox stands before the huge desk of R. Janus. It is raised on a thick platform, so that even a tall man has to look up, as if he were a child.

"What do you want, Paulson?" Janus demands. He is a massive man, built like a rhinoceros and just as strong. He is 67 years old, bald, with broad shoulders and a barrel-shaped physique composed almost exclusively of muscle. He is dressed smartly but conservatively in a dark grey three-piece suit, with a blood-red tie.

"It... it's Pollox, sir. Uh, I believe I've found an error in the census statistics," Pollox says hesitantly.

Janus scowls. "That's *it?*" Brusquely, he resumes work on his PDA, ignoring Pollox.

"Sir, I believe it to be highly relevant..." Pollox says nervously.

Janus sighs irritably, and puts down his PDA. He makes a slight palm-up gesture while pursing his lips and raising his eyebrows, then leans back in his chair and crosses his arms.

"It – it appears there is a vastly disproportionate ratio of RePurposings in Old Society compared to New Society," says the Commander, looking down at his tablet, his features illuminated by the screen.

"There are many more OS residents, proportionately." Janus replies dismissively.

"Yes, but correcting for that using birth rate statistics, there are more OS residents being RePurposed. Most of the NS deaths are listed as "accidental", and it is roughly equivalent to the birth rate. The only conclusion I can come to is that senior citizens who should have been RPd as Sub-As or -Bs are instead dying unproductively from old age, or rather, *accidentally*..."

Pollox trails off mid-sentence. Janus looks bored; he stares through Pollox to the floor behind him. Pollox feels a surge of anxiety; he begins to sweat.

41

"My – my report clearly shows that most New Society residents are neglecting their RePurposing obligations. This is the same problem we have in Old Society, but the difference is, we're *not* collecting New Society citizens. So, either this is a statistical error, or we need to tighten the belt on our policy enforcement."

The Chairman scoffs. "Don't be so naïve."

"Come again, sir?" Pollox can't hide his surprise.

"Last year the population of New Genesis was nearly 2 billion. We're packed in like fucking sardines here, and every one of these fat, self-entitled assholes eats about two tons of food a year. If we used the richest soil imaginable, it would still be impossible to produce that volume, let alone this dead, irradiated sand we're trying to grow in. If humankind wants to live, we need to cull the herd. We can comfortably lose about a billion people."

Janus produces a bottle of synth whiskey and a glass from his desk and pours himself a couple of fingers.

"Even *if* we were somehow able to have the factory running at full capacity, it would take thirty years to get humanity down to a manageable level. The truth is, Pollox, the people of this city owe us their *lives*, and we're calling in the loan." Janus swirls the glass and takes a drink.

Pollox shakes his head. "But if we're so hard up for numbers, why don't we enforce RePurposing for New Society citizens?"

Janus slowly leans forward, looking down at Pollox over the edge of the desk. When he speaks, his voice is quiet.

"Because they are the *real* citizens of New Genesis, Paulson. The lower class proletariat are just scum: worthless fodder only good for one thing, and they outnumber us substantially. We need to severely cull the population of those animals so that New Society – the *true* society – rightfully becomes the *only* society." He tosses back the rest of the glass. "That is what the entire RePurposing operation was designed for in the first place. So get back to work, and leave the numbers to the professionals. You're a soldier, not a statistician." Janus says brusquely, terminating the conversation.

"... Yes sir," says Pollox, and retreats from the room, his neck burning.

Pollox's credit chip is maxed, again. He discovers this when he tries to buy a quart of milk from the vending machines in his apartment building but is greeted with the familiar symbol of denial: a blinking red dollar sign with an X over it.

He digs through his kitchen drawer, producing a small bag with some of the antique coins they still use in Old Society. It is a 40 minute walk to the nearest OS corner store; he can't afford a gravcar.

The clerk looks with mild disdain at his New Society outfit, but takes his money without a word. On the way home, Pollox has to stop to rest his throbbing ankles. He sits heavily at a bus stop, forcing himself to ignore the visible grime on the bench, the smell of urine in the corner.

"Look at that," says a voice. A rough-looking individual addresses his companion, motioning to the large shatterproof flat screen display on one wall of the enclosure, which looks bizarrely out of place within the surrounding dilapidation. Pollox squints at the overly-bright screen. A wall of text is scrolling by – daily news headlines.

40,000 Dead in Ventilation Malfunction

Thousands of citizens lost their lives yesterday due to a system error which resulted in improper ventilation of toxic gas from chemical production facilities, incorrectly rerouted into the air circulation system of districts 600-607. Exact numbers of fatalities are not yet known, but preliminary data estimate at least 40,000 dead. Investigators are working to identify the source of the error.

"Weren't no malfunction," said the man. "I been working maintenance on those systems for 22 years, and it just ain't possible." He spits on the ground.

"Huh." says his friend, inattentively. He is squeezing the black, greasy leaves from several ersatz cigarette butts, his fingers stained dark yellow.

"I been watching," continues the other man. "I seen it comin' a mile away. New Society needs room for more mansions and shit. What Janus wants, Janus gets."

His friend remains silent as he piles the reeking leaves into a pipe thickly coated in tar, then lights it, the ember glowing red in the waning light of dusk.

"But what about the evacuation?" asks Pollox, confused. The man turns to stare at him. Several seconds of awkward silence follow; Pollox can feel the other man studying him, his NS outfit, his combed hair, his polished military boots.

"Weren't no evacuation," the man mutters gruffly, then turns back around.

Pollox stares through him. He shivers despite the balmy heat. His palms have become cold and clammy, again.

Had something gone wrong??

The television blinks and roars into life, once again flooding Pollox's apartment with light and sound. He collapses onto the sofa. The screen displays the rolling splash logo of the talk show, then disappears to reveal the two men from before. The host straightens his tie and speaks into the camera.

"Hello, and welcome back to *Goodnight New Genesis!* You all know me; my name is John Emmett Clifford, and once again I would like to welcome the illustrious Newt Moreau back to the show. Newt is a journalist and political analyst with *Hogarth Finance & Metrics*." The large man in the guest's chair smiles and nods. Clifford turns to him.

"So, Newt, you've obviously heard about the incident that happened yesterday, regarding the ventilation malfunction which resulted in the tragic death of thousands of Old Society citizens across eight districts. As I'm sure you well know, there has been a massive uproar about it on social media. People are saying that it's an outright lie, that it's a diversion and a shifty cover-up for some clandestine ulterior motive. What do you make of all that?"

Moreau adjusts his glasses. "Well, John, I have certainly heard a few theories about the validity of the official report – " he begins.

"Wait, wait, you mean *conspiracies*, not theories." Clifford interrupts with a wave of his hand.

"No, John, I don't. A conspiracy is nothing more than a suspicious *idea*, but a true *theory* demonstrates *verifiable evidence* as a plausible explanation for observed phenomena. In this case, there is legitimate evidence which supports the claim that the official report was completely falsified."

Clifford laughs drily. "Come on, Newt, you're telling me you actually believe this tripe? The internet is crawling with insane quacks off their rocker with paranoia and delusion. You can't believe everything someone tells you."

"I can't argue with that, John, but you could say the same about the narratives we're fed through the propaganda machine. The objective fact is that we have had engineers and academics coming forward in droves to protest, demonstrating objectively conclusive evidence that there is no possible way this "malfunction" could have occurred."

"*Really*. Like what?"

"The first argument is that the only place toxic gases could be found in such large quantities is the industrial section. Obviously, toxic waste ventilation must be kept completely separate from the air supply system. It just doesn't make sense otherwise! Why *in the hell* would those systems be contiguous? It would be like feeding your sewage pipe to into your water main.

"Secondly, the poison that killed all those people was found to be gaseous Hydrogen cyanide, which is not a by-product of *any* industrial process employed in New Genesis. There is literally no way that this chemical could have been produced in *any* quantity, unless it were intentionally synthesized." Moreau shows his hands, palms up. Clifford makes a wry face and rolls his eyes.

"Alright, alright, Newt, well, you know, if you can show me actual figures, *maybe* I'll believe you. But let's move on. Let's suppose for argument's sake that you're right, and R. Janus really did decide to just randomly murder 40,000 people, just for fun. Why would he do that?? I'm sure he has better things to do. There's just no motive!"

Moreau scoffs, incredulous. "Like hell there isn't! John, *you* live in New Society; you know how crowded it has become! There are more people than ever who want unnecessarily spacious real estate; and in the last five years alone, 82% of all NS parks and public recreational spaces have been bulldozed to make way for mansions and shopping malls, and now, these spoiled rich kids are pointing fingers and whinging that they deserve *more*."

"Wow, Newt, did you forget to take your wheatgrass puree this morning? Have you seen Old Society? It's a thousand times worse!"

"So what? The NG-RPEB doesn't care about those slums, John! *Some people believe that New Society wants to expand, and will absorb ground at any cost.*"

"*Ho-LEE,* that's a far-fetched conspiracy, but if that's the case, why don't they just gas the entirety of Old Society and be done with it? Then *everyone* can have a backyard swimming pool and, you know, their own personal ice cream parlour! Am I right?!" Clifford turns to the studio crowd and waves his hands encouragingly. The audience cheers in response. Moreau stares in disbelief.

"Surely you can't be serious!" he splutters. "There's *no way* they could get away with that! There's no plausible deniability! With something this small, the public can be easily convinced, but it's impossible that anybody would believe that the ventilation system would conveniently fail in all of Old Society, while New Society just so happens to be spared."

"But if New Society really doesn't care about Old Society, then there would be nobody left to protest! The opposition will have been wiped out!" shouts Clifford dramatically, evidently enjoying the attention of the crowd.

Moreau speaks as if Clifford is the only person listening, and his voice is quiet and intense.

"John, you know as well as I do that we're talking in generalities. These decisions aren't in the hands of the People, they're up to the policy-makers, who comprise a very small percentage of the population! The citizens in New Society are for the most part *good people* with families, and a strong moral code. Do you really think that if we just decided to gas *millions* of people, that there wouldn't be some sort of civil repercussion?" Moreau leans forward in his seat, his eyes wide. Clifford sneers, rolling his eyes.

"*Pfffft.* Of course! But look at what's happening now! *Evidently*, this incident is causing civil unrest and cynicism, despite the plausible deniability you yourself attributed to the scenario. But *so what??* The truth is, those in power enforce the law! What are the People going to do, rise up with pitchforks and torches?" He laughs nastily.

"Well you never know, John... it wouldn't be the first time." says Moreau quietly.

Pollox switches off the television and numbly shuffles to the vending machine for a bottle of synth whiskey.

He wakes up with a pounding headache. His mouth feels like cotton and tastes like feces. He's lying on the couch, fully clothed. The room is spinning. He lurches to a sitting position. The clock has triplicated and is gyrating around itself. He squints. *07:42.* Shit. He's almost ¼ of an hour late for work. He notices in a detached manner that this bombshell just doesn't instil in him the same panic it normally would.

He has a cold shower to clear his gyrating head, then stands naked in the bathroom shivering, trying to maintain his balance enough to towel off. He slowly clambers into his uniform, knots his tie, and, despite his pounding headache, polishes his boots and the medals on his jacket, until they gleam. Some habits never die. Now he stumbles through the dark room, into the kitchenette, and fumbles with the kettle.

As the coffee is brewing, the clock, which has ceased its mischief, beeps *08:00.* The television turns on automatically, and the only time it does that is in situations of mandatory public address. Sure enough, the screen resolves showing the stern, robust figure of R. Janus, chairmen of the NG-RPEB Board of Trustees. He is wearing a dark grey suit which gives off a reflective sheen at the folds, and a crimson red silk tie. The flag of New Genesis, a golden phoenix shown ringed in flame on a blue background, is visible behind him.

"My dear friends," he begins as usual, "I am sorry to interrupt your morning programs, but I have important news regarding the tragedy that occurred only two days ago in districts 600-607. I consider myself the voice of the People, and you, the citizens of this fine city, have expressed doubts about how this horrific misfortune came to pass.

"I have been deeply moved by these concerns, and have not slept in two days: I had the case reopened and have *personally* been working around the clock with investigators to probe further into the incident. We have concluded our investigation, and it is my great shame to announce that we have discovered proof incriminating our own Commander Marxus Pollox of the NG-RPEB."

A picture of Pollox flashes on the screen. He drops his coffee cup, which shatters all over the floor. He can only stare at the glowing rectangle.

"Evidence has come to light that Pollox entered into an agreement with a real estate developer to expand the territory of New Society in order to gain a cut of revenue made on property sales. Emails and documents have been found confirming this arrangement. These emails also revealed Pollox's plans to intentionally poison the relevant districts in order to render them vacant and viable for appropriation. Finally, it appears the fatal order was authorized by Pollox himself on the day prior to the incident." A document is flashed on screen which bears Pollox's name and signature. Pollox vaguely recognizes this as the order drafted by Granger.

Janus clasps his hands together on his desk, and lowers his head for a moment of solemn silence. When he looks up again, his expression is one of deep sorrow.

"This is a heavy blow to New Genesis, and to the NG-RPEB. Pollox was new to the position, and he should have been screened more thoroughly. I am deeply ashamed to admit I have let *you* down, the good people of New Genesis..." Janus lowers his gaze and sighs heavily, his shoulders slumping. After a moment, he straightens up and directs his piercing gaze into the camera once again.

"However, I am a man of the People, and I promise you that Pollox will be found, and put to justice. This atrocious crime against humanity will not go unpunished. I think of each and every one of you as my *friend*, and I can't allow someone to treat my friends like this! There will be retribution! I ask for your grace, and I sincerely hope we at the Board of Trustees can again regain the trust of the citizens of New Genesis. Thank you."

The television once again goes black. Pollox is reeling with vertigo; there is a high-pressure ringing in his ears. The floor is littered with jagged shards of porcelain. The percolator bubbles away unheeded.

He reaches numbly for the medals on his jacket to try to rip them off. They won't give. They're stuck; the embroidering is sound; he is weak.

His eyes are glassy; he feels hollow.

What does a person do, when they realize their own absurdity?

The transport van is dark. There are no windows. The only light oozes weakly from two luminescent strips running the length of the cell: a heavy wash of deep blue. Commander Marxus Pollox is crammed shoulder-to-shoulder with a dozen other faceless wretches. The vehicle shudders and vibrates as it rumbles over the dark desert sand.

After a long time listening to sniffles, coughing, wheezing, farting, and the countless other reverberations and loathsome stink which manifests when many humans share the same dank space, the transport vehicle slows to a stop. The rear doors open with a creak, flooding the interior with light.

"Welcome to Omega!" says a young woman from within the white glow. "My name is Jade. This is the start of a new life, a new beginning!" Her words are upbeat, but her voice is cracked and strained.

Omega. Home of the resistance group The *Omega Faction,* who, for the last seven years, have been infiltrating New Genesis and intercepting OS citizens from the RP lists. Officially, they're terrorists. Unofficially, Janus considers them as doing him a favour: they're helping him clear his city of the vermin he desires so badly to exterminate.

As soon as Pollox saw the public address, he knew he was a wanted man. In fact, if it were not for his drunken oversleeping, he would have been apprehended at HQ a half hour before the address was broadcasted, which was evidently the intent.

Realizing this, he immediately changed into civilian clothes, threw some bare travel supplies into a bag, and high-tailed it into Old Society. He knew that he would not be recognized out of uniform.

He used an old public audiophone terminal to ring a New Society bytehead hacker who owed him a favour, and was known to have OF ties. The hacker used an encrypted frequency to put him in contact with a woman named Jade, the founder of Omega Faction. He requested political asylum under a falsified name. After two days of hiding out in an OS hotel, Pollox was picked up in the dead of night by an OF extraction squad.

Pollox climbs out of the van. His back aches so badly he can barely stand. He is given a change of clothes, a protein bar, and a bottle of water. *Please go to Tent 86. This is only temporary, you will be transferred to permanent residency as soon as one becomes available!*

He allows himself to be carried along by the crowd, into a large canvas tent. It's been divided off into small squares about as wide as he is tall. Makeshift walls have been created using blankets hung from strings. Shadows dance within them. Men, women, children. Several people are crying, weeping in exhausted despair. Not many of them are children.

He sighs raggedly, and looks around at his fellow refugees. Their lives are gutted and ruined, and have fallen to rubble, just like his. Their faces are empty and dilapidated; Pollox can see himself reflected within their dark, sunken eye sockets.

[2018]

The Omega Faction

(*3009 A.D.*)

The walls were shrinking by the second. It was dark; there were no windows. The only light oozed weakly from two luminescent strips running the length of the cell. It was a heavy wash of deep red. Images of violence pressurized within her skull, bursting forth in an anguished sob, a terrified wail. It was too loud; it hurt her ears. She was hyperventilating; she couldn't breathe.

She curled up on the floor and cried. She knew about the RePurposing plant, but until now, it was merely an interesting bit of trivia, an idle threat parents used to coerce unruly children into submission. She never thought it could actually happen to her.

But it wasn't like the whispered stories told at sleepovers, where your future implodes down to that single moment when they kick in your door, screaming at you, proton rifles shoved in your face.

It wasn't like that at all.

Eirene awoke that morning to a shining, golden puddle of sunlight flooding through her bedroom window. It illuminated the card she had placed on her dresser, which read *Happy 18th Birthday, Daughter!* She smiled. Her dad was so dorky and awkward sometimes. She yawned and stretched, basking lazily in the warm, fuzzy remnants of sleep. Eventually, she sat up, rubbed the sleep out of her eyes, then padded to the bathroom in her bare feet and pajamas. She sang in the shower. As she was stepping out onto the soft bathmat, she heard a light tapping on the door. She smiled.

"Come in, Astraea," she said. The door opened and a little girl entered, turning around and closing it with both hands, as if she were pushing a large boulder. Astraea was 6 years old, with shimmering blonde ringlets cascading down over her shoulders and in her bright sapphire eyes. She was wearing cotton-candy-blue and -pink fleece pajamas which were slightly too big for her, so that only her fingertips peeked out of the sleeves, and her feet disappeared completely.

She stepped over and hugged her sister despite her still being wet, and Eirene laughed, looking down and brushing the child's hair out of her eyes. "What's up, baby?" she asked. She could barely make out Astraea's reply as the girl spoke directly into Eirene's bellybutton.

"I had a bad dream," she said in muffled syllables, only her eyes and nose visible as she peered up the undulating dunes of her sister's body.

Eirene wrapped a towel around her shoulders and sat down on the bathroom floor. Astraea happily scrambled into her lap.

"Another one? Like the others?"

Astraea nodded. "The dragon men," she whispered.

Eirene wrapped her arms around the girl and kissed her wispy golden hair, breathing her sweet musky scent. For months, almost every night, the child had woken up screaming. She dreamed about men like dragons who threw her into a deep black pit, to her death.

"It's just a dream, honey." Eirene said gently. "There are no bad men here. We live in a good neighbourhood, where that kind of thing doesn't happen." *Thank God for upper-middle class New Society status,* she thought. "Now, why don't you go get dressed, and I'll make you some breakfast, okay?" She kissed Astraea's soft, warm cheek, and the little girl nodded and whispered "Okay, Reiney..." before toddling off to her room.

Eirene was an only child until she was 12, when her mother died, just after Astraea was born. She had gotten sick, her father said. Throughout most of her life, Eirene was a solitary, melancholy child, without any good friends to speak of, preferring to be alone and read. Her father would sigh and shake his head. They never shared a close bond, so when Astraea came along, Eirene was delighted, and instantly assumed a maternal role. For the first five years of Astraea's life she slept with Eirene, curled up in the curve of her belly, like a kitten.

Eight months ago, when Astraea turned 6, their father decided that she should grow up a little, and forced them to have separate rooms. Astraea cried herself to sleep for weeks, and soon after, the nightmares began. Eirene would sneak into her sister's bed, and sing to her in whispers until she quieted, her breathing becoming smooth again.

As she dressed, Eirene felt the soft rays of the sun warm her skin, and imagined that, back before "The Great Nuclear Holocaust of WWIV", she just might have heard the twitter of *birds* and the chatter of *squirrels* in *trees* outside. She had read about all these things on *GenNet,* but had never seen any of them in "real life".

She found Astraea in her room, pulling lacy socks on, and together they walked downstairs, to the kitchen. She thought she would maybe make them eggs fried within little holes cut in toasted bread, before walking Astraea, then herself, to school. But when she entered the kitchen, a bewildering tableau lay before her. Sitting all around the table were armed, armoured military personnel, chatting convivially. One of them was drinking coffee from a cup she had painted many years before. It said:

"I LUv YU DADY"

in red lettering on white. In the midst of it all stood her father, in a plaid housecoat, laughing. That one image was instantly etched into her mind: *His head thrown back, his eyes squeezed shut. His teeth not quite white, his mouth a dark, gaping hole. Those red letters.*

The room fell to silence. Every head turned to stare at the two girls, who stared back. The floor felt cold on Eirene's bare feet. She curled her toes. Then, the man drinking the coffee carefully placed the mug upon the counter, then walked casually across the room and laid a heavy hand on Astraea's shoulder. The little girl shrank and tried to pull away, but was held firm. She cried out, her voice small and pitiful. Eirene tried to move to Astraea, but another soldier stepped in between them.

"Girls," father said, "I have something to talk to you about."

The three of them sat in the living room, in three chairs arranged in a triangular formation, about a meter apart. Eirene noticed that soldiers were blocking the doorways. She shivered.

"Astraea, honey," Dad said in a honeyed voice to the child, who was scowling and rubbing her shoulder while glancing trepidatiously at the soldiers. "You know we live in a wonderful place, right?" She nodded. "Well, in order to keep it so wonderful, every person has to be productive – they have to do good things that help the city. That is because there is not enough food for everyone. The people who can't be productive have to help provide food for the other people. It is the most wonderful thing anyone could do for New Genesis, and *you* get to do it *today!*" He grinned exuberantly.

"What d'you mean?" Astraea asked, scrunching her face up.

Eirene frowned, but said nothing.

"Well, sometimes people are broken, and so they can't –" Father began.

"She's not *broken!*" exclaimed Eirene. Father turned to her.

"Honey, just *listen.* As you know, children in New Genesis start school at age four, and by the end of their sixth year, it is expected that they at least knew the alphabet and several sight-words. Astraea's tests have indicated that she has what is known as dyslexia – she can't read letters properly, and sometimes they go upside down –"

"I *know* what it is."

"Well, that means that she may probably never be able to read properly, so she'll never be a truly productive member of society, and will only be a burden on New Genesis. Therefore, she is obliged to serve the state by RePurposing as a Subsection-G. It's hard for me too, but it's necessary!" Dad spread his hands and shrugged.

Eirene opened her mouth, but had no idea what to say. She had the bizarre feeling that her body was not her own, that she were just controlling it like a marionette, from a dark cave far away, deep inside. Her eyes drifted to the coffee stain on Father's robe.

"Honey, don't look so forlorn!" he said, bringing her back to attention. "Billions of people are able to eat, because of the selfless actions of a few! Besides, it is a service we must *all* perform eventually, myself included!" He nodded emphatically. 'We must show gratitude to the ones who have previously given their lives for ours, by willingly reciprocating!"

Eirene felt dizzy. *Was this a joke?!*

"She's just a little girl!" she whimpered, suddenly feeling very small. "Look, just take me, and leave her. As a trade."

Father looked chagrined. "But, honey…" he said, tightening the knot of his housecoat, "…you're going, too. I've designated you an RP_Sub-D."

Eirene's vision shifted subtly. Everything had a bizarre, unreal quality. It developed halos, turned dark and hazy around the edges. She could hear her blood pounding in her ears. Everything seemed sharper in the middle of her field of view, but hazy and dark off to the sides. It all looked like a cartoon.

"*For years you've been diseased with depression and anxiety*," her father's voice echoed distantly. "*The doctors say it probably won't get better. According to the rules, anyone with a chronic mental illness is designated a RePurposable Subsection-D.*"

Eirene couldn't breathe.

"*I love you*," father said, "*but we* all *have to make sacrifices. Today is a great day! Today you have the opportunity to serve mankind! Eirene, honey, you should be proud!*"

The trip in the transport vehicle was a hellish eternity of terror. *Where is Astraea?* The two of them had been separated and put in separate containment vehicles. *Are they taking her to the same place? What is going to happen?* Abruptly, the transport lurched to a stop. The doors swung open, and a bored-looking soldier encouraged her with a shock stick to exit the vehicle. He removed her gravcuffs.

"Over to that pen." He pointed in the direction of a massive iron door in a vast expanse of grey featureless wall. *The mulching factory.* She looked up the smooth face of the building and began to feel dizzy. Familiar sensations were returning: shortness of breath, pounding heart, sweaty palms.

"Move!" the soldier commanded irritably, shoving her from behind. She stumbled but kept her balance, and moved anxiously toward the door. Several other transport trucks were unloading people like her; they were all funnelling towards this door. She saw dozens of men and women of a wide range of ages, but one common thing about them was their clothing. They did not wear the standard issue grey coveralls of New Society, but a motley assortment of ragged garments typical of citizens of Old Society. In fact, she was the only NS citizen there. Most of the people appeared frightened and shocked, like her, but she saw one man struggling and protesting as he was dragged from the van. A soldier promptly thrust forward his shock stick, and the man shrieked before collapsing in a heap, and was dragged the rest of the way.

Eirene didn't really notice this, however. She was frantically looking in all directions, scouring the two dozen or so transport trucks and a few times as many people, looking for Astraea. She was nowhere in sight, and as the flow of people narrowed, Eirene's vision was occluded, and she was swept through the door.

Behind her, the door slammed shut with a ground-splitting explosion of sound which made her wince, and reverberated into infinity. The world disappeared; day became night. She abruptly felt dizzy; she couldn't breathe, her heart was pounding painfully. She broke out of the swarm of people and huddled on the floor, shaking.

"Shh, shh, shhhh, you're okay. Come over here. You're alright." a kind voice said to her. She looked up, startled. In the darkness, she saw only a shadow, but the voice sounded like it belonged to an old man. She allowed him to lead her across a vast, murkily lit room. It was some sort of a warehouse, with no furnishings of any sort on the smooth concrete floor. There were no beds or chairs, and the only amenity she could see was a row of metal toilets along one wall, without walls or dividers. One woman was self-consciously sitting on one of them, while a bare-chested man stood in front of her, holding wide his shirt as meagre cover. Eirene had an uneasy thought: this is only short-term holding. She won't need beds or human dignities where she's going.

The warehouse was full of people. Most clustered together in ragged groups, standing or sitting on the cold floor. Some lay with clothes bundled under their heads or over their eyes, trying to sleep. The perimeters of the room had the highest density of people, as this was the only way one could sit while leaning against something, or lie down against the wall for some bare sense of security. Many were weeping, while others stared coldly into infinity, or sat silently holding their heads in their hands. Most appeared exhausted and were filthy, and Eirene wondered if they had actually been here for some time, or if they arrived in such a state.

She saw dozens of children. Several were crying. Many clung helplessly to their parents, but a great number huddled in groups of two or three, evidently alone. She anxiously scoured their faces for Astraea, but she was not among them.

"We're – we're just over this way," said the small man who had taken hold of her hand. He was very thin, and had soft white hair and beard stubble. Every so often, his face contorted with a grimace and he gritted his teeth, his lips twisting, and he regularly twitched his head and emitted a strange sound.

The man noticed Eirene watching him. He hung his head. "I – I have – I'm a Sub-D."

"*...Me too.*" the young woman whispered.

The man guided her to a group of older adults. He said something to one of the women, who approached Eirene, smiling gently.

"Hello. My name is Marcy. That is Angus, whom you just met, and these are Katherine, Emmanuel, Suzy, and Franklin." She motioned to the others in the group: a shabby, ugly bunch, looking more dead than alive.

Eirene had lived her whole life in the New Society districts, where life was generally the same every day. Comfortable, safe. Most people were fairly healthy, if not somewhat overweight. New Genesis officially had food restrictions, but, in practice, that only seemed to be applied to the Old Society districts where food supply trucks were few and far between, and fights often broke out at supermarkets.

Eirene was not accustomed to seeing the vulgar, dismal, revolting people of Old Society. It was something she had always pointedly avoided. Why would she want to intentionally surround herself in an environment of filth and slovenly self-decay like the lower classes? Yet, now, her own father had discarded her into an OS dung heap, and these people... were caring for her. Her cheeks and neck began to feel hot.

"I have to go find my sister!" she protested.

"Oh, I'm very sorry; I understand! May I help? What does she look like?"

"Six years old, blonde curly hair, wearing pink leggings, lacy socks, a blue and red superhero shirt, and bright red shoes!" Eirene whimpered. "Her name is Astraea."

"Well, let's go see if we can find her," Marcy said in gentle tones, still smiling reassuringly.

Eirene lay on the floor at the back corner of the pen, alone. She had been there for hours. Her throat was dry; she hadn't had anything to eat or drink since last night, when she sat down to dinner with Astraea and her father. They had spaghetti and meatballs; it seemed like so long ago...

She stared at a single lamp far away on the ceiling. She had felt darkness before, but this was so much worse.

Why do they leave us to wait here? Why don't they just get it over with? Waiting for the guillotine is worse than the final blow.

She closed her eyes, letting the heavy blanket of apathy smother her, but in the scarlet void she saw Astraea reaching out to her, tiny in the huge hands of a faceless soldier. She saw her father, his blue plaid housecoat, his fuzzy flip-flop slippers, those off-white teeth, his eyes crushed shut, laughing as if he had just heard the funniest joke in the universe.

Eirene opened her eyes. She gritted her teeth and stared at the bright light above her, willing herself into a state of defiant indifference, but despite her best efforts, her vision fractured into a jagged, radial effusion of light, smeared details growing less distinct, until her eyes overflowed and her body was wracked with deep sobs which provoked a violent fit of ragged coughing which shredded her dry throat. After a while, it all subsided. Anguish melted into numbness, and the indifference she had been searching for coated her like a thick slime.

A voice abruptly brought Eirene back to herself. "You ok?" it asked. She turned to see a girl sitting beside her. She was thin and pale, wearing a faded turquoise floral print dress, and looked to be around 15 years old.

Eirene did not answer. Instead, she pulled her legs up to her chest and wrapped her arms around her knees. *How could I possibly be okay?!* She thought.

"I've made a little club of children," said Melody. "Every time I see another child arrive alone, I ask if they want to join. They've all been torn from their families…" She looked forlorn.

"How long have you been here?" Eirene's voice was barely a whisper. Her throat felt like sandpaper.

"Oh… about two or three weeks…" Melody murmured, shrugging apathetically. "I don't have a way to keep track… I don't know when we're supposed to go to the… umm… or why we're waiting. It's torture, honestly…"

"Look, have you seen a little girl named Astraea?" interrupted Eirene, and described the child.

Melody thought for a moment. "No, I'm sorry… is she your sister?" Eirene looked at the floor and nodded. "I'm *really, really* sorry…" Melody whispered, hesitantly placing her hand on Eirene's shoulder.

Eirene didn't respond immediately to Melody's offer. Instead, she laid listlessly on the bench, allowing time to pass by in a daze. However, eventually, she decided that she *should* help the other children here. Like Astraea, they were probably terrified and lonely. So, she wandered over to where Melody and the group of children were huddled, and quietly sat down. Melody smiled and introduced her to the timid children. Over the next couple of days, Eirene sang to them and played with them and hugged them when they cried, and tried to ignore the fact that every one of them reminded her of Astraea.

One girl was named Annabelle. She was 5 years old and wore a faux-satin purple dress with yellow trim. Her hair and eyes were chestnut brown. She alternately clung to both Eirene and Melody, and constantly asked when she'd be able to go home to her mommy and daddy. Eirene felt a sense of purpose and comfort in consoling the child. In the same way that Annabelle declared that Eirene was her temporary mommy, so too, was she Eirene's temporary little sister. Of course, this did not prevent Eirene from scouring the warehouse several times a day for a child with golden curls and a red and blue superhero T-shirt... without success.

The abducted children were distressing enough, but on top of that, Eirene saw countless parents whose own children had been forcefully removed to... *somewhere* else. They yelled, raged, pleaded, and cried, beseeching and begging the impassive NG-RPEB guards to be reunited with their children, or even for mere *information* about their children's wellbeing. In most cases, they were simply ignored, or were told that the requested information was not available. In several cases of fathers becoming irate and even violent, they were either tazed, or were implicitly or explicitly threatened with physical or sexual abuse of their children or spouses. In every one of these cases, the men would immediately capitulate. One man crumpled to the floor while hiding his helpless tears behind his hands.

Eirene soon found she couldn't watch these exchanges. It was just too much for her to handle. She had to ignore them.

At some point, she found her way back to the initial group who had initiated her into the pen. She thanked them for reaching out to her. Then, they shared with each other why they had been designated RePurposables.

Angus had Tourette's. Suzy was 52, with the mental age of a seven year old. Emanuel was convicted for the murder of a New Society prom queen. He swore he didn't do it, that he was framed. Katherine had cerebral palsy. Franklin had schizophrenia. Marcy was a successful OS counsellor, with hundreds of patients, but someone found out she had Asperger's, and there she was.

Here we all are. Totally expendable.

The thought plagued her until she drifted into a disturbed, fitful sleep.

On the fourth day, Eirene was sitting with a group of young girls (they never went around alone anymore), preparing a salad of sorts, sorting through rotten lettuce and yellow peppers upon which large sections had turned brown and slimy. She did her best to salvage the good bits and discard the rest, but it always seemed that after all the rot, there really wasn't much of anything left. She sighed.

"...'Reiney?" a tiny, weary voice, barely a whisper, resounded from behind her. She froze, her breath catching in her throat. Her heart skipped a beat, then started pounding. She twisted around. Behind her stood Astraea, looking pitiful and exhausted. Her face and arms were filthy, her clothes stained and torn, and both her shoes and one sock were missing.

Both girls erupted into heavy sobs. Eirene pounced on Astraea, pulling her into a massive embrace. Astraea collapsed into her arms, holding so tightly around her big sister's neck that Eirene couldn't breathe. The warmth of Astraea's little body against hers felt a million times better than a hot shower on a cold day. She whispered comforting words into the child's ear, rocking her back and forth, her eyes closed. She could still hardly breathe, but now it was for the shock of relief. She was crying silently, her tears wetting the face of the smaller girl, washing some of the dirt away.

"Are you okay? What happened to you?" she asked.

The little girl hiccupped and wiped her snotty nose on the back of her hand. Then she wiped the back of her hand on Eirene's shirt, and hiccupped again. That brought fresh tears to Eirene's eyes, but this time, they were tears of joy and laughter.

"You're awesome, Astraea. Here. Blow."

She lifted the hem of her shirt to the girl's tiny button nose. Astraea blew hard. "Again." When she had finished, the little child curled up in her big sister's lap, rested her cheek and a hand on Eirene's soft breasts, and simply lay there, her breath nearly silent, her chest moving like gentle waves on a calm sea.

After a while, she told Eirene her story. She had been taken in a big car that was real dark inside and red and real scary, then some men made her go into a big room like this one and she didn't know anybody and she felt sad. She tried to make friends with some other kids, but they were mean to her and pushed her down and sat on her and shoved her face into the floor and spitted on her. They wouldn't leave her alone for forever and kept hurting her when she was tryna sleep, by pulling her hair and pinching her. One time one of the kids stole her shoes and didn't give them back and she cried a whole lot. She was real hungry all the time because most of the other kids wouldn't let her have any of the food, except for a nice boy named Marvin and a nice girl named Lucy, who had real pretty green ribbons in her hair, and can she get some ribbons too maybe someday? Blue ones, or maybe yellow? Anyway, she was scared of mosta the kids but the adults even more. But then today, mosta the people in the room were brung somewhere, and the ones that were left were brung into here and then she saw her big sister and was super happy.

"I missed your boobies cuz they're like real soft warm marshmallow pillows." She said, giggling and snuggling her nose between Eirene's breasts. Then her tummy growled menacingly and she squirmed.

Eirene smiled sadly and ruffled the girl's hair. A flood of relief washed over her, and she held her sister even tighter.

For the next nine days, Eirene was inseparable from the children. Most of them were very young, and terrified, and spent much of the time crying or curled up in silence. Melody and Eirene attempted to distract them with games and lessons, and when they got tired (there was no difference between day and night in the pen) the two young women bundled them all together and cuddled them to sleep, singing songs and telling stories. It was at those moments the kids sometimes smiled and laughed, and forgot where they were and what had been done to them. The warmth and closeness of bodies, of people who need each other: it was something Eirene had never experienced ever before, except for with Astraea.

If we suffer, we are the same.

Several days later, Eirene, Melody, and some 300 other RP's were standing in a line up, at the top of one of the belt shafts. They were waiting for their turn on the final carnival ride to oblivion.

Eirene didn't know where Astraea or any of the other girls were. They had all been separated. Only by luck was she able to find Melody in the crowd, and cling to her. They were standing single-file, and a soldier was travelling down the row, handing each person a small pill.

"This is a medicine that will make you feel relaxed as you travel on your final journey to benefit glorious New Genesis it is a great day all of humanity is indebted to you." He droned listlessly at them..

Eirene watched as her cellmates glumly swallowed the pill and went back to staring inconsolably at the ground. *I can't take that pill. I need to keep alert. I need to find Astraea! I need to get out of here!* she thought. The soldier drew near. Two people away, a commotion ensued. A man was refusing to take the pill. He was yelling about fascism and murder and bastards. Another soldier stepped in, and they began to physically force the pill down his throat. The man was struggling and grabbing onto the soldier nearest the two girls, pulling his shirt out from the beltline.

Eirene had an idea. Amidst the chaos, she reached out and grabbed the soldier's gravcuffs and control fob from his belt, and stuffed them down the front of her shorts. At the same time, she began shouting as loud as she could at the objecting man.

"You *traitor!*" she screamed. "After all New Genesis has done for you, *this* is how you repay us?! You are defiling this great honour! I have been waiting for this moment my *whole life!* I don't even *want* to be tranquilized! I desire to experience every exquisite moment up until the *last instant!*"

She fiercely jabbed her elbow into Melody's ribs; who, although bewildered, took up a similar tirade, yelling and shaking her fist in a dramatic show of indignation. The struggling man was no longer struggling after a jolt with a shock stick, and the soldiers shoved the little yellow pill to the back of his throat and held his mouth and nose closed until he swallowed it.

The soldier continued down the line. When he arrived at the two girls, an unusual sight greeted his eyes. Together they stood at attention, sombre, tall and proud, boasting the greatness of the moment and sticking out their chests.

"Please, sir, we want to be fully sensate as we serve New Genesis." Eirene's gaze was levelled far away, at the horizon. "It is our great honour to experience *everything.*"

After a bemused moment, the soldier shrugged. "It's your funeral." he muttered, and moved onto the next person, who was looking at the two girls as if they were lunatics, even as he swallowed his pill.

They were loaded onto the belts, into hard plastic chairs with restraining bars which swung down, pinning them to their seats. The belt slowly moved down the incline, and they began to descend into darkness.

"What are we doing?" Melody hissed. "I wish I took the pill! I don't want to..." her voice trailed off as she stared into her lap, wringing her hands anxiously.

"Look, we're finding my sister and we're getting out of here, alright? I just have to find a way." Eirene strove with all her strength to lift the restraining bar, but it was locked in tight. Sucking in her stomach, she wriggled up in the seat, and back and forth. The bar ground painfully against her hips, but, eventually, she was able to slip free. Melody was much thinner, and followed her example easily.

"Okay, uh, now we... *Marcy!!*" she exclaimed, as she saw, several seats behind her, the kindly woman she had met the first night. Hopping from seat to seat, she clambered back to the doctor and beseeched her urgently to try to free herself the way they had.

Marcy merely looked at her with half-closed eyes and shrugged. "Don't worry! It's just a nice ride!!" she said, beaming stupidly.

Eirene tried several more times to rouse the woman, all in vain, before making her way back to Melody, who was waiting in quiet panic.

Eirene looked around her. The floor of the shaft on either side of the belts angled steeply downward. It was dangerously smooth. Anyone who stepped on that would end up in the pits faster than if they stayed on the belts.

"Okay, we can't go on the slope, we'll have to jump over the people." Together they tried to clamber over the chairs, looking frantically for a little girl with blonde, curly hair, but suddenly, Eirene's foot slipped into the gigantic chain below, getting caught in one of the links. She struggled desperately, to no avail. Melody was curled up in the lap of an old woman, whimpering. She was looking ahead of them.

The yawning mouth of the pit approached. One by one the chairs swing under the belt, ejecting their occupants and folding to begin the long return upwards.

From her crablike position between the seats, one foot stuck in the chain, Eirene shouted at Melody, "Take my hand!" The girl reached out to her, shrieking as the seat folded under, the restraining bar lifted, and the woman she was sitting on dropped headlong into the deep chasm. As she fell, her weight forcibly dislodged Eirene's foot from the chain, just as it began to disappear under the belt. She felt as if her ankle had been broken.

The two girls plummeted, screaming, into the pit. To their surprise, their landing was soft, cushioned by a rainbow-coloured pile of live bodies. That human pool was slowly funnelling down to a hole in the center of the pit, where it cascaded over the edge, flowing down into the mulching machine below.

The girls tried to run up the pile, but there was nowhere to go. The pit was 500m in diameter, and the vertical sides were of smooth alloy. There was no way out. With each second, they were slipping ever closer to the hole. Eirene looked frantically around. *Where is Astraea?* Her eyes scanned the motley ocean of RePurposables, looking for her golden hair, her red and blue shirt. *Nothing.* They were drifting closer and closer to the hole. When they were only a couple of meters away from the edge, she peered over the side. She could hear the crashing of the massive hydraulic plates of the mulcher, far below. A vile stench wafted upwards from within the bowels of the machine, carried upon a rising column of damp heat.

Through the cascading stream of bodies, Eirene suddenly saw something: a ladder. The hole the bodies were flowing through was actually a short vertical column descending a dozen meters or so, before evacuating into the mulching room. Tucked under the lip of one edge was a ladder extending down the column, interspersed with little hatches. *A maintenance shaft!*

She hesitated. She couldn't leave until she found Astraea! Desperately, she scanned the sea of bodies again, to no avail.

Perhaps she's not even here yet! Eirene thought. *Perhaps she's still in one of the pens, and I can find my way back and rescue her!*

She had to believe this was true; the hole was growing nearer.

Quickly, she explained the plan to Melody, who nodded but stayed frozen in place. After a rough shove, she clambered around to the other side of the hole, then up the pile a ways. Eirene climbed around to the other side and upwards, mentally preparing herself for the task ahead. Only a meter or so from the opening, she saw something that made her scream and lunge forward, but just as quickly, the moment was over; it was forever gone, and she forced herself to refocus on the task at hand. As she flowed over the edge, she reached down and, after a moment of blind fumbling, grabbed hold of a handgrip on the underside of the lip. Her body careened over, and she found herself dangling in midair with all her weight on one hand. Her fingers were slipping. She quickly swung her feet over, hooking them in the ladder, then locked her right elbow and knee into rungs of the ladder. With her free hand, she reached into her shorts where she hid the gravcuffs.

A gravcuff unit is a disc four centimeters in diameter which, on contact with electroconductive surfaces on each side of the disc (such as a person's wrists) creates a capacitive charge discrepancy which triggers a high-intensity localized gravity singularity, instantly binding the surfaces together with an attractive force of around 1000 times normal earth gravity.

Eirene already knew how to use gravcuffs. She was fortunate enough to have gotten to play around with them many times during the frequent educational initiation events sponsored by the NG-RPEB at New Society public schools from kindergarten through graduation. She activated the disc. A luminescent strip around its circumference shone blue. She touched one side of it to her wrist. It instantly stuck in place, and one half of the strip turned red. She braced herself just in time; a half second later an arm pierced the flow of bodies, reaching downwards, frantically waving, fingers outstretched. Eirene grabbed it just above the wrist. As Melody's skin contacted the exposed side of the gravcuffs the other half of the band turned red, at which point wild hellbeasts couldn't tear them asunder.

Melody's body did a flailing arc through the air and she cried out as she impacted the ladder below. When the girl was secure, Eirene pressed a button on the little handheld unit in her right hand. The red band of the gravcuffs went black, the disc fell down into her hand, and Melody regained possession of her arm.

They clambered down to one of the hatches and climbed inside. It was devilishly hot, and the noise of the crushing machines below reverberated, like rocks in a tin can, throughout the shaft. The only available light shone from individual luminescent orbs set into the top side of the shaft at intervals. It created eerie puddles of light outside of which matter ceased to exist, swallowed by total blackness.

Within one of these voids of oblivion, Eirene collapsed in a heap against the wall and wept. She wailed in anguish and enraged fury, punching the side of the shaft over and over again, creating irregular indentations smeared with blood. After a few minutes, she silently collected herself and began to move forward through the tunnel, silently followed by Melody.

After quite some time of crawling aimlessly, the shaft came to a five-way intersection. Two pathways extended to the left and right, two extended vertically, and were perpendicularly intersected by the shaft they were currently in, which terminated at the junction. Eirene wagered they had crawled through the pit floor all the way to one of the outer edges, and the lateral shafts would travel around the circumference of the circle. The lower vertical shaft would certainly travel downwards to the mulching room. Therefore, the only way to go was up, hopefully to freedom.

They climbed onto the ladder and began the ascent. But it was not so simple. After only 10 meters or so, the column abruptly ended, levelling off on a 90° angle. It travelled horizontally in the same direction they had been going, then twisted and turned several times, until Eirene was totally disoriented.

As they crawled onwards, knees sore and backs aching, drenched in sweat, the girls heard a roaring sound growing nearer. The shaft vibrated beneath them, and this sensation grew in intensity and volume. It sounded like a waterfall, but with an undercurrent of a deep rhythmic thrumming.

The shaft turned left, then terminated abruptly a few meters ahead, at a grate through which light was spilling. Upon reaching it, the girls discovered it was handled and hinged to swing outwards. On the wall beside the hatch, a sign shouted: *"WARNING: Do not enter ventilation shaft while turbines are active. Death or serious injury may occur."*

"Well, that seems like an appropriate invitation," Eirene said wryly. She swung the grate open, poked her head out of the shaft, and looked around. As she glanced down, a spell of vertigo nearly pitched her over the edge. She was protruding into a shaft about 25 meters squared, and at least 60 meters deep. At the bottom she could see massive spinning turbine blades flickering in the inky blackness. To one side of the hatchway, another ladder waited invitingly, extending upwards towards a little glowing square of white light some 125 meters above. An upward wind surged past the tiny shaft. It was hot and damp, and smelled vile, carrying the putrid stench of the Mound.

Eirene withdrew, trembling, and sat with her back against the wall.

"What do you think?" she asked Melody, who was sitting beside her. She was speaking about the turbine shaft, but Melody answered differently.

"I'm thinking about the children. In particular, Annabelle. She would look up at me with her big brown puppy dog eyes and tell me earnestly that, until she was allowed to go home to her family, I should be her mommy. And, when would she get to go home? And why had she been taken and brought here? What was going to happen?" Melody dropped her gaze to her feet, and heaved an anguished, ragged sigh, then looked back up to Eirene, her eyes brimming with tears, "And all I could say to all of this was *I don't know.* The biggest, bewildering, terrifying questions ever to dominate the poor girl's young mind... she looked up to me, and all I could say was *I don't know.* I failed her!"

Eirene spoke gently. "You're not a failure, Mel. You were there for every one of those children when they had nobody. You made that horrible place liveable."

Melody shook her head abjectly. Tears dropped into her lap. "I *am* a failure. Three dozen kids counted on me, and I let them all die."

Eirene was quiet for a moment, fingering the hem of her shirt, the little crusty patch where Astraea had blown her nose. When she spoke, her voice trembled.

"I... I saw my sister when we were in the pit..." she whispered. "She was drifting along with all the rest of them, conscious but heavily drugged, and when she saw me she smiled and reached her arms out. Her hands were so tiny... And then she went over the edge... and I couldn't move fast enough to catch her!" She dissolved into tears, crying silently, staring down at her hands.

Melody was quiet for a moment. She looked up, her eyes hard with resolution. "You ask me what I think? I think that there is no risk greater, no fate worse, than what we already deserve. So let's go." She crawled to the edge of the shaft, and stepped out onto the ladder, into the raging updraft. Wordlessly, Eirene followed her.

They climbed for what seemed like hours. The stench of the air pervaded them, nauseated them. They were saturated with sweat; it ran into their eyes and slicked their grip on the rungs of the ladder. The muscles of their limbs ached and burned. Yet, at last, the opening above them was close enough that they could see the blue of the sky. *The home stretch!* Eirene felt her heart quicken, her breath catch in her throat.

The rungs were dampened by Melody's palms, and perhaps, in her excitement, she stepped too hard on the next one, just onto a spot where her sweat-soaked grip had glistened the metal. Her foot slipped. She cried out and groped frantically for the rungs. But they simply slid from her fingers, and she fell, narrowly missing Eirene's face with her boots.

When she saw the slip, Eirene ducked forwards against the ladder. Now, as Melody fell past her, screaming and flailing incontinently, Eirene reached out and grabbed her by the front collar of her dress. Melody slammed into the ladder below, but didn't grab it. Instead, she panicked, clutching at Eirene's left arm with both hands. As Melody struggled, Eirene felt the dress slipping from her weary grasp, and as the fabric slipped through her fingers she grabbed the girl's forearm, but they were both tired, and their bare skin was slippery. Slowly, Melody slid down Eirene's arm, and neither of them could do a thing about it.

They locked eyes for one last desperate moment, the updraft whipping their clothes violently. Eirene saw fear and sadness in Melody's eyes, then, her friend's hands slid over her own, and she plummeted downwards into the dark, yawning shaft. The updraft of the turbine below caught her dress and billowed it out like a wingsuit, but that did not stop or slow her fall; it merely spun and cartwheeled her body end over end as she pitched deeper into the roaring, thrumming darkness.

With a cry of rage and frustration rolled into one giant sob, Eirene hung from the ladder limply. After a moment's breath, she turned and slowly dragged her way upward again.

At the top of the ladder, the deep shaft terminated in a massive grate, beside which was another hatch. She opened it, and looked out. She was sticking out of the top of one of the bubble domes, 900 meters above the ground. She squinted in the bright desert sun and climbed out onto the top of the dome. She flopped onto her back and stared up into the cloudless blue sky, utterly exhausted.

Now what? She had no time to even think about what had just happened. She needed to keep going, but she was stranded on the top of a giant dome. Of course it was out of the question to go back down inside. Perhaps she could slide down the outside of the dome, to the ground? No, the angle of the dome quickly became dangerously steep, at which point the orbital velocity would fling her off the slick glass surface and she would plummet to a sticky death about 200m below (which is the height of a 66 storey building). She shuddered at the thought.

She roasted in the desert sun, trying desperately to force her sluggish neurons to fire productively. She couldn't stay there much longer, in this heat. She had to get *somewhere.*

She perchance glanced at her hand, where it rested upon the dome. A crackling arc of static between her fingers and the glass surface.

The radshield! It creates an electroconductive surface!

Eirene fished out the gravcuffs, attached one side of the disc to one of her wrists, and placed the other on the glass. It immediately stuck fast. Then, she used the control device to dial down the strength of the gravity singularity, until she could shift it just slightly by pulling on it. She crept down the surface of the sphere until gravity began to force her into a slide. With one hand, she controlled the strength of the singularity as she slipped downwards, slowly at first, then more quickly, attempting to ski on the edges of her shoes, lifting her body up to avoid friction burn.

As the ground rushed up towards her, she dialled up the strength of the singularity once again, and gently alit on the ground. As far as her eye could see, the bubble-wrap array of the domes of New Genesis stretched into infinity. Behind her, the same infinity applied to dunes of yellow sand, the desert of the wasteland Outside. The heat of the midday sun caused the air to shimmer.

She suddenly felt very small. If she went back home she would be arrested immediately. There are no homeless people in New Society, due to enforced RePurposing, and trying to survive on her own in the chaos of Old Society would be a grim proposition. She had a better chance out there in the irradiated desert.

She started walking.

The sand was soft, and sinking into it made the trek wearisome. Three hours later, Eirene was in the middle of the desert surrounded by imminent death in the form of absolutely nothing but sand and sun.

She wearily dragged herself ever onwards, her limbs heavy, drained of every ounce of strength from the long ladder climb. After around five hours of walking, the radiation sickness began to kick in. She felt dizzy, and horribly nauseated. Every few minutes she stopped to wretch. Eventually, she collapsed in the sand, her breathing ragged, her body evidently trying its hardest to evert.

She had a tremendous headache, and her thoughts weren't making any sense. She closed her eyes and tried to still the spinning in her head, but it was to no avail, she collapsed headlong onto the blisteringly hot sand. It burned her cheek, but she wasn't paying attention. She was looking at all the tiny grains a few centimeters from her eyes. How strange it was that from a distance they all looked the same colour, but up close, they were all different colours. How they're all tiny pieces of huge rocks. How maybe that desert used to be a massive mountain range billions of years ago and it slowly eroded away. The shiny particles were apparently shell fragments from when the globe was mostly ocean, before the continents broke apart.

The light was rapidly fading; the blue sky beginning to turn grey. The temperature was dropping. Something nagged at her mind, but she couldn't place it. She lost consciousness.

Bartlomiej Maksymilian was 24 years old. His blonde hair, bleached white from the desert sun, burst in chaotic tangles from beneath a tattered Australian bushman hat. He was dressed in a full-bodied outfit of deep yellow synthetic material, complete with boots, cargo pants, utility belt, long-sleeved jacket, and gloves. A large pair of goggles covered the top half of his face. The rest was streaked with sweat and grime.

He was riding his nuclear-powered dirt bike along the crest of a dune, spraying sand behind him. He stopped for a mouthful of water from his canteen. With a gloved hand he wiped his lips. He squinted. A black dot in the distance caught his eye. He pulled the fission sniper rifle from his back and surveyed the horizon through its scope. He saw a strange sight. A dangerously underdressed female clambered atop a dune, then tumbled down the other side and lay still.

Max approached the girl curiously, killing the engine of the dirt bike and dismounting. He squatted down, his large boots with their knobby treads sinking into the sand next to her head. He reached out and turned the girl's face to him. She was unconscious. Cute, too. He scooped her up and sat her on the gas tank, allowing her to slouch forward across the handlebars.

He gunned the throttle, and headed home with his catch.

Eirene slept for two days, tossing and turning under sweat-soaked sheets, feverish from dehydration, heatstroke, and radiation poisoning. Every few hours someone came in and changed her IV drips, one which contained saline, electrolytes, and nutrients, and another containing a compound known as Prussian blue, which bound to radioactive isotopes in her body, allowing them to be excreted in her urine. Her sunburns were treated with a cooling salve.

It was in the late morning; Bartlomiej Maksymilian was outside cleaning his dirt bike, when he noticed the barefooted figure of Eirene stumbling unsteadily out of the medical clinic. Her head spun nauseatingly, and she clambered to a chair in the courtyard and slouched there, unmoving, staring through the ground.

"Feeling better?" Max asked.

The girl didn't move or answer immediately. She seemed to be lost somewhere beyond reality. Finally, she spoke in a weak, cracking voice.

"Where am I and what am I doing here?"

"You are in the encampment of Omega. I found you passed out in the desert"

"Oh." she said listlessly, without looking at him.

"I'm Bartlomiej Maksymilian." he said. She gave him a baleful, apathetic stare.

"You can call me Max, if you want. What's your name?"

"It doesn't matter. Thanks for rescuing me, Max, but I think I'd rather just go back to the desert."

Max looked cynical. "You're gonna die out there."

Eirene ignored him. She climbed from the chair and began to walk away, but nearly collided with a young woman approaching from behind her.

"Oh, it's you!" the woman exclaimed. "You're finally awake!"

Eirene stumbled, grasping the girl's shoulder for balance.

"My name's Athena. I was the one changing your IVs. I didn't know if you'd make it." She was 17, had blue eyes, and hair the colour of fresh straw.

Eirene turned and ran, weaving unsteadily and stumbling several times. She ducked into a secluded alleyway, and burst into choking sobs. That girl looked just like Astraea might have, if she had lived. Eirene's tears stung her eyes and blurred her vision.

*My only responsibility was to protect her! It should have been **me!***

And yet... it *hadn't* been her. She was still alive. Strong enough to escape the pit, the factory, the wastelands...

What now? Does she just go back out into the desert and die? Or does she live bleakly, without meaning, carrying out her existence as before, every day the same, until the end?

She sat in the cool shade of the alleyway for a long time, thinking.

Astraea, Melody, Annabelle, and all the rest: she *owed* it to them to do everything she could to prevent other children, other *people*, from being destroyed by the vast, stinking death machine at the heart of New Genesis! She must repay her debt of undeserved life, by saving the lives of others.

Eirene wiped her tears with her fists, opened her clear, green eyes, and took a deep, shuddering breath.

Max was sitting with Athena and an older man, at a round stone table, beside a phenomenal floating silver sphere in the center of town. At the approach of a shadow, they looked up. Eirene stood above them.

"You're back," Max said wryly. He gestured to his companions. "You've already met Athena, and this is Doctor Maksymilian, my father."

Dr. Max stood awkwardly. He had a few days of beard stubble and unbrushed hair. In fact, it appeared that his entire person had somehow gone unbrushed. Yet despite his just-awoken appearance, his eyes were bright and alert.

"Hello, I am Omega's head nuclear physicist," he said genially. "It is good to see you up and well."

"What are you doing to stop New Genesis?" Eirene blurted, her voice trembling.

Dr. Maksymilian looked perplexed, running a hand through his hair. An awkward silence ensued.

"I beg your pardon? Why do they need stopping? They *used* to come with their airships and shell us, but they couldn't penetrate our force field, and quit trying. We're no threat to them."

"Don't you *know* what they're doing?!" Eirene stammered. Father and son looked blankly at one another.

"No," replied Max, showing his palms and shrugging. "Why would we?"

As calmly as possible, Eirene told them what had happened, in excruciating detail.

"My sister was only *six!*" Her voice cracked, and fresh tears came to her eyes. "Dozens of other kids, too! Hundreds or thousands of other people! Every day!"

The other three listened in silence until it was clear Eirene was through.

"I..." Dr. Max began, then lapsed into silence, his mouth opening and closing like a fish. Finally, apologetically: "We haven't known what's been going on in New Genesis for centuries," he admitted, "They didn't do that when my Great Grandfather left to start Omega. It was bad, but not *that* bad... I... we... uh, well, maybe you would like to take some medicine to help you calm down? We can talk more... productively," he said delicately.

Eirene shouted hysterically. "No!! No fucking way! They gave us something to help us "calm down" before they *slaughtered us!!*" She burst into tears again.

Athena approached Eirene and gently placed her hands on her shoulders. "It's okay... This is just a mild sedative, a benzodiazepine to stop the panic attack so you can think clearly and rationally again."

Eirene gasped a choking breath and avoided looking into Athena's concerned blue eyes.

"No," she said. "I'll deal with it on my own."

Eirene was in the bathroom, staring at her own reflection in the mirror: her red hair and green eyes, her freckles. She tried to find the person who had looked back at her only a week or so ago, but she was gone. Staring from the glass was someone new. There was something haunting and frightening deep within those jade eyes. It gave her goosebumps, and she quickly turned and walked out.

"Hey, what's your name?" Athena asked, when she returned to the others.

She stared silently into the distance for a long moment.

"It's Jade." she said finally. *Eirene is dead.*

"Well, welcome, Jade, to our humble town." Dr. Max said politely.

Jade looked around at the people and buildings around her. "What is this place??"

"This is the colony of Omega. It was founded three generations ago by my Great Grandfather Tormond Maksymilian, to escape the political and economic corruption of New Genesis. Since then, it has been home to his descendants and those of about thirty-something other families who came with him at the time. We are a peaceful community of farmers and scientists, mostly. Our scientists are primarily geneticists, who have modified the seeds of many plants to grow in extremely poor conditions, as well as nuclear physicists who work to advance the field of anti-radiation and nuclear weapons technologies."

"The radiation! How can you avoid it without bubbles – domes?" Jade asked.

Dr. Max smiled. "New Genesis is a laughable anachronism, now. Do you know those bubbles are more than 400 years old? Antirad tech has changed a lot since then. Would you like to know how our anti-radiation shield/forcefield works?" Jade nodded.

He indicated upwards, to what appeared to be a modern art piece in the center of the colony. It was a gigantic sphere of smooth alloy, 20 meters in diameter. It floated, seemingly suspended by nothing, above a base of six interconnected hexaradial metal legs flush against the ground, each 1 meter wide by 6 meters long, tapering inwards at the end. These formed a peculiar sort of V-shape with the bottom side flat on the ground, and the top side curved upwards to mirror the shape of the floating silver sphere.

"This is our shield and power generator. Ironically, we are using volatile nuclear technology in order to protect ourselves from the failures of past uses of volatile nuclear technology." He chuckled.

"Look here." He indicated to Jade a circular perimeter denoted by a metal ring set into the ground. "This ring's only function is to remind us where the boundary is. Otherwise, it is very difficult to detect until you're upon it." He extended his hand into the thin air in front of them. Jade cried out in surprise. The air had become a solid wall in front of her. When touched, intricate patterning radiated outward in jagged, rainbow-coloured fractals, then faded back into invisibility.

"This is our dual forcefield/radshield. The forcefield is a result of some minor but successive modifications of the original prototype developed by Elwood Ralson way back in 1951. The radshield is our own design. It works upon the chemical principle whereupon unstable molecules such as radioactive isotopes will neutralize given excessive opportunity to decompose constituent molecules to properly fill their orbitals, and *POOF!!* No more radioactivity!" Max Senior grinned like a child.

Jade smiled politely.

Jade, the Maksymilians, and Athena were all gathered in the research center's cafeteria, eating a late lunch of spinach salad with walnuts and cranberries, with freshly sliced peaches. These tasted incredible to Jade. Back in New Genesis, they had fruits and vegetables, but they were tasteless and unappetizing.

"So, I think we should try to stop New Genesis..." Jade ventured, through a mouthful. The others exchanged glances.

"You're joking, yeah? We're farmers and scientists." scoffed Max. He refilled his cup of green tea.

"But some, like yourself, have combat experience!" Jade insisted with wide eyes. "And you have weapons, and technology!"

"Our weapons are few, and serve adequately the basic self-defense we train for, not some sort of militarized offensive," said Dr. Maksymilian. "And our technology is that of passive defense, and agriculture."

Jade was quiet for a moment. "Okay, so we don't have enough for assault. But I know New Genesis personally, so we could do, well, covert operations, where we rescue children and their families from being RePurposed!"

Max grimaced and shook his head. "This is moronic. It's fucking suicide to piss off New Genesis; their military is equipped with proton weaponry – have you seen what that does to living flesh?"

"But no one will see us! The soldiers don't bother patrolling Old Society, except for RePurposing. It's a microcosm. We could figure out how to breach the domes somewhere in OS at night, and be in and out quickly!"

"But you said the factory was in New Society," Athena interjected, pushing her empty plate away. "And it would most certainly be highly fortified."

"That's true," replied Jade, thinking quickly. "We couldn't rescue the people already in the factory. But we can intercept the NG-RPEB before they abduct people."

Dr. Maksymilian still looked skeptical. "Surely it is impossible to speculate accurately which citizens are likely to be targeted."

"You're right," admitted Jade. "And that is why we will need to pirate the RP lists." The three others looked blankly at her. "The RePurposing collections are targeted according to predetermined lists of citizens. I know a bytehead, a hacker – well, mostly just a computer nerd – but he hacked the NG-RPEB servers; I've seen the lists with my own eyes. They include all personal details relevant to finding the targets."

Jade looked beseechingly at the others, who exchanged wary glances.

"Jade," Max began, "It's just too much risk for the payoff –"

"You're willing to sit idly by while *innocent children* are *murdered?!*" Jade exploded. *"My LITTLE SISTER –"*

"Jesus Christ," muttered Max, rolling his eyes. Athena shot him a murderous look before turning to Jade.

"Okay, Jade, I understand," she gently interrupted. "And I'm really sorry that happened..." She looked to the others. "Look, maybe we can at least *see* if we can put a plan together? I can canvas for volunteers in our militia. It may be small, but I know of at least a dozen men and women who would gladly get behind rescuing children from being murdered."

"We can't sustain a major influx of people," Max protested loudly. "We're a small town!"

"Just a few!" Jade promised quickly. "Just until I've made it up to Astraea..."

"Oh, and how many people do you need to rescue to assuage your massive guilt complex? 10? 100? 1000? *Pfft.* You'll *never* –"

"Max, back the fuck off!" snapped Athena.

Dr. Maksymilian donned a thin smile, raising both hands disarmingly. "Guys, let's just cool it." He turned to Jade. "I'll have to run it by the council, but maybe we can draw up a plan," he conceded. "but we only go ahead with it if the calculated risk is low."

"Yes, of course!" gasped Jade, suddenly short of breath. Her heart was racing. "What should we call ourselves? *The Resistance?*"

"Oh, for fuck's sake," muttered Max. He roughly grabbed his dishes and stomped back into the building. Athena watched him leave, pursing her lips and shaking her head.

"How about *'The Omega Faction'?*" she suggested, turning back around.

"Awesome!" Jade breathed, her eyes alight. Dr. Maksymilian shrugged and flashed a thin, manufactured smile, then left the same way his son had gone.

"We'll figure something out, Jade," assured Athena, then walked away.

Eirene was alone.

Her heart was pounding; her palms were sweaty; she felt nauseated; she couldn't breathe. Yet, unlike usual, more familiar panic attacks, this feeling of terror was infused with excitement. Hope mixed with desperation.

Her terrible burden of guilt shift was still no lighter.

She must do *more!*

[2015 – 2018]

The Lamb

(2151 A.D.)

Molochai's arm stump is on fire, again.

Not literally, of course, but it feels like it: that burning feeling that happens if he falls asleep lying on it. He sits up with a groan and rotates his elbow stump from the shoulder, rubbing it with the other hand, trying to get the circulation back. Grimly, he wonders to himself why it is he has any circulation at all; at 62, he is a living, breathing, blood-pumping miracle. Most people these days don't live past 40 – that is, if they make it to adulthood at all.

Another pitiful noise escapes his lips as he hauls himself to his feet. He lights a lump of tallow-and-cloth, and shuffles through the scattered aluminum racks upon which some hangers still hang, perhaps, in some anthropomorphic world, still yearning for the day when they might be clothed again. But, that day will never come.

The old department store is nearly black inside. Only a few shafts of light stream in through the thick dust from the cracks in the plywood and other makeshift board-up material, and even this light seems sick and dying, like absolutely everything that remains now, or what's left of it. Long coat racks, circular shirt racks, neon pink sale posters exuberantly proclaiming savings, all are coated with a layer of dust and filth which has accumulated for decades.

Gritting his teeth, Molochai pries loose one of the boards and peers out. Snow blankets the urban street outside, piled at least a meter high. A savage wind is tearing it up, lifting it meters in the air in white tornadoes and flurries. Beautiful and deadly. He has expected this, however. This is how it's been, ever since the metaphorical shit hit the fan, some 40-odd years ago – ever since the devastating nuclear holocaust and the resulting unending winter, and death.

Molochai replaces the board and hobbles back to his bed, which consists of several thick woollen blankets, and one of his backpacks as a pillow. Slowly, wearily, he begins to pack up. He's been here for two days. It's time to go. Can't stay in one place too long. It's dangerous to get too comfortable. He's not alone.

Many people survived the nuclear blasts, but what life remained was barely liveable. Humankind necessarily regressed to a dog-eat-dog, brutalistic barbarism. It was inevitable: destroy an animal's natural habitat, freeze it, starve it and wound it, and its natural response will be one of savagery, a base instinct of survival.

When he has packed and loaded everything onto his back and sled, Molochai steps out the back door of the department store into a bleak alleyway deep in the heart of what used to be New York City. Overhead, the clouds in the sky boil crimson. Long-term exposure to radioactive compounds caused a bizarre alteration to the already mangled hydrologic system. Acid rain and radioactivity polluted and ate away at the earth and everything on it, exposing vast amounts of minerals and metals, which dissolved into the water, and was carried upwards, in the form of gaseous aerosols, into the ever-present clouds. The result was a sky permanently stained blood-red.

Molochai Abrams is a tired old man. His long, matted grey hair falls in tangles over his shoulders. An unkempt grey beard explodes from his lower face, giving him the appearance of being constantly electrocuted. In addition to his arm, he is missing several teeth and an eye; in its place is a ghastly black hole. He used to wear a patch, but he doesn't bother anymore. If anything, a frightening appearance really comes in handy. There are no such thing as friends anymore. He even doubts there are really all that many good people left at all. They're all mutants and looters, murderers and rapists and scavengers.

...Well, to be honest, *everyone* is a scavenger. They have to be if they want to live. And, to be fair, there *are* good people left. He's known some wonderful ones. They just seem to be dwindling so rapidly, however, in proportion to the bad.

With a sigh, he trudges forward. He isn't wearing shoes; his feet are wrapped in many layers of wool, bound with animal skins and strips of leather. His outfit is of a similar fashion, composed of scraps of old clothing augmented with hide or coverings made of other clothes or old blankets. In his pocket, he carries a worn brass compass with a cracked glass face.

Rounding a corner, he emerges out onto what used to be Times Square. At one time, long ago, these buildings used to be alive with neon lights, electronic billboards advertising Revlon, Sony, Victoria's Secret, Virgin Mobile – all of life's urgent necessities, featuring smooth models with perfect teeth looming several stories high, guaranteeing a better life for whoever bought whatever shit they were selling.

Now, everything is dark and lifeless. Jagged glass still protrudes from the edges of the old screens. Exploded circuitry hangs high in the air, suspended by dead wires. He looks up at the tall skyscrapers. They stand silent and ominous. Their windows are blown out black holes, seeming to suck the life out of anything which draws near. There are few plants or trees. No birds. Almost no arthropods. Some arachnids. No cephalopods, cnidarians, or molluscs. Only a few species of highly mutated reptiles. Some mammals, other than humans. Doubtless still protists, bacteria, and viruses.

But they have all been devoured, destroyed, or transmogrified to some degree – at least in New York state, which used to be a massive metropolis and a major commerce center for the United Continents of America, before WWIV, which truly was the war to end all wars.

In the early 22nd century, global politics had reached a supercharged state of tension and rivalry. After World War III, the United States of America took advantage of the weakened state of the globe, to expand its borders. In a massive conquest, it overran the entire Western Hemisphere under the guise of "protectorates" and "liberators". These countries were doing poorly, they stated; their economies were on the verge of collapse; they faced a clear and present danger of being taken over internally by terrorist sleeper cells within their very borders. They needed a strong, independent force to take charge. So they did, albeit unilaterally, despite global outrage, and protests accusing them of violating every UN sanction in existence. Yet, no one did anything about it. Then, they took the entire continent of South America, and collectively renamed their newly expanded empire the United Continents of America. Still, the rest of the world waved a complacent, dismissive hand at them. Centuries passed, during which time, the UCA grew into a terrifying fascist state, cloaked under the illusion of democracy and the Newspeak concept of "Homeland Security." Then, in 2111, they finally set their sights on the Eastern continents.

The problem was, for the UCA, that they had very few independent resources. Most of their food and crude oil came from the East. They needed to control these resources, so they tried the same tactics as before.

You poor Eastern countries are in a bad way. Let us help you, they wheedled.

Hell no, was the response. The East was wise, and had been for centuries.

Then you're all terrorists, was the response of UCA, *and we will fight to free the citizens of your countries from your oppressive regime, unless you submit peacefully.*

No chance. Bring it on.

Have it your way.

In 2112, without even warning their own citizens, the UCA launched an offensive of hundreds of nuclear warheads from remote locations over the state, towards the East. This was anticipated, however. The countries of the East had already been conferring with each other, making unlikely allies. England shook hands with Iraq, Syria cooperated with France, Ireland with Afghanistan. China with Russia. They weren't friends by any means, but they had a common enemy. Even Switzerland had renounced its neutral status and had been waiting at the ready. They formed the Eastern

Alliance. Almost immediately, a counter strike was launched. Then the whole world literally went to hell.

With his gloved thumb, Molochai absently polishes the smooth brass back of the compass in his pocket, feeling the engraving there, almost rubbed out by time. He trudges on. He is so very hungry; he hasn't eaten in many days. There is very little to eat. Of the few species of animals left, the easily edible ones make themselves scarce, while the more challenging ones consider themselves the predators, and everything else the prey, including humans.

Usually Molochai gets by eating cockroaches and rabbits, two species which evidently retained their impressive reproductive capabilities even throughout the nuclear fallout, although they have experienced some interesting mutations. Usually, evolution takes millions of years, but the blast of atomic radiation affected a massive speciation event in the form of an overwhelming number of random mutations, and, as a result of the genetic drift brought on by the near-extinction-level event, natural selection worked fast and hard. In a period of merely 40 years, the cute, fuzzy rabbits and bunnies of Molochai's youth have become ghastly creatures. The size of large raccoons, these creatures have long, shaggy fur, an outcome of the selective pressures of the constant winter. Their characteristically long herbivore peg teeth have been replaced with the savage incisors, canines, and premolars of wolves and wolverines, and a taste for flesh in the absence of any remaining edible plant life. The rapidly hostile environment has selected for vicious claws around three centimeters long in fully-grown adults. The cockroaches are mostly similar to how they were before the Event, except they are now the size of an hefty loaf of bread, and their mandibles can remove a human finger as if it were made of soft cheese. Understandably, even these animals, among the more tame of those remaining, are difficult for many people to catch, especially Molochai, now that he is an old man with one eye, one arm, and a bad limp. He makes traps, but lately, he has had nothing to bait them with. Usually, he'll lure the rabbits with the cockroaches, but they're not cooperating at this time.

Every so often he'll come across some ammunition in a store or a home which has somehow escaped looters. He only ever finds a handful of bullets at one time, so he carries three bolt-action hunting rifles of different calibres, a .45 ACP revolver, and a 9mm handgun, with the hope that whatever ammo he may happen to find will fit one of these five weapons. They're old, worn down, rusted, heavy and cumbersome, and usually useless, but if the opportunity arises, it can mean the difference between life and death – an easy meal, or defense against enemies.

The old man's stomach growls irritably, reproaching him for even thinking of food. Shuffling slowly along the street, he suddenly stiffens, and flattens to a wall. Up ahead he can hear voices. Orange and yellow light dances on the walls of an alleyway. Someone is there, and they have fire.

Pressed with his back up to the cold stone wall, Molochai's heart jumps. He swallows, his throat dry. He never knows how to feel, when this happens. To meet other people is always a life-or-death situation. Does he risk it, or move on? Does he go in bluffing, with an empty pistol raised, or does he approach smiling and friendly, with his hands raised in truce, hoping he won't be shot in the face, or even worse, beaten to death?

He carefully peeks around the corner. Sitting around the fire are two men and a woman, looking to be in their mid-twenties. This means that they did not know a life before all of this vicious hell-on-earth. Survival is hard-wired into them. For Molochai, it is not innate – this puts him at yet a greater disadvantage.

He prepares to move on. He is badly outnumbered. Even a bluff would never work. He begins to walk away, but suddenly freezes in his tracks, as the delectable scent of roasted rabbit grabs him fully by the nostrils. His stomach groans and snarls so loudly he is afraid they may have heard. He grimaces and curses under his breath, shaking his head.

I must try! Do I have anything to trade?

He searches his possessions. A knife, a whetstone, some rope, his compass, some matches, a lump of tallow candle, a bit of fire starter, a little tub of lard he slowly sucks a fingertip of, when the hunger becomes too unbearable. Nothing really expendable. Not the knife or whetstone; that would be suicide. Likewise for the matches and fire starter. Maybe the candle? Definitely not the compass. Possibly the rope. The guns are too valuable in their *potential* use, despite their age and dilapidation. And there is no use trading a food substance for a food substance, particularly when his is awful and theirs is delicious. All things considered, however, Molochai really has nothing to lose, and everything to gain. There is no telling when he might find more food, and, admittedly, getting shot or beaten to death would be a much quicker and less painful retirement than starving.

First, he backtracks a short distance, and hides his sled containing his bedding, his guns, his matches, fire starter, and lard. The compass never leaves his person, but he does stuff it down into his underwear, behind his testicles. He does his best to cover his tracks, then, back at the entrance to the alleyway, he reaches into his pocket and pulls out a filthy rag which, at one point, was white. Keeping the vital parts of his body behind the wall, he calls out, "Young travellers!" and extends the handkerchief beyond the wall, waving it pitifully.

As expected, the group around the fire explodes into alarmed action. Molochai can hear rapid movement, the click of pistol hammers being drawn back. "Who is there?" one of the males says, his voice firm, but quiet. Naturally, he does not want to attract more strangers. "You, with the rag. Show yourself."

Molochai slowly rounds the corner, his hands raised high. He flashes a grin he hopes looks disarming, harmless, and pathetic. He attempts to mollify them, and allay their suspicions. "I am an old man, half blind, three quarters lame, freezing and starving. I do not desire a fight. Please, I would just like to share your fire."

"We're all freezing and starving, old man. Why should we care? Are you armed?"

"In a sense. I carry a short hunting knife which I use to skin and prepare animals and perform other necessary survival tasks. It is not intended as a weapon, only a tool. I carry a whetstone, some rope, and a bit of candle." He has stopped several meters away from the group and stands still, his hands raised.

"That's it?? Why do you have a candle without fire starting materials?"

"Alas, I used the last of my matches, but I hope to discover more, so I keep the candle. Please, I only want to share the warmth of the fire. It costs you nothing. May I approach?"

"Slowly. You will be searched. Make no quick movements and do not resist."

His companion searches the old man, removing the knife and whetstone, but leaving the other items. Molochai submits, under the watchful eye and ready pistol of the one who had spoken. He knew his knife would be confiscated. He could have hidden it, but in the case that something went wrong, it was more useful here, in his vicinity, where he might be able to retrieve it, than back there with everything else. If they are good people, they will return it to him. If not, he has very little chance anyway, even if he does manage to grab it.

He is invited with a dismissive motion to an overturned barrel near the fire. He limps slowly over to it and sits. The party of three remains across the fire from him. The young woman is about 19, and is huddled between the two men. The one who had done the talking is still brandishing the pistol. He seems to be the oldest. For several minutes, the four of them sit in silence, warming themselves, watching the crackling flame cough and crepitate, its licking yellow tongues craving the dead sky.

Above the flame, a flayed rabbit is impaled on a skewer. The younger man rotates it slowly. Molochai is nearly hysterical with hunger. He just stares, and would drool, if his mouth weren't so dry. He would eat snow, but it's unsafe before it's been boiled.

The gunman clearly follows Molochai's gaze. "I suppose you'll be wanting some of our food, then?" he says in an ambiguous tone.

Molochai is unsure of how to respond. *Is this an offering, or sarcasm?* He equivocates. "Well, uh, I can't imagine what reason you would have to share," he states politely.

"None whatsoever. Unless you have something to trade."

"Well, I have some rope, and a candle..."

"We've been through this already, and you have nothing we are interested in, except for this knife, which we already have... although I *was* planning on returning it when you leave *soon*." The emphasis is not lost on Molochai. He lowers his gaze, his stomach churning painfully.

He changes the subject. "So, what is your story? How do you come to be here?"

The man replies without looking at Molochai, spitting his words out with disdain. "This is our life. This is how we live. This is how we have always lived. Your question is stupid." After a moment's pause, he says in a voice only slightly less hostile, "I am Victor, this is my woman, Ophelia, and my brother, Francis."

"Ophelia! Shakespeare, eh? *'I shall obey, my lord!'*" Molochai says dramatically, executing an exaggerated bow. The cold, blank death within the eyes of the young woman instantly freezes and kills Molochai's smile. He shudders a little, and looks away into the darkness. It is obvious they have no idea what he is talking about.

"Ahem... never mind... My name is Molochai Abrams. I have lived since before the Event. I was about your age, when it all happened..." the old man begins to exposit.

Victor abruptly looks up at him with wide, intense eyes, a curled lip, and a hardened jaw. Molochai stops mid-sentence, his mouth hanging open.

He gets the picture. *Shut up or get lost. This isn't 'happy fun story time around the campfire'. This is survival. This is life.*

The morning was cold enough to condense his breath in the air, but the sky was a rich blue, the sun warm and golden, and the grass of Central Park green and luscious. A young, strong Molochai, recently turned 23, rode his bike along the pathway, weaving through the Sunday-morning early birds. He dodged silver-haired old ladies out for a casual stroll with rubber-tipped wooden canes, and he made a rather thorough inspection of a young woman in neon blue spandex who was jogging briskly. He coasted along behind her, admiring her superlative assets, until she turned and swore at him. He grinned and winked at her, pursing his lips together in a distal kiss, before slithering past her and continuing along his way.

Molochai was on his way to his girlfriend Amy's house, but he was obligated to stop for an anniversary present of some sort. He sort of forgot it was yesterday. *She's probably pissed. Oh well. What's the worst that can happen? Plenty of fish in the sea.*

He exited the park and pedaled into traffic, inciting a screech of brakes and a barrage of epithets as he weaved in and out and of thousands of yellow taxis and commercial transport vehicles. He surfed through a wave of pedestrians, then skidded to a stop in front of a florist's.

A few minutes later, a dozen long-stemmed red roses were protruding from his backpack, and he was back on his bike. Abruptly, while torquing up a hill, his chain broke, and he careened wildly out of control, colliding with a side of a passing truck and tumbling to the concrete. The roses scattered everywhere. The driver got out and began yelling at him, but Molochai wasn't paying attention. As he slowly climbed to his feet, he was staring at a television set in a store window, around which a growing crowd of people were gathered, chattering loudly. Molochai read the text scrolling in large print across the screen:

BREAKING NEWS – WARNING TO ALL CITIZENS – UNITED CONTINENTS OF AMERICA UNDER ATTACK BY EASTERN ALLIANCE. **NUCLEAR IMPACT IMMINENT**. ALL CITIZENS URGED RETREAT CALMLY TO UNDERGROUND SHELTERS OR BASEMENTS... **BREAKING NEWS –**

Molochai was shocked. *Certainly this is a hoax!* But no sooner had he thought it, a helicopter roared overhead, its downdraft scattering newspapers from a vendor's rack. Over loudspeaker, it began blasting the same message, interspersed with a frenetic wail of sirens between each repetition. Abruptly, the streets exploded into hysteria. Molochai was already running.

His knowledge of university physics told him that an intercontinental ballistic missile can travel seven kilometers per second. His knowledge of geography told him that it is around 5,500 kilometers across the North Atlantic Ocean from the UCA to the EA. His knowledge of how to operate a smartphone had just told him that this means he had an estimated 13 minutes until impact, but who knows how long has passed since launch? Molochai ran like hell.

His uncle's house was a 15 minute walk away. He had a deep bomb shelter from the 1950's cold war nuclear scare. But what about Amy? There was no time. All he could hope to do was save his own ass.

As he ran, he looked up into the blue sky and saw a white streak arcing downwards in the distance. He ran faster, shoving people aside to be trampled underfoot by thousands of panicking citizens. When the crowd became too dense, he switched to running and leaping atop the rows of now-abandoned cars choking the roads.

Suddenly, he saw a brilliant flash of light ahead of him, and a second later was hit by a deep concussive sound which rattled and shattered the glass in shop windows. A massive white mushroom cloud was billowing into the sky, with an angry bubbling fireball expanding outwards from the bottom at a phenomenal rate.

He dove wildly over his uncle's fence, hit the ground hard with his shoulder, sending shards of pain stabbing through his body. Ignoring the pain, he scrambled to his feet and flung open the door to the cellar, stumbled down three flights of stairs, opened the aerospace pressure-locked door, and slammed it behind him. A moment later, the lights flickered, then went out completely, as the earth shuddered violently above him.

"Uncle Jerry??" he whimpered into the inky blackness, the words choking in his throat. Beneath his ragged breathing and the blood pounding in his ears, there was total silence.

He was absolutely alone.

A fiercely agonizing hunger pang shocks through the old man's body, bringing him abruptly back to reality from faraway memories projected upon the muddy canvas of his inner eye. He winces and contorts, his abdominal muscles spasming painfully. He looks up to see the three strangers gnawing hungrily upon the bones of the rabbit, less than an arm's length from him.

Its scent torments him. It is too much. He can't stand it. Obviously they are not going to share. Willing his aching joints to obey, he pries himself off the barrel, forcing a smile and a courteous disposition.

"I thank you for your hospitality, young travellers, but now I must go! My knife, please."

Wordlessly, the younger brother hands Molochai his knife and whetstone, and he begins to limp slowly away. The cold of the day quickly grabs hold of him, stealing what meagre warmth he had gained. He fantasizes the travellers will call him back, invite him to stay, tell him they have changed their mind and offer him a little bit of rabbit in exchange for the fantastic story of his real-life experiences in a massive cataclysmic event which occurred long before their time, nevertheless shaping their lives completely.

But they don't. Food is too precious a resource to waste on the tall tales of a dying old man.

The last vestiges of fire-warmth shiver from his miserable core. He hobbles painfully back to his sled, and decides to bed down again. What reason is there to go out into the cold, brutal blackness? He would just kill himself all the sooner. He may as well relax, warm-ish in a blanket, rather than freezing in the snow.

Molochai lights his tallow-and-cloth candle, and takes a very old, very worn book from within his things. He lays down heavily, and sighs. His whole body sags. As he closes his eyes for just a moment, he regrets recalling his past. It is more productive *not* to remember, lest he become mired in depression and apathy. But the words on the yellowed paper of his novel are occluded by the oppressive images within his mind; he can't stop remembering. He retrieves the compass from his pants and clutches it furtively in his hands, his thumb rubbing ceaselessly over the engraving on the back which gleams a brilliant gold as the candlelight dances and sparkles upon its highly polished brass surface.

Many hours passed, while Molochai huddled beneath the earth in the blast shelter lit by the flickering light of an oil lantern.

What has happened to the world??

A horrified, morbid curiosity gripped him. He was compelled by the urge to ascend to the world above, to see for himself the true nature of things. He found an old army footlocker at the back of the shelter – it contained four bright yellow hazmat suits and four Geiger counters, as well as flashlights, batteries, glow sticks, a flare gun, an old revolver, and a box of 100 bullets.

He *had* to go out. He *needed* to know. He suited up.

The aerospace door opened with a hiss, and a massive wave of heat overwhelmed him. He crept up the concrete stairs to the gaping hole in the earth which used to be the cellar. He looked around. The sky was black; it was night. The house was gone. *Everything* was gone. Ash coated every surface. The landscape had been reduced to a wasteland of rubble and twisted metal. Massive sky-scraping office buildings had been completely stripped of all materials, even concrete. All that remained were mangled steel girders. Some were twisted almost into helices, others had been crumpled like paper. Fire raged *everywhere.* The only colours remaining were shades of yellow, orange, and red. He stood, dumbfounded, turning in circles amidst a wild jungle of flames. He was afraid the heat would melt the hazmat suit to his flesh. The Geiger counter was reporting so rapidly it sounded like a continuous buzz. He turned it off, and ventured forward into an expanse of death no longer even remotely resembling the suburban neighbourhood of mere hours ago.

All around him, vehicles were piled high, as if they had been lightly swept there. A van was lodged several stories up in the twisted wreckage of a building, its tires aflame and dripping molten rubber. He peered into the vehicles on the ground. Their interiors had ceased to exist, leaving only encrusted, blackened shells. Several of the newer cars not made of steel had literally melted into the ground.

Yet, this was not the worst. Oh, no. Above the roar of the flames, a constant wailing could be heard – thousands of human voices, screaming in agony and terror. Charred bodies littered the streets, recognizable only vaguely by their size and shape. Some of the more intact bodies were twisted into grotesque sculptures, their arms and legs stiff, reaching up and out at odd angles. He stopped above a huddled black form: an adult, curled into the foetal position. Tucked into its embrace was a tiny corpse, merely a lump of black ash. Molochai shuddered, and walked on.

As he wandered further from the blast location, the suffering increased – many had not died, unfortunately for them. Molochai saw humans – *people* – bald, completely naked but devoid of any distinguishable features, their skin a mottled texture of black and bright red, like the cooling surface of magma. He couldn't tell if he was looking at men or women: even their genitalia were consumed, completely burned off or hidden beneath a blackened crust of cooked flesh. He watched, horrified, as one of the still-living dead dragged itself pitifully through the ash. Many were writhing and convulsing, their skin burned so deeply he could see striated muscle tissue through the spider web of cracks in their charred skin, like the surface of a desiccated lake bed, but these fissures were bright red and raw, oozing blood and clear glistening plasma. Their faces were twisted into ghoulish caricatures, their lips melted from their faces, exposing their white teeth. They had no eyelids left, their eyeballs milky and blistered over.

They all were screaming with every cubic centimeter of their rapidly approaching last breath. A horrible, harmonious crescendo rose towards the lightless, Godless heavens. Molochai was drenched with sweat, and staggered forward, light-headed and nauseated. Looking around through his transparent visor, he saw an endless horizon of blackened, living, dying, shrieking bodies amidst a firestorm which reached its hungry, licking tongues and grasping fingers towards the eternal cosmos.

Truly, this is hell.

Abruptly, he vomited, the acrid, chunky liquid spraying the inside of his helmet and streaming down his torso, arms and legs, inside the hazmat suit, eventually pooling in his boots and the fingers of his gloves. He turn and ran blindly, gripped with an all-consuming terror, a desperate need to get back to the bomb shelter, to hide like a frail child quaking under his blankets, attempting to will away the terrifying monsters outside. He tripped over a corpse on the ground. Its head crumbled into powder as his boot swept cleanly through it.

An eternity later, he found himself back at the shelter. He didn't even know how – he had no way of orienting himself in this nightmare; he should have been lost forever, dead like the rest of them. Maybe he soon would be: he did not know how strong a concentration of radiation his hazmat suit was designed to stand. Regardless, he was as good as dead already. What – or who – was there to live for in this world, now?

Months passed while Molochai hid underground, afraid to venture outside into the haunting nightmare above. He ate canned food sparingly, drank bottled water even more sparingly, and played solitaire for hours on end, not even seeing the cards. He hated sleeping, and avoided it for as long as he could.

The moment he drifted off he was back outside, surrounded by immolating humans in a lake of fire. But, in his dreams, the barbecued corpses were still alive and in agony, or undead and crawling after him. He looked to their faces and saw Amy, his friends, his uncle, his parents. They all reached out to him. He couldn't move. They surrounded him from all sides, their crispy black flesh oozing carmine blood through its crusty surface. Their eyes were hollow, empty sockets, their mouths gaping black holes framed by lipless teeth, their noses merely hideous triangular holes in the centers of their faces.

They screamed ceaselessly, their jaws vibrating, spastic, their rasping, tormented voices growing ever louder the closer they came. Soon, their arms were intertwined around his throat. Their teeth were touching his ears and cheeks, quivering with the force of their agony. Their ghoulish wails rose to a violent crescendo; his eardrums burst with their horrible reverberations, blood flowing from his ears to stream in jagged rivulets down his throat. Their breath smelled like death and decay. Those empty, eyeless black pits were centimeters from his own, and he couldn't look away.

Then, he spontaneously combusted. He looked down at his body and saw roaring flames consuming his flesh. He lifted his hand in front of his eyes and watched as his skin blistered and bubbled, then burst with sprays of bloody pus, literally melting from his hand. The muscles and tendons were tightly interwoven around his bones, which soon were all that remained. He could hear a noise that terrified him to the depths of his soul: an agonized shrieking, louder than the rest. *It emanated from within him.* Then, he was outside himself, forced to watch as his eyes sunk into his skull, his lips pulled away from his teeth, and he became yet another blackened corpse.

Every night he woke up drenched in sweat, screaming hysterically. Early on, he urinated on himself or voided his bowels, vomited as soon as he woke, or came to with his face lying in a puddle of acrid bile and partially digested food. After a handful of these revolting experiences, from which he had only limited capability of cleaning himself, unless he was willing to waste a great deal of water, he somewhat solved the problem by eating and drinking very little, only after awakening. By the time he fell asleep he had nothing remaining to accidentally eject while sleeping.

He huddled in the tiny, stinking lair, breathing unventilated air ripe with the pungent, repugnant stench of his waste products, which he was, at first, too terrified to dispose of outside. They accumulated in bottles and buckets in the corner, but eventually, the reek of ammonia, stomach acid and feces made his eyes burn and his head reel. He coughed and gagged with increasing frequency, until he finally resigned to emptying the containers into the concrete corridor which extended between the door and the stairs to the world above. It soon formed a fetid swamp, but the lip of the doorjamb was raised nearly six inches, enough that the rancid filth did not rise high enough to leak into the shelter each time he unsealed it.

Molochai spent his waking moments yearning for psychological distraction. He liked the science fiction books lining the shelves on one of the walls. He could escape into them. He could laugh bitterly at the predictable irony of the post-apocalyptic plotlines. But after a time, he'd read them all twice or thrice over, and his anxiety could no longer be assuaged by them.

Perhaps a year had passed since the incident. He didn't know, but he knew he couldn't survive in the shelter forever. Food and water stores were dangerously low: he was down to a liter of water, a few cans of green beans, a jar of lard, and a bar of black, bitter, waxy chocolate.

He couldn't stay there. If he did, he would slowly die. If he didn't, he would probably also slowly die.

Death is life now. It is in everything. So, what is there to lose?

He gathered everything clean he still had, which was not much – some clothes, a few blankets, the water and food, a portable liquid purification device, a hunting knife and whetstone, the flare gun and the other materials in the footlocker. He also brought a couple of the other hazmat suits, in case something happened to the one he was wearing. The first one he had vomited in was laying long discarded in the corner, putrid and mouldy: he had not wasted water on cleaning it.

As it had before, the shelter door hissed open and Molochai apprehensively climbed the concrete steps. But this time, when he reached the surface, the world had changed yet again. The twisted metal structures of mangled buildings still remained. The desolate wasteland persisted. The Geiger counter still chattered frenetically, though the ticks were individually discernable now.

Everything was still dead.

Yet, now, it was quiet, save the sound of a strong wind howling through the ruins. There was no more screaming. There was no more fire. On the contrary, It was *cold.* As cold as it had been hot before. A deep layer of snow obscured every surface. The sky rumbled and boiled above him, a deep scarlet which flashed angrily with intermittent, interspersed lightning charges.

Yet, seeing all this, he felt an unexpected sensation of peace wash over him. It was as if the dreams that had been haunting him had been swept away; they were now proven false. Hell had never existed outside of his overactive imagination. There was merely this beautiful, serene, impossibly quiet winter wonderland. Slowly, he began trudging through the snow, off to... wherever.

The old man is jolted awake with a violent start, and finds himself staring at a pair of cracked leather boots. He looks up. Victor is squatting in front of him, holding something in his gloved hand, rotating it over and over in the flickering light of the wasting tallow candle. It is his compass. As soon as the realization hits him, Molochai lunges forward with his only hand, but clutches at empty air. Victor had easily moved the item out of his reach.

"This is a very nice piece, old man. You also found some matches, it seems? And some guns? Blankets! All of these things you did not tell about before! No matter; it is to be expected. I understand." He nods and looks matter-of-factly at the old man. "This is a nice piece. I will trade you a whole rabbit for this piece."

"*NO!!* That's mine! Give it back!" Molochai shouts hoarsely, aware his voice sounds weak and pathetic. "I have guns! I will trade you one!" His eyes are wide, desperate. Victor scoffs.

"*These* guns? You must be joking. They are so old I would fear for my own life to fire them." He reaches over and picks up one of the rifles. "Look at this piece of shit! It is practically falling apart!" As if on cue, the wooden butt of the rifle falls off, landing with a clatter on the concrete floor. Victor scoffs and tosses the rifle back on the sled.

"I will trade you one rabbit for this. As you have seen, I am not a bandit. I do not steal. We are *good people*." He places the compass down gently in front of Molochai, who pounces on it. "If you change your mind, we will be over there, in the building to the south. But we are leaving within a few hours, so you'd better make up your mind quite quickly." He disappears into the darkness.

Molochai hugs the compass tightly. In the flickering orange light of the meagre candle flame, he looks at its cracked glass face, the red-and-white needle inside teetering gently on its pin. He flips it over, and, as he has done thousands or millions of times, he runs his thumb gently over the two words engraved into the golden brass underside. It is all he has left by which to remember his son.

Eight years had passed since Molochai ventured into the snowy wasteland from the depths of his nightmare-haunted tomb. He was grateful for his Scouts survival training. Without it, he would be long dead. He was then 31 years of age. There was no enjoyment in life anymore. Everything came down to *live or die*. Kill or die. Murder was still murder, but the diagnostic criteria had narrowed, and the possible legitimate justifications were incommensurable. Steal a potato: die. Steal antiradtech, medical provisions: die. Steal anything: die. And then there were those with no moral code whatsoever: Have something I want? Die. Sexually attractive? You'll wish you were dead.

There were three invaluable characteristics to improve the chances of living a longer life: Ability, brutality, and deceit. After a while, Molochai had become a skilled marksman and a ruthless fighter, always looking out for number one. Like everyone, he lived nomadically, travelling from zone to zone, scouting for food, weapons, batteries, water, medical supplies, books, things to trade.

There were dead zones, live zones, and grey zones.

Dead zones were those with radiation levels above 400 REM – acute illness and rapid death in 60%-95% of organisms exposed, after 30 days: *Lethal Dose 60-95/30*. Even heavy duty antirad suits could not ward off these high levels of radiation for more than a few minutes.

Grey zones were those between 100-400 REM – mild to serious illness: vomiting, diarrhoea, fatigue, compromised immune system, internal haemorrhaging, marrow and intestinal destruction *(LD 10-70/30)*, which were comfortably safe in antiradtech.

Live zones were those up to 100 REM, within which it was possible to live without antiradtech, albeit with a compromised immune system, a very high risk of cancer, and severe birth defects. Unfortunately, these quickly became, by necessity, tolerable side effects – totally radiation-free zones just didn't exist anymore, and most people did not have antiradtech. As a result, cancer killed many thousands of people, ghoulish mutations at birth killed scores more before they reached adulthood. Often, mutated newborns were simply abandoned, buried in the snow to freeze or suffocate to death. It seemed the most practical and humane solution to a ubiquitous problem. Finally, simple illnesses like the common cold, flu, and hypothermia ravaged thousands more.

Society and economics were a thing of the past. It was every man for himself. There were no more governments. No monetary system, no legal justice system other than the arbiter with the biggest gun. Crime was rampant. An ever expanding gang of thugs, bandits, thieves, rapists, pedophiles, and murderers formed within two years of the Extinction Level Event. As a blatant mockery of their late government's "liberating" foreign policy, they called themselves the Protectorates, and constructed massive fortresses all over the state, equipped with automated sentry guns and ten-meter-high walls. Within these fortresses, black market commerce traded rare and illicit goods and services. Protectorate scouts would hunt down whatever defenceless survivors they could find in an area, and take them for slaves, kill them, or, in the case of the mutants, throw them in cages and make a sort of circus out of them.

Anyone who valued his hide made damn sure never to be spotted by the Protectorate, and if they did, they made sure that those particular Protectorates would never spot anything ever again. By the time he found the boy, Molochai had killed more Protectorate than he could keep track of, as well as a great many other ordinary citizens who had somehow crossed him or got in his way. He couldn't afford to show compassion or mercy – any vulnerability or perceived weakness could leave him compromised, and dead.

It was a dark, grim day – there were never any other type, beneath the bloody sky – and Molochai sat hunched in an LZ somewhere in old-world Manhattan, rotating a giant cockroach on a spit. If he cooked it, the gooey green slime inside solidified somewhat, becoming more gelatinous, and slightly more palatable. Still vile, but what else could a person do, aside from eating other persons?

He had just finished this delicious supper when he heard the growl of engines. Peering out from within the dilapidated office building within which he was holed up, he saw a couple of dirt bikes tearing through the snow toward him. They were not interested in him, however, but in what appeared to be a nuclear family of a father, mother, and young child. They trudged along in the snow, looking miserable and quite close to death.

Upon seeing the Protectorate thugs approaching, they stopped, visibly alarmed. The father raised his hands warily. The mother was carrying their child, a boy of about three. The dirt bikes skidded to a stop in front of them, spraying them with snow. The father pleaded with them; he didn't want any trouble; they had nothing of value!

This was a lie, he was told. It was observed they were wrapped up in a heavy woollen coat, shawl, and blanket, respectively.

Take them off, now. They belong to us.

The man pleaded: *Please, it is all we have to stay warm, you can't take these; it will kill us!* But that was not the Protectorate's problem. The thug aimed a shotgun at the mother and child, and the father immediately consented, telling the woman to remove her outer garments.

But I beg of you, let the boy keep the blanket! he pleaded.

No, the Protectorate needed that blanket. It simply couldn't be helped.

The mother lowered the child to the snowy ground. Then, the man knelt down as if he were about to remove the boy's blanket, but instead whispered something to him, stood, and turned to face the bandit.

Look, can't we just talk – he began, stepping close to the man, hands raised apologetically. As he did this, the boy bolted. The thug tried to raise his weapon, but the man was standing too close to him, so, he lashed out with the butt of the shotgun, shattering the father's eye socket, sending him flying backwards to the frozen ground. The mother cried out and knelt down beside him, looking from him to the fleeing boy, panic-stricken.

The Protectorate thug levelled his weapon and fired a shot just as the boy disappeared behind a nearby building. The wall erupted in a spray of concrete. The man cursed and wheeled on his companion, berating him for standing idly by. The other yelled back abuse, arguing that he had been focusing on the parents, who were more important. The first bandit spat in the snow at his feet, and turned to the man and woman, demanding they remove their clothes. The woman took off her shawl, and removed the coat from her husband, who was lying unconscious, his blood a shock of crimson upon the snow.

ALL OF YOUR CLOTHES!! the man shrieked, his eyes wide. He was livid and shaking with rage. After an agonized, helpless hesitation, the woman obeyed, stripping naked in the snow, first her husband, then herself.

Molochai crouched behind his wall, watching all this. He adjusted the grip of his revolver in his hand. He could easily take out these two; they were not more than ten meters away. Yet, he hesitated. The two bullets would be wasted: what benefit would it be to him to save these people? Thousands died every day. He felt no particular affinity towards them. He would rather the bullets went towards saving his own life, whether it be through self-defense, or hunting for food.

So, he watched, and did nothing.

The husband regained consciousness presently, dashing madly to his feet, then staggering and falling again. His wife constricted him in an embrace, whispering tensely to him. After a moment, he relaxed slightly, then looked up at their persecutors. Blood streamed from his crushed orbital rim. They both shivered violently. Molochai could hear their teeth chattering. The two naked humans huddled pitifully in the snow, clinging to each other.

Cold? asked the bandit, *Here, you must let me help you.* He reached into the side bag of his bike and pulled out a glass bottle full of a transparent, slightly brown liquid. He unscrewed the cap and crammed a rag into the bottle. Then, he produced from his pocket an antique Zippo lighter, and flicked it open. He looked up at the couple and smiled.

They moved too late. As they turned and frantically stumbled through the snow, scrambling like animals toward where the boy was hiding, the thug lit the petrol-soaked cloth, and hurled it at them. The bottle hit the father in the back of the skull. He dropped like a sack of bricks as the glass shattered, spraying accelerant all over him. As he hit the ground, it ignited with a *whumph*. He lay face down, insensate for a few seconds, but as the fire began to consume his back and head, he began to scream and writhe in the snow. As he rolled over onto his back, the snow choked out the fire with a sizzle, and he stopped screaming for a moment, but no sooner had that happened, he was hit in the chest with another Molotov, the glass shards and burning diesel cascading into his face. He resumed shrieking and rolling madly in the snow, but by then the fire was out of control, and in a few seconds, he lay still, immolated.

The woman was lying close by, where she had tripped and fallen as she turned in surprise to witness the terrible event. She beat the snow with her fists; she wailed and cried and sobbed, appearing torn between crawling to her husband, or running to her son. She never got the opportunity to do either. The Protectorate walked calmly up to her, shoved the two barrels of his shotgun against her eye sockets, and pulled the trigger. Her anguished weeping abruptly stopped in an explosion which echoed through the urban wilderness, as her head disappeared in an arcing spray of bone, brain, and blood, fanned out all over the snow behind her. Her naked body dropped inertly onto the ground, blood spraying from her neck stump, soon reducing to a pulsating flow. The bandit reached down and cut off her ring finger with a knife, then approached the husband and simply ripped the digit from his smoking, blackened hand.

He then plodded slowly through the bright red snow, towards the building where the son had escaped. He peered into its dark hollows, looked around for a moment, then shrugged, walked back to his dirt bike where his companion had gathered and packed the clothing, and with dual roars, they sped off into the distance in a spray of dirt and snow.

Molochai sat, breathing hard. Even after almost ten years, seeing that sort of thing still set his heart racing. The rasping of his breath was deafening upon the cold silence. No sound existed but a distant howling of wind. After a moment, he arose from where he had been crouching and made his way through the building, towards the other building, within which the kid had disappeared.

He found the little boy four stories up, beside a window overlooking the carnage, shaking violently despite the warmth of the blanket around him. He looked up at Molochai in terror, his eyes red and swollen. Molochai knelt down and gently took the tiny human into his arms, rubbing his back, rocking him, humming softly, until the child, after more than half an hour of bawling, relaxed and fell asleep out of pure exhaustion.

The boy did not speak, ever. Molochai didn't know if he spoke before, but in the entire time they were together, not a single word emerged from the child's lips. Only by chance had he discovered the boy's name: the mother had screamed it hysterically, as the boy ran away. His name was Isaac, but Molochai soon came to simply call him Zac.

Over the next seven years, the two roamed the wastelands together. Molochai taught Zac how to fight, how to use his opponent's own strength and body movements against him. He taught him how to hunt, how to make and bait traps and snares. He taught him how to skin and prepare rabbits, how to preserve them. Zac learned how to kill roaches, using a large club to crush their exoskeletons. He learned how to use a long-range rifle to take down hellbeasts, the massive mutagenic hyenas with seven rows of razor sharp teeth and ten infrared-sensitive eyes.

Zac learned how to build shelter, make fire, and, of critical importance, how to barter. Interpersonal skills were very useful in a post-retail world. A person needed to know how to play the game: when to stick hard and fast to a price, when to acquiesce, and when to decline altogether a deal which somehow nagged at his intuition.

The two of them often saw other survivors. Some, like themselves, had become tough wilderness outlasters; others still clung pitifully to a life they remembered from the past. Many times they came upon grotesque frozen bodies, mostly newborns and children. They often had bizarre defects, caused by prenatal DNA mutations. They saw a baby with a head three times the size of normal, a child with eyes set on either side of its head, like a horse, possessing a nasal structure resembling that of a pig. Some had giant, swollen limbs, some were missing limbs or had extra limbs, some had abnormally long or short limbs. Many had oddly proportioned facial features, like real live Picasso paintings, with one eyeball huge and the other tiny, or a massive jaw or forehead. The worst mutations did not even look human.   They saw a baby that had a second head growing out of its mouth, hairy, with malformed features. Another mutant was a child whose face appeared to have literally sagged and melted, as if it were made of wax and had sat too close to a fire. One newborn they saw haunted Molochai's dreams for months afterwards. Its face consisted of one huge, bulging, lidless eyeball in the center, below a knobby finger-like structure with nostrils, and above two ears set horizontally underneath the chin, right next to each other. The baby's skin was a waxy whitish-purple.

All they could do was stare, or avert their eyes and walk on. Molochai knew that many more of these frightening aberrations survived, captured and confined in brutal circuses by the Protectorate. Several times they came across Protectorate fortresses: massive structures with huge walls thick enough to walk on, rimmed with razor wire and sentry guns, hundreds of torches burning around the perimeter at night. Guards patrolled the walls and outer boundaries, armed with high-powered rifles and automatic machine guns. Occasionally, Molochai and Zac would sit and watch a fortress for a day or two, hidden from view within a desolate building. They would see dirt bikes and ATVs entering through the huge main gates, containing Protectorate forces. Often there would be trailers hitched to jeeps with barred windows, through which, even from a distance, Molochai and Zac could see ghostly human-shaped shadows.

One thing was for certain: food and resources existed within those fortresses, and barely anywhere else. There were even rumours that successful agriculture and animal husbandry was occurring within these places, but no one could get in who was not a prisoner, in which case, you would want nothing more than to get out.

Life in a constant nuclear winter was hard. They were often stumbling into Grey Zones and Dead Zones – sometimes it was only apparent by the rapid onset of fatigue and nausea, at which point they would pull out the radiation monitor and discover, yes, they would soon die if they didn't leave immediately. It wasn't possible to have the monitor on all the time; good batteries were scarce. They did wear antirad suits, but these didn't help in the DZs. Food and shelter were always a problem, too. What ill would come from eating thoroughly irradiated food? Molochai did not know. They were constantly battling frostbite, chill, hypothermia, fever. Blankets and warm clothing meant the difference between life and death. During the day, the temperature hovered at around -15°C; at night it could drop to -40°C, easily. But the man and the boy slept curled up together to conserve warmth. Many nights, Zac would wake up in a cold sweat, screaming, but Molochai would hug him tighter and sing songs from his own childhood, and after a time Zac would fall back to sleep. Sometimes this would happen multiple times per night.

It took months, even years, for their relationship to grow close. At first the boy was distant and wary, moody and angry. Later, he came closer to Molochai. He would walk or stand directly beside the man; it was unclear whether it was for warmth, or out of affection. Yet, at some point, his small hand reached up and grasped the larger. Every so often Molochai would receive an unexpected hug. By the time Zac was seven, Molochai had a son.

Soon after Zac's eighth birthday (according to the tattered, scribbled "birth certificate" Molochai had found wrapped in plastic in the boy's pocket), Zac returned from exploring with a burlap bag full of items, including an old novel with curled pages, a fork, a couple of batteries, some rifle bullets, a length of rope, and a compass, which was Zac's favourite. It was the size of a hockey puck, made of shining brass with a glass front, and an interior design of alternating black and white triangles radiating outwards from a central point, with elegant, pirate-style letters at the poles. Molochai congratulated him; it was an excellent find.

Zac took the compass everywhere. He became the official navigator. Molochai even found an old map of New York State, although its usefulness was limited, since the primary navigational landmarks were roads which no longer existed. But Zac loved it, and would fastidiously track their progress as best he could, with salvaged pencils, or a sharpened stick burnt to charcoal. During the evening, huddled around the fire, Molochai would point to locations on the map and describe what they used to be like. He described 22nd century life: Jumbo hot dogs with onions and ketchup. Electric heaters. Stovetop ranges. Cars. Cotton Candy. Fruit. Cheese. Vegetables. Flowers. Trees. Baseball (which made no sense to Zac). Hockey (which felt a little more familiar). Newborn deer. Libraries. Kittens. Puppies. Bicycles. Television. Toilet paper. Smartphones. GPS. Zac loved the idea of GPS. *A map which updated itself??* It was inconceivable! No matter what Molochai described, Zac would sit and listen in rapt astonishment: none of these things ever existed in his life. Submarines? Subway trains? Airplanes?? *Outer space rocket ships???* It was all just too much to believe or even comprehend.

Although Zac did not speak, his eyes and expressions communicated his thoughts to Molochai, who could usually guess what he was thinking. So of course he had asked, in this roundabout way, *why do we not have these amazing things anymore?*

So Molochai told him about nuclear war, the Event, and what had happened to the Earth. He taught him about governments, fascism, and the fallacy of democracy. He described the Cold War of the 20th century; how this life they were living right now was exactly what they were trying to avoid by means of the Arms Race. Zac looked confused. *So why did they do it?* he asked with his eyes. *If it is so bad for everyone, why?*

It was a question that had chased Molochai for years. What would have motivated the UCA to make such a rash decision? Perhaps they did not know the EA had nuclear technology? That sort of ignorance was unlikely. Perhaps they thought they would, with a surprise attack, be able to destroy the EA before a counterattack could be coordinated. Or perhaps it was no more complicated than some single, irrational, emotional human had, in a fit of illogical rage, decided to push The Button.

He didn't know. Nobody knew. No one would ever know.

Zac scowled, and curled up, his brow furled, trying to unravel the mystery. He soon fell asleep.

Around a year later, on Molochai's 37th birthday, Zac presented him with something bundled up in a dirty cloth. He unwrapped it. It was Zac's compass. Upon the back, two small words had been scratched into the brass:

DAD LOV

Tears welled up in Molochai's eyes. *Thank you,* he whispered, and hugged the child so tightly he couldn't breathe. From that moment onwards, this compass was Molochai's most prized possession. As Zac had done, Molochai never let it out of his sight. He fell asleep with it in his hand, his arm wrapped around the boy. It was the singular evidence that someone in this terrible world gave a shit that he was alive.

The momentous catalyst to the awful apogee in their lives together came when Zac was eleven years old. The two of them had been rooting around an old military base for any supplies. Zac was going through the bunk rooms, while Molochai was raiding the med bay and weapons locker. Most of the goods had already been looted, but there were still some useful things.

The crucial moment came when Molochai walked into a bunkroom to see Zac looking perplexedly at a fragmentation grenade. This sort of weapon had never been introduced to him before, so he had no idea what it was. But he did see an inviting ring, so he pulled it. This was the instant Molochai walked into the room. He immediately shouted and rushed towards the boy, which was, in hindsight, absolutely the worst thing he could have done, because in surprise, confusion, and guilt, Zac dropped the grenade. As it fell, the spring-loaded trigger popped up and off, spinning through the air. The smooth steel-cased hand grenade hit the concrete floor with a thud, then rolled toward a bed.

Molochai should have simply grabbed the boy and dove for cover, but in his panic he thought only of the grenade. He intercepted it with his foot before it rolled under the bunk; he bent down, picked it up, spun around, and threw it in the direction of the open door behind him. He was too late, however. A few centimeters after it had left his hand, the grenade detonated. The explosion sent him backwards, crashing into Zac, and both of them hit a bunk bed, knocking it over.

Molochai lost consciousness for a moment. When he became sensate, he tried to climb to his feet, but the arm he reached out to support himself with was no longer there, and he fell onto his face. Bewildered, he somehow arranged himself into a sitting position, then was aware of a sticky warm liquid all over him. He looked down to see his arm had been blown off at the elbow, and was squirting blood at a phenomenal rate.

He screamed at Zac to quickly cut a tourniquet from one of the pillowcases in the bunk, and bind his arm. The boy did this with admirable speed, and tied it around the arm, pulling on one side while Molochai himself pulled the other. The wound quickly stopped bleeding. Molochai collapsed onto his back in the large puddle of blood, breathing raggedly in fear, shock, and relief.

But they were not out of the woods yet.

Molochai directed Zac to help him as he pulled several shards of shrapnel out of the flesh of his stump, then bandaged up the arm. He did this quickly, while he was still in shock, and couldn't feel most of what was happening. Then, he loaded up a syringe of local anaesthetic, jammed it into one side of the bandage, and unloaded it. He did this twice more over the surface of the stump, then wrapped tape around the whole thing.

He leaned over and vomited, before collapsing against a wall, wheezing. A panic began to seize him. They had no more medical supplies, and if he was going to survive, he would need more bandages, cleansing ointments, coagulants, antibiotics, and more painkillers – if he wanted to get luxurious – not to mention stitches of some sort. The only place he knew these things existed for certain, for kilometers around, was the nearby Protectorate fortress. They would somehow have to break in, get the supplies, and get out somehow, all without being noticed. He explained this to the boy, who looked terrified, but took a deep breath and nodded silently.

They were crouched behind an embankment a few hundred meters from the fortress. From what Molochai had seen, there was no way to scale the walls, and the main entrance was the *only* entrance. If they were to get in, it would have to be through that gate. This meant they would need to appropriate a Protectorate vehicle and disguise. They crept parallel to the dirt road leading away from the fortress, until the road curved and was out of sight of the snipers on the walls. Molochai explained his plan to Zac, who disappeared behind a snowy embankment.

Molochai sat in the middle of the road, and waited, shivering, for a Protectorate jeep to arrive. In a matter of minutes, he saw one approaching, on its way home. When it was about 50 meters away, he climbed awkwardly to his feet, and began weaving drunkenly, staggering towards the vehicle, arm and stump outstretched. He hoped the jeep would stop, and not just plow right through him. He prepared to dive out of the way.

Luckily, the vehicle slowed to a stop in front of him, exactly where he wanted it to. The driver shouted something to him, but before Molochai could respond, a high-pitched whining noise zipped through the air between them. The driver registered surprise, and looked in the direction from which the bullet had come, just in time for another shell to enter his left eye socket. The back of his skull exploded all over the face of the soldier in the forward passenger seat, whose head likewise erupted in a spray of blood, bone, and brain matter. Molochai ran up beside the jeep, grabbed the shocked Protectorate thug in the back seat, who was frantically fumbling for his gun, and pulled him out onto the ground before plunging a long, curved hunting knife into the mercenary's neck. Then, he quickly tore the front passenger out of the car, while Zac ran up to the other side, dropped his rifle, and dragged the driver out, dumping him on the roadway.

It was very important to do this all as quickly as possible, to minimize the amount of blood that soiled the vehicle. Ideally they would have not had any bloodshed at all, but given the severity of Molochai's wounds and the number of men in the vehicle, this was not a practical solution. Their next action was to remove the shirts and jackets from the bodies, then drag them off the road, burying them in snow, before effacing all traces of blood with more snow. Next, they drove the messy vehicle a few kilometers away, melted snow over a fire, and used the shirts of the men to wipe out the vehicle as well as possible, which would hopefully not attract attention at a quick glance. If a more thorough inspection was done, they would be completely fucked.

Molochai then chose the least messy of the jackets bearing the Protectorate insignia, cut one of the arms off, and donned it. Then, he bound and gagged Zac and placed him in the back seat of the jeep, before driving towards the fortress. Zac was instructed to look terrified and scream as loud as he could through his gag, while thrashing around in the back seat. This was to divert as much attention as possible from the front seat, which had seen most of the carnage.

At the gate, the Protectorate guard waved them to a stop. He greeted Molochai as "Brother", and they exchanged the Protectorate salute. Then, he glanced at Zac in the back, who was performing his part well, and gave an ugly, crooked smile, revealing decayed or missing teeth.

"Looks like you found a fighter, eh? He will gain good odds in the ring, I think!" he exclaimed.

Molochai heartily agreed, leering as evilly as he could muster, feeling rather like a pirate in a children's movie.

The guard gave a hand signal to some invisible thug, and the gigantic gates, literally made of tree trunks bound together with thick steel bands, opened inwards slowly.

Molochai drove the jeep through the gates. As soon as they were through, Zac ceased his struggling; drawing attention now was exactly what they didn't want to do. He sat up in his seat to have a look around.

The inside of the fortress was literally a village. Housing complexes were arranged around the periphery of the 1,200 meter diameter fortress, with security centers located around the perimeter, providing stairway access to the top of the wall. In the center of the fortress, in a triangular configuration, was a huge marketplace, a circus, and an arena. The arena consisted of a dirt ring surrounded by rows of crude benches containing onlookers. Within the dirt pit, two boys Zac's age were literally beating each other to death with their bare hands, spurred on by the desire to live, and the cheers of the crowd. The circus contained "exotic specimens": pitiful, sorry mutants made to live a life of exhibition, public humiliation, and beatings.

Yet the marketplace was what amazed Zac and Molochai the most: it was full of artefacts of a bygone age which Zac had never seen before, and Molochai thought he would never see again. Toasters, mini stovetop ranges, washing machines, all hooked up to solar power. More books than Molochai had ever seen. Frying pans, utensils, cooking knives, hunting knives, guns, ammunition, you name it. All the modern conveniences. The currency appeared to be various types of metals or alloys weighed in grams and kilograms: in increasing order of value: nickel, aluminum, iron, steel, copper, silver, gold, bismuth, indium, zinc, antimony, and titanium. These metals could be used to make machine parts, weapon parts, and different types of solder for reparation of electrical circuitry. Gold, which had historically been a precious metal merely for its attractiveness, was now used as conductive plating for wires and circuitry.

Both man and boy gaped incredulously at this spectacle, and had to remember to keep their outward composure. Molochai pulled over and asked for directions to the nearest infirmary from an ordinary-looking street vendor. When they exited the vehicle, Zac's ankle bonds were cut and his wrist bonds were loosened, so he could easily shrug them off, if the need presented itself. Molochai grabbed him roughly by the collar, and dragged him into the infirmary.

An attractive nurse greeted him with a smile. She couldn't have been more than 20 years of age, and had blue eyes and straight blonde hair tied back into a ponytail, with chaotic wisps escaping around her ears and along her hairline.

Molochai was totally caught off guard. He had expected the entire fortress to be composed of murderers, rapists, thieves, perverts, and other rogues, not sexually compelling young women. It also completely confounded his plan, which was to kill whoever guarded this place. He just couldn't bring himself to slaughter her. Virtually hovering in front of him was the first youthful-looking female he had seen in 14 years. She reminded him of Amy.

The nurse asked how she might offer help, but then saw Zac's wrist bindings, and her smile instantly disappeared. Molochai loosened his grip on the boy, and decided to tell an omissive truth: he had had an accident with a grenade while out scouting, and he had blown off his arm, and badly needed medical attention.

"Have you kidnapped a child from the wastelands to sacrifice to your barbaric arena?" Her tone was icy. "Because if you have, you can go rot in hell. And I don't care if you are Protectorate." She set her jaw defiantly.

Molochai balked; again, this was completely outside of what he had been prepared for. He stammered, and explained that he had actually *rescued* Zac from the arena, and was trying to smuggle him out. The girl looked at him as if he had just told her that he was going to flap his arm and fly away. Molochai insisted, and beseeched Zac to show her his false bindings. The boy easily pulled his wrists apart, and the rope fell to the floor.

"You blew your arm off, but just so happened to stop for a casual rescue mission on the way back??" the girl asked, clearly unconvinced.

Molochai pursed his lips. "I know it sounds foolish. The truth is, I passed by, at first, but I turned back. I knew I couldn't have lived with myself if I had turned a blind eye." he said wearily, then added, "Please... I barely made it here, and if you send me away, I won't make it anywhere else."

The girl peered long and hard at them both, then motioned them to follow her into the back. Molochai breathed a sigh of relief, only just then aware he had been holding his breath. He sat down on an unbelievably clean inspection bed. Zac sat silently in a chair in the corner, while the girl peeled the tape and bandages off Molochai's mangled stump, as gently as she could. His eyes watered; he gritted his teeth as the gauze which had embedded in the wound pulled free. When the stump was uncovered, the girl whistled softly and grimaced. Molochai could see his lower humerus bone protruding jaggedly from the ragged flesh. His skin below the tourniquet was a sickly white. A putrid smell emanated from the pus-filled wound. He actually felt embarrassed in front of this gorgeous young woman, as if it were extremely important that she not consider him the wretched, filthy, ugly old man he knew he was.

She excused herself politely before returning with an experienced-looking doctor, who, after a moment of peering and poking, informed him that he would have to undergo surgery and have a skin graft taken from his thigh. Molochai was alarmed, he had expected to kill everyone and furtively flee with an armful of supplies. He felt very distrustful of being incapacitated like this, especially if they were to put him under.

He was still thinking it over, when a loud noise resounded from the lobby. The nurse looked alarmed, and rushed out to investigate. Aggressive male voices were heard, then protests from the girl. A moment later, the door slammed open, and a man immediately identifiable by his uniform and insignia as a high-ranking Protectorate officer barged in, followed by the ordinary-looking vendor, and a low-level thug. He stopped and surveyed the scene, his hands flexing on his automatic weapon.

"Who the fuck are you?" he asked Molochai. "And why are you..." he observed the name on the sleeve of the bloody jacket. "Ah. That is why Carson never reported in. Well, let's go have a little chat, shall we?" He produced pair of handcuffs and advanced, then paused, looking at Molochai's one arm, then at the handcuffs, appearing slightly perplexed. Unexpectedly, the girl stepped in between them, protesting that he had an open wound; at least let her clean and bandage it. He would bleed to death or succumb to infection before sufficient questioning, otherwise.

"Fine. But make it quick." The officer stepped back, but still aimed his weapon at Molochai. Zac sat in the corner, rigid and alert.

Once local anaesthetic had been administered, Molochai felt the constant ache of suppressed agony fade into numbness, and he felt wonderfully relieved of what he hadn't even been aware had been a substantial burden upon his consciousness, like a constant throbbing migraine.

He kept shifting his attention between the officer standing guard, and the unjustly gorgeous nurse working on him who stirred a sensation in his loins he thought gone forever. She looked up at him and smiled, her face registering concern. She obviously fully believed his rescuer story now. With his body positioned between her and the officer, she indicated with her eyes and a quick tilt of her head, to the counter behind her. Molochai looked, and saw she had conveniently placed there a long-bladed scalpel.

She finished with his arm and silently nodded to him, then turned to the officer, and announced, "I've got the wound bandaged, but I've run out of tape to bind it with, and I have to get more. I do appreciate just another moment of your patience!" Then, she turned and walked quickly into the back room.

At that point, Molochai leaped off the bed, grabbed the scalpel, and rushed the officer, swiping diagonally downwards, cutting a wide gash in his cheek. The officer looked shocked, and swore, partially releasing his grip on the rifle, as one hand automatically rose to cover the wound. Molochai lunged forward and gripped the rifle by the handguard, pulling it from the officer's grasp and swinging the butt, hitting him in the left ear. The officer stumbled, cursing and groping at his head. Molochai flipped the gun under his arm, then dropped it, catching it by the pistol grip and bracing the butt stock against his shoulder. He ignored the cowering vendor and swung the barrel of the rifle menacingly towards the guard, who backed off, and Molochai rushed past him into the lobby, not looking back.

Suddenly, behind him, he heard a yell. He whirled to see the boy with a pistol to his temple, in the grip of the guard, who was bleeding profusely from his face and ear, and yelling at Molochai to *"Drop the gun and get the fuck on the ground! DO IT NOW!!"* After a moment's hesitation, Molochai complied, and was dragged by his collar, struggling and cursing, through crowds of onlookers who turned with mild interest from their daily routine, and onwards, to the middle of the arena. There, both he and Zac were thrown violently into the dirt.

They lay in the mud, breathing heavily, surrounded by half a dozen armed guards. Several minutes later, the officer appeared above them, his cheek stitched up. He stood, and decreed that for the lives they had taken from his soldiers, a life must be taken from them.

"Choose!" he shouted at Molochai, who frantically looked over at his adopted son who lay beside him, breathing hard and staring with wild eyes that implored his father to do something superhuman and save him.

Molochai's mouth went dry. He looked up at the officer. "For Christ's sake, take me; don't kill the boy!" he cried.

"Very well," said the officer. He played to the crowd of spectators, raising his arms theatrically, and turning full circle.

"THE OUTSIDER HAS CHOSEN TO DIE IN PLACE OF THE BOY!" he shouted. A mixture of cheers and boos effused from the crowd.

He turned to where Molochai was lying on his back in the dirt, and knelt on one knee above him. He produced a long dagger, showing off its fine, curved blade, its handle of silver and jade.

"Let it be done." he stated with finality, and, with both hands, raised the knife above his head, ready to bear it down into the heart of the man beneath him.

Staring up at the officer who formed a shockingly black silhouette against the boiling red sky, Molochai couldn't breathe. He saw the blade raise, a sharp extension to the long arms of the towering shadow. Instantly, he was overcome with the same panicked, hysterical feeling of absolute terror that had struck him the moment the bombs dropped, a lifetime ago.

He was overcome with a crushing sense of anxiety and helplessness: he felt like a pitiful, helpless child again, cowering in snivelling tears beneath his father's fist. An intense sensation of nausea overwhelmed him, and he was compelled, as he had been on that day, 14 years ago, with a beastly desire for self-preservation at all costs. As the knife began to make its downward, seemingly slow motion descent, he twisted madly to the side, raising his arm in front of his face, and heard his own screaming voice as if it were not his own:

"NO! STOP! Oh, God, no! Not me! Please! Not me! The boy, the boy!" He crumbled into weeping as the knife halted a few centimeters from the soft pocket of flesh above his collarbones, below his throat.

The officer stood, and shouted to the crowd: "The outsider has changed his mind! The *boy* will now die!" A roaring cheer erupted from all around them.

Without a word, he walked over to where Zac lay on the ground and knelt above him. Knife raised, he looked over at Molochai and shouted imperiously,

"Have you chosen well??"

Molochai could hear nothing except the pounding of his living blood in his veins, in his ears. He could see nothing except the stricken look on Zac's face: one of absolute bewilderment and terror, pleading helplessly with his father: his betrayer, as death loomed above him.

The child looked up at the officer, seeing the same silhouetted, jagged bringer of death as Molochai had moments before, and his mouth dropped open, his lips trembling. Tears rose and overflowed hot down into his ears, as he crushed his eyes shut, wincing and trying desperately to shrink away from his imminent, inexorable slaughter.

The officer struck downwards with the dagger, swiftly and strongly. The blade was met with little resistance, and in mere milliseconds, was buried up to its hilt.

Molochai curled up into the foetal position and wailed and sobbed like a toddler, trembling violently despite the heat of his clothing. His vision was completely blurred, but very clearly he heard the voice of the officer:

"Get up. You are Protectorate, now. This son of a bitch doesn't deserve to call himself your father."

Bewildered, Molochai stopped crying and wiped his eyes and nose with his wrist. He saw Zac reach up to the officer's extended hand, to be pulled lightly to his feet. The dagger remained where it had struck, sunk deeply into the dirt on the far side of the boy.

Zac stared down at Molochai with an expression of unspeakable hurt and disdain, then violently spat in the dirt beside him. Eleven seconds previously, Zac had been eleven years old, but now, to Molochai, it seemed like their ages were reversed. He watched the boy escorted silently away without looking back, then he sat up and shivered pitifully, feeling dizzy and nauseated.

The Protectorate officer turned and looked down on him.

"You scum-sucking sack of shit," he muttered.

He wound up and booted Molochai in the face, sending him sprawling onto his back in the mud. He flickered out of consciousness for a moment; when he opened his eyes, he saw, scattered in the dirt, merely a centimeter or two in front of his face, several bloody teeth. Then, the officer was kneeling heavily on Molochai's chest, one hand covering his face, crushing his head into the earth. Through his one uncovered eye, Molochai saw the flash of the dagger, saw the blade rush towards him... then saw nothing. The point of the blade sunk into the edge of his eye socket, and, with a twist and a gouge, the Protectorate officer tore the eyeball from his head. He lifted his hands away. Molochai saw, through his remaining eye, a bizarre spherical *thing* impaled on the end of the dagger's blade. It stared accusingly at him, blue like the sky used to be, red like it had become, his optic nerve dripping blood, dangling uselessly from the back of the globe.

Molochai covered his face with his hand and screamed. He wailed pitifully as they dragged him to a blacksmith's shop, the flesh on his knees scraped raw along the stones. He howled in terror when he opened his eye and saw a red-hot kiln, centimeters in front of him, the heat searing his face. He shrieked so hard he gagged, when they ripped the bandages from his arm and jammed the raw, bloody stump against the glowing, near-molten metal. When three thugs held him down and secured his head, and he saw a glowing red poker slowly approaching his eye-hole, he began crying, incoherently babbling, begging abjectly for mercy. The white tip of the poker dipped gently into his skull. There was a sizzling noise, then, everything disappeared.

The old man lies beside the tallow-and-cloth candle, turning the compass over and over in his hand, remembering.

His stomach growls fiercely. He hasn't eaten in so long. He will die soon. He has been dead for decades.

With a heavy sigh, he rises wearily to his feet, and slowly drags his mutilated body the few meters to the building across the alleyway. Victor is happy to see him. In silence, his eyes averted, Molochai relinquishes the shining, engraved compass, and receives, in return, a small chunk of charred meat.

[2015]

"Quality Protein-Rich Meat Products"

(3015 A.D.)

It's the meat. I can smell it in the air as soon as I open the door: I can tell that something is very wrong. I figured it might come to this at some point, but I didn't expect it so soon.

It went from good to awful, literally overnight. In only a matter of hours, the whole thing degraded into a putrid, rotting mess. I couldn't do anything about it. I didn't even realize it was happening until too late. And of course, no one takes responsibility. *It's not our problem,* they always say. *Sorry.* Bullshit. What an utter waste. I throw down the phone and look again through the door.

Goddamnit!! I just got that pork rump roast yesterday; I was going to eat it tonight, but I got up this morning and discovered the motor on the refrigerator had blown: everything had been festering in the artificial tropical heat of the bubbles, all night long. This pisses me off, because we only ever get meat on ration once a month. A bit of pork or beef or chicken. Eat within five days, wait another 25 days, eating wilted lettuce and maybe a bit of oats or old, stale bread discarded from the affluent New Society bakeries. Perhaps some shrunken, withered apples, or rubbery potatoes riddled with sprouting eyes... but usually just bars of compressed protein paste, and carb crackers.

Meat day of all days! And management won't even vouch to replace the ration! They'll send someone to repair the fridge sometime between Monday and Friday within the hours of 8am and 6pm, and would I be available during that timeframe? How does one even respond to that??

I responded by hurling the phone at the couch (can't afford to break it) and slamming the fridge door. Because you know what? Soon, I'll be out of this dump. I'm moving up in the world. I got a call saying I have been accepted as a lab technician in the *New Genesis Family Farms*, helping to supply meat rations to the citizens of this fine city... hopefully they have working refrigeration systems. Personally, I don't give a flying fuck about this shithole, but if it gets me out of these Old Society ghettos, I'll worship it as if it were literally a sacred cow.

I grab a stale dinner bun out of the bag in the cupboard, and find it dotted all over with green fur. Great. I look around at my pitiful apartment. It is an ancient relic, decomposing and crumbling around me. The floors are rotten hardwood, gone spongy probably before I was even born, and threatening to break through in a few places I take care to avoid. The ceiling fan stopped working long ago. I tread upon a shabby tapestry

103

carpet, stained or worn through in several places. The wallpaper is so crudely painted over I can still see the floral print embossed underneath the paint, if I look closely. The green paisley sofa (which functions as my bed) has foam bursting from the cushions, and an infestation of black mould, with a population rivalling New Genesis, advancing up the back. And, on top of everything, thick layers of dirt coat literally every surface. Who can afford a vacuum cleaner? It would suck precious electricity I'd rather use to heat my water in the morning for a shower and a coffee. Even then, if I use up my allotted kilowatt hours too luxuriously, as I always do: I spend the last week of the month with shockingly cold showers and revoltingly cold coffee. But no more.

Fuck this place.

I heave my bag over my shoulder and step out of the apartment, locking the door behind me. Down the outdoor hallway, all the other doors look just like mine: cracked green paint curling from the damp wood of the door, thanks to this constant contrived tropical biosphere.

I curse at a rat with glowing green eyes I see scampering along a wall. A goddamned nuclear war, and rats just *had* to survive, and they're the size of cats now (which are unfortunately extinct, else they might curb the rat problem. Then again, they might be the size of horses.). Fucking terrifying. The walk to the farm is long, about 45 minutes, through the slums of Old Society District 56HR. Derelict buildings of glass, brick, and mortar loom above me, their surfaces cracked and crumbling, the windows dark. We haven't had *proper* (read: legal) industry in OS for almost a century. Now, everything is abandoned and left to decay, just like we do, on our feet, in the ground, or decomposing on the Mound, deep in the Pits. I can see gaunt faces peering out at me from the windows: the homeless-by-choice. It's smart, really. If you have no door, the NG-RPEB can't kick it in spouting bullshit about how *you've been found to blah blah blah and this qualifies you for RePurposing as a Subsection_whogivesafuck,* even though everyone knows it's a total fabrication. We Old Society filth are the cattle for the New Genesis elite, and when the agents of deception have the power, it is the victims who end up wearing the lie by force.

So, many live off the grid. No telephones, no electricity, no radio, no monthly meat rations, and no homes. They just fucking live and die like cowardly blind mice, trembling for fear of the farmer's wife.

Well, not me. I'm taking charge of my destiny. And speaking of farms, I took the liberty of accessing *GenNet* to research what a farm is and what to expect, and I must say, I'm pretty damn sceptical. Apparently, farms are delightful places where animals are raised lazily together in cow barns, chicken coops, luxuriously muddy pigpens, and wide-open horse pastures.

The pictures were lovely, although I know they were from the 20th century, back before the *Extinction Level Event* that made the world what it is today.

Will I have the opportunity to milk cows and pick eggs and feed baby pigs with a bottle? Unlikely. It sounds *too* lovely, as if, with a name like *Family Farms*, maybe I'll be able to finally feel safe, and at home. But I know it's just another face of the *New Genesis RePurposing Enforcement Bureau*, and R. Janus, the sociopath who runs it.

The border between Old Society and New Society is blatantly obvious: it is a checkpoint where we are intrusively searched, and looked down upon like we are the scum of the earth.

"Stop! State your identity, destination and business." The soldier stiffly blocks my path with a proton rifle.

"My name is Persephone Anance, OSFem#4583871; Residence OSD56H8; en route to NSD23B, for employment."

"Employment in a New Society district?" He steps forward, empowered by his crisp grey uniform with its red trim. "How about I employ you to conceive my child, whore? I'll pay you with your *life*."

He towers over me. I maintain a strict poker face, but inside I'm shitting my pants. I know this kind of thing happens daily. Any OS resident can be "detained for questioning" without reason or rights, indefinitely.

"Wenkler, step down." booms a steely voice behind the soldier. "Wenkler" leers at me, then, before I can react, he reaches out and grabs my left breast with one hand and reaches between my thighs with the other. I do my best to contain my breath through gritted teeth – *this is just a checkpoint – the real goal is farther ahead.*

"See you next time, sweetie." he croons, and turns away.

Behind him stands a man in a black and red uniform with more shiny bits on it. He stands a full head taller than the soldier. The giant NG-RPEB officer approaches me. I grasp one hand with the other to keep them from shaking. He looks down on me, and, to my absolute surprise, he speaks gently.

"Relax... we're not all assholes. Stay safe, miss," he says, and he stands aside.

The wide, clean streets of New Society lay before me.

My chest feels like it is tearing apart – I realize I've been holding my breath. My heart is racing; I'm sweating; I feel like a tiny boat of emotions in a dark, raging gale of helpless terror. Words are beyond me; I hug my bag to my chest and force myself to walk with calm, wooden legs, through the checkpoint. As soon as I am out of sight, I lean back against a wall, gasping raggedly, feeling the blood pounding in my temples. I've been assaulted before, only there were three of them, and nobody to come to the rescue. It was a long night.

The Farm looks like none I have ever seen on *GenNet.* Occupying at least two square kilometers, the facility is a towering cluster of geometrical shapes. I gawk openly as I wander through it, feeling like a little lost kid. The complex is divided into multiple roads in a grid system. To my left are rows of hundreds of silver cylinders two or three stories high, with sharply funnelling bodies. They look like the vats used in the old brewpubs for brewing and aging beer. Across the road are tall rectangular buildings of brilliant white ceramic and steel. Across yet another road are rows of what appear to be greenhouses with triangular roofs. The facility stretches onwards to the horizon. A group of men in white coats walk by and openly sneer and laugh at my threadbare clothes.

Oh, shit! I almost forgot!! I duck behind a building and, hoping to hell there are no cameras, I quickly strip off my clothing, down to my bra and panties, then pull on a tight skirt, a low-cut suit jacket that makes my breasts look twice as big as they are and threaten to spill out, and some flat-bottomed slip-on shoes. I draw the line at high heels. This female clothing is so goddamn uncomfortable, and I feel like a sexual billboard, as if I dress this way just so I can give men massive erections with which they feel entitled to assault me. I fucking hate it. But this job means *everything* to me! I quickly twist my hair into what I hope looks like a casually professional updo, securing it with bobby pins.

I kick the bag out of sight under some sort of ventilation unit, then, furtively clutching a little canister of aerosol defensive spray, I make my way to the main office, by the helpful directions of the same workers who scorned me a moment ago, and who now insist on leading me there, one of them holding his hand on my lower back, a little too low for comfort. They call me "baby" and "cutie", and assure me they will see me again. I shudder and open the wide glass doors by massive brass handles shaped like wings.

A wide red carpet extends down the center of the elongated lobby, which stretches at least 50 meters. Marble pillars line the walls, supporting balconies extending six floors up. Some sort of green plant exists in pots all over. I think they're called ferns. I didn't even know they still existed. I finger a leaf. It's fake.

I walk up to the wide, oaken desk (probably fake, also) with its glistening, waxed surface. A bored-looking man sits behind it. Upon seeing me he points a long index finger, waving it dismissively.

"Look, lady, you've obviously got the wrong place. Your kind aren't welcome here. Leave immediately."

"*My kind?* I'm here for the job –"

"Right... Look, sex kitten, you "ladies of the night" may "work the streets," but that's not a *real* job. If somebody here called you, kindly deal with your business off the grounds."

"Excuse me?!" I snap. *Keep calm, Persephone. Think about the fridge at home.* "Look, I am here for the job interview– Assistant Geneticist – with Mr. Tomakin."

"Pfft." The guy scoffs and attempts to stare me down with a cold, steely gaze. I won't look away. "There is only one person listed as an interviewee, and he will be arriving any moment, so I would appreciate it if you would quit fouling my air. I have summoned security, and they will *escort* you off the grounds, forcibly if necessary." He looks smug, and leans back in his swivel-chair, placing his feet impudently on the desk.

I force my voice to remain level. "I *am* that person. Persephone Anance. Percy."

The receptionist immediately removes his feet from the table, straightens up, and accesses his computer. "*What?* We thought you were a man – Percival."

I give a little feminine shrug, and look meek. Of course, it's just an act. I knew they would mistake me for a man. Nobody calls me Percy, but it's the only way I could think of to actually get an interview. Obviously, I am not going to tell them that. I just do my best to look innocent and bewildered. He doesn't seem to buy it.

"Listen, *ma'am,* falsifying information on a resume is a federal offence, eligible for immediate RePurposing." He motions with his hand. I look behind me and see two armed guards approaching.

"I didn't falsify anything!!" My voice sounds too shrill for my liking. "HEY! Get your fucking hands off me!" I snarl, forgetting my plan to be ladylike and charming. The security guards are looming over me now, their huge meaty paws on my upper arms.

"She's resisting," states one. The other nods, and I see their hands move towards the stun batons on their belts. *Oh, God... Those things fucking hurt.* I am so scared, I'm almost peeing myself. I hold my breath and try to keep myself from trembling. My anxiety is rising like a pressure cooker; my hand reaches slowly into my pocket for my defensive spray…

Abruptly, the intercom on the desk buzzes loudly. The two guards pause, and look over to the secretary, who presses a button on an earpiece, listens for a moment, then mumbles something, before pressing the button again. He looks up and, with the tiniest wave of his hand, the two guards release their grip on my arms. Apparently some order in my favour has come down from heaven. I seize the moment to regain my composure: I haughtily pull my arms away and look highly indignant.

"If you'll excuse me, I'm late for my appointment!!" I say testily, smoothing the wrinkles from my jacket. I turn my nose up at them, and stomp towards a door which I hope dearly is the right one. My knees keep trying to collapse under me. My limbs are stiff; I feel like I have two wooden legs.

The large double oaken doors are carved in undulating spirals, with the chiral image of a long, twisting, Oriental-style dragon slithering up their entire three meters; they open just before I get to them. A little man stands before me; he has the figure of a cartoon stick man and is wearing peculiar spectacles with odd hexagonal lenses. His dark suit is undoubtedly tailor-made, but still fits him like a cigarette tube. His dress shoes are black with pointed toes gilded in shining, golden, swirling oriental patterns. He has a tiny, razor thin moustache sharpened to pencil points on each side.

"Mr. Tomakin?" I extend my hand tentatively. The man looks down at it with obvious disgust, but, after a moment's hesitation and a barely perceptible flash of a grimace, he takes my hand, briefly vibrates it, then returns it to me as if it were diseased, and he must now go boil his arm up to the elbow.

"*Miss* Anance, I presume. How *creative.*" He glares disdainfully up his nose at me, and, with a dismissive motion, orders me to a chair in front of his desk. I sit, or rather, perch. It is absurdly tiny, and uncomfortably hard. He sits in his own massive luxury chair boasting a back which easily extends half a meter above his head.

"So… you are interested in the position of Assistant Geneticist. Okay, let's see here. Age twenty-seven… Says here you grew up in NSD, but attended a university in OSD??" His brow furrows as he digests my dissonant half-lie. I could falsify my district of birth – that was just a small hack into the right circuits of *GenNet,* but the educational records are much more complicated, and, frankly, beyond my skill level.

"Yes. My parents were hit with hard times. My father discovered he had Parkinson's – genetic screening wasn't mandatory when he was born – and dutifully RePurposed himself, but the social RP supplement was not enough to afford my entrance into an NS University." Total bullshit, federally offensive.

"And it says you received... an honours Undergrad, and Graduate's degree... with a double major in Biochemistry and Microbiology?!" He looks stupefied. "You can get that in Old Society?!"

I smile coolly and stare straight ahead, unblinking. "If one is diligent enough, yes. You will find the high quality of my work speaks for itself."

Tomakin clears his throat, and regains his composure. "Ahem, well, I regret to inform you that in New Society, we do not honour OS degrees. *Regrettably,* this means that –"

That you'll work me harder than anyone else, and pay me less.

"...you will have to start at a lower pay grade and work your way up, but I have *every confidence* that in no time at all you will reach pay equity."

Yeah, right. I can practically see the glass ceiling and escalator from here. But still, even shit wages here are at least twice as much as what I make now.

"Of course, Mr. Tomakin; I understand. I am *sure* it is merely protocol, *entirely* out of your control." My words are liquid honey.

He shrugs and turns his hands upwards, in a great show of reluctance. "Well, now that we have that settled, Senior Geneticist Jean-Claude will give you a tour."

At first, the genetics labs appear pretty unspectacular – the usual collection of microscopes and culture dishes, centrifuges, rotary evaporators, IR and NMR spectroscopes, and the like. "Senior Geneticist Jean-Claude" is in his late forties, with snow-white hair and a neatly trimmed goatee. He shows me through several identical labs, spouting irrelevant bullshit the whole way along. *The Farm is committed to providing the highest quality products, blah blah blah.* I'm bored.

"So, when do I get to see the livestock?" I interrupt him. He goes red in the face and looks at me irritably.

"Ahem. There is no *"livestock"*, Miss Anance. All original-source viviparous and oviparous animals – and many ovoviviparous species – have been extinct since the Event, or did they not teach you about that in your *community college*? (I bite my tongue.) The meat products are derived from stem-cell cultures grown in a nutritious substrate. *Surely* you have heard of the process of somatic cell nuclear transfer?" His tone is blatantly condescending, as if he has just asked me if I know what a chair is.

"Yes. It is the process used to create embryos which are genetically identical to the parent organism: forced asexual reproduction, if you will, commonly known as cloning. It involves isolating a female gamete from the parent, and from this egg removing the haploid nucleus with half the usual number of chromosomes. This is replaced with a regular diploid nucleus from a parental somatic (body) cell. The cell then initiates mitosis as if it were a regular egg cell which has already united with a male gamete, a sperm, and fertilized. This forms what is called an embryonic stem cell, and growth proceeds as normal, the cell having been "fooled into thinking" it has created a genetically distinct zygote via the usual channels of sexual reproduction and meiosis." *I know what a fucking chair is.* Senior Geneticist Jean-Claude looks somewhat peevishly disappointed.

"Ahem. Indeed. I will show you the embryos."

We enter a much larger room, the size of at least two school gymnasiums wide and three long. Arranged upon workstations extending the length of the room in long rows which seem to converge into infinity, are countless glass beakers about the size of a human head, which contain bright green liquid. (Later, I learn that the scientists call them "pickle jars".) Within these float tiny creatures – animal embryos, hooked up to nutrient tubes which occasionally emit bubbles from the areas where they seem to impale the frail little bodies. From the labelling, I can see each row is segregated into a single animal type: some are cows, others sheep, pigs, chickens, etc. They look like little aliens in the gelatinous green liquid: amorphous blobs with gigantic heads and dark purple bulges for eyes. I can see through their skin to bones no wider than a needle, and miniscule organs. I see hearts beating asymmetrically through gossamer-thin striated muscle tissue. *Fascinating! Definitely beats my current job at the state-augmented, state-taxed MegaMart.*

All along the rows of stasis vats are computer terminals monitoring heart rate, temperature, emergence and patterning of brain activity, and other displays I'm not familiar with. The flashing lights and scrolling text make me think of the original Star Trek television series from the 20th century I dug up on *GenNet* – if it has lots of little flashing lights, something important must be happening.

"We have scores of these rooms. At any given time we are growing hundreds of thousands of cloned animals for consumption by the citizens of New Genesis." JC says, in a bored tone, as we pass into another room, this one containing much more advanced specimens. Now, the foetuses actually look recognizably like the animal they are supposed to represent.

"What are these?" I ask, pointing to several narrow tubes which all converge at the region approximating the heart of the animal. They appear murky and almost black in the green liquid of the vat, but following the tubes out, I can see that each of them is a different colour, with varying opacities.

"IV lines," JC explains impatiently, "*Obviously*, the animal is too small to locate veins in any traditional sense, so the needle is plunged directly into the heart, and even that is only the size of a kernel of short-grained rice. The needles therefore are extremely fine – in the region of micrometers. Only a single molecule of each compound can pass through at a time, but they do so continually." He looks up at me and answers my next question before I ask it. "The compounds are nutrients, steroids, growth hormones, antibacterial agents, and antifungal agents. The latter two are to decrease the chances of unproductive death, which is a total waste of valuable resources, and the former three are to encourage extremely rapid development. A cow, for example, has a natural gestation period of 274 days, that is, 9.13 months – similar to that of a human. This is completely unreasonable in terms of a sustainable aggressive animal agriculture practice. As a result of the compounds we pump into the zygotes via the brine, and the foetuses via IV, we have been able to reduce this period to 73 days, just over ¼ of the original timeframe."

"But these animals look normal. Wouldn't that introduce complications?"

"*Obviously*." he rolls his eyes.

We enter an elevator and descend further into the bowels of the farmhouse. Upon exiting, I see that each of the vats in this room is big enough to contain an average-sized border collie, had dogs still existed. JC points to the closest one. The calf in this tank looks normal and healthy, in terms of morphology, but it is obviously very dead – a preserved specimen.

"This is a normally developed specimen, most of the way through gestation." We walk down the row, surveying the living creatures. "These are our consumable specimens, at an equivalent stage."

I'm shocked. Several of these animals have multiple body parts, including heads. Some have limbs in the wrong places, and most of them have abnormally large torsos but nearly nonexistent legs.

"After they're "born" we amputate the legs, because otherwise, they tend to break them by thrashing, which leads to infection and death, so we just remove them at birth. The animals survive just fine like that."

I don't have to believe him, because he shows me. Another level down the rooms are jammed floor to ceiling with wire pens, barely larger than the grotesque sausage-like animals lying in swampy puddles of their own excrement. Their bodies are covered in bright red, raw patches. JC tells me it is a combination of the equivalent of bedsores, as well as the caustic effect of the chemicals excreted in their waste products.

*And we **eat** these things?!*

The worst thing about this room, however, is the oppressively loud, disturbing cries. All of the animals are screaming hoarsely. All they can do in their lifelong prison is writhe, their spinal columns twisting with the force of their endless agony. They quiver their tiny little flesh stumps and shriek, lying half-dead in an acrid puddle of piss, diarrhoea, and blood.

It's *horrible!* It's too much! I'm reeling with a wave of panic which crests over me and crashes like a tsunami. I suddenly gag and heave, spitting bile onto the lab floor. I wipe the blur from my watering eyes, and literally run back to the elevator. JC follows casually, a shit-eating grin on his face.

On the way up I tell him I'm fine, that it was just a shock, that I'm still on board. He merely looks indecipherably at me, and the rest of the ride is spent in silence.

He leads me back to Tomakin, who produces a thick contract and slams it in front of me like a first year biology textbook. Still nauseated, sweating cold, I read through it as best I can, while in my left ear his wheedling voice narrates the "important bits" each page contains, which he conveniently appears able to sum up in about 1/16th of the actual printed words. I'm not a lawyer; I can't comprehend most of this stuff.

But I *need* this goddamned job, so I sign on the dotted line, in red ink.

Over the next few weeks I learn the ropes of the position. My job mainly consists of nuclear transplant and initial development monitoring. I feel like God in a way – I create the initial organism, and watch it grow, checking for any significant developmental difficulties early in the process. Sometimes a clone will go afoul immediately. Possibly the transcription factors are messed up in the nuclear transplant process and the genetic instructions aren't carried out properly.

The most common problem occurs in formation of the morula. This is the initial cell division process that forms a multicellular organism from the single celled zygote. The unique feature of this process is that the cells will multiply exponentially, but the little ball will never get bigger, until a certain point is reached. The zygote will multiply from one cell, to two, four, sixteen, and so forth, forming a multicellular ball: the morula. After a short time, it will become hollow in the middle, forming the blastula, and this differentiates into different types of cells: mesoderm, endoderm, and ectoderm, which will become muscle, organs, and skin in the developed animal.

The issue that occurs is when the zygote becomes, in a sense, cancerous. The cells multiply, but in an unregulated fashion, and rather than staying the same size, the ball of cells expands exponentially with the number of cells. This results in a large tumour which will eventually form a severely deformed creature, which usually dies. If I notice this happening, I terminate the process immediately. No sense wasting resources.

It's really cool, watching the tiny cell become living animals! It's magical in the sense that it is mind-blowing, but it is not a miracle, because it is all explained by biology – except for that first cause which set it all in motion. This still perplexes me. In any case, I've been having a great time down in Sublevel 1, with this stuff. Luckily, I don't have to go down into the further Sublevels – the mutant foetuses and tortured animals give me the creeps. At least at the point I am working on, before the immense chemical cocktail has taken effect, the creatures I'm working with are still natural creatures, albeit clones. I'd rather not think of the later stages.

But I *can't* not think of them. Those screams, the wild, desperate, rolling eyes, foaming mouths, lolling tongues, and the smell of vomit and excrement – it haunts my dreams. And, I now forgo the meat ration I so coveted before... Irony, right?

On the walk home, in my ratty OS rags (I don't dare to wear my good clothes past the border: that's just *begging* for a violent rape and mugging in the vile slums I call home) I look up at the giant billboards posted all over town. They show images of a peaceful, idyllic farmland with rolling green pastures, trees, and a beautiful orange and yellow sunrise. Cows, pigs, and chickens idle listlessly in pastures, pens, and coops, without a care in the world. The caption reads: *New Genesis Family Farms: Quality Protein-Rich Meat Products For You and Your Whole Family!* I scoff. Quality, sure, but exactly what quality? The meat products we churn out are the afterimage of a life of medieval torture and the creation of chemical Frankenstein's monsters. I discovered this old 19th century book on *GenNet* last week. A mad scientist creates a single abomination out of dead flesh. We, however, create millions of abominations out of living flesh...

When the animals reach slaughtering age, we don't bother wasting chemicals euthanizing them, we do it the old-fashioned way, tried and true, perfected back in the early 21st century:

A worker grabs an animal by the head with an electrified clamp, which stuns them. Then, they are impaled by meat hooks and strung up, and their throats are slit, but lots of times they wake up too soon, so when they're strung up and bleeding out, they're still conscious, spraying blood everywhere, twisting and screaming and choking, and bubbling and frothing like they've just eaten a bar of soap: very, very red soap. Or, the bleedout operation might be botched, leaving the animal fully sensate and alive when it's dropped into a tank of boiling water, which makes the skinning process much easier – just like potatoes.

Sick or dying animals are kicked and beaten and electrocuted by the workers, for sport, then impaled through the brain with a thick, pressurized, pneumatic bolt. Baby animals close to death are savagely brought the rest of the way: they have their heads smashed repeatedly onto the concrete floor until they're just a pulpy mess, or they're stuffed into a decapitation machine, but if it's done carelessly, they might just end up partially decapitated, with only their snout and half their face sheared cleanly off. When that happens, you can see their one remaining eye gyrating wildly, and their pink jelly brains are visible through the gaping hole in the front of their skulls.

Other stuff happens too. It's really horrendous. As an "Assistant Geneticist", I don't have to do it myself, I just wear a white lab coat and supervise impoverished Old Society citizens paid below-subsistence wages with no benefits and long hours. And because I've been there, *I get it:* I fully understand why they unleash their indignant rage upon these helpless creatures. I see the bitterness and spite in their eyes as I perform my "administrative tasks" and boss them around – I feel like a hypocrite. I think, *"Guys, I'm actually just like you, just smarter, cleverer, and a better liar; tough break, sorry about that."*

I admit, it *does* get to me. But everyone in lab *agrees:* they're only dumb animals! The truth is, I have my own life to think of! I *really **need*** this job! Besides, it's not forever... just until I get settled into my new apartment. Then I'll find something different.

I promise.

"Have you prepared the substrate for batches #BVS_64B, #4500 - #4700?" My lab partner, Assistant Geneticist Mason, asks me. He is a little younger than I am, with messy brown hair, a perpetual couple days beard stubble, and walks with a loping slouch. He looks like Shaggy, a character from a 20th century cartoon about a mystery-solving quartet with a Great Dane.

"Bovine Serum 64B... uh... yes. They're ready to go." We are preparing for another nuclear transplant operation. Mason and I have been working together every day since I started here, 13 months ago. He showed me the ropes and after a while we became sort-of-friends outside of work. We go back to his place and play video games. I don't have anything like that at my place, but his New Society apartment is awesome! There is a holographic media room that places you directly in the middle of a game, as if you are really there. Special eyewear allows you to see normally, but also overlays personalized aspects of your user experience upon your own body, such as outfits, gear, gadgets, and weapons. Motion capture sensors track your movements and put you directly in the action.

I have a home entertainment station, too. It is a kitchen chair with metal legs and covered with paisley vinyl coloured avocado green and amber-alert orange, with yellow foam everting out of several rips and gouges. Beside it is a bookshelf which is missing a shelf, and upon it are a couple dozen books from the 19th-21st centuries, from back when they still made books with paper (before Apple gained an imposing position in government and passed a bill outlawing paper because of "environmental concerns"). I've read all the books so many times I can nearly recite them. Mason's place is way cooler, and, soon, I'll be able to afford a place like that, and an immersion chamber, too!

"Um, I need more Formalin; I have to go down to SubLevel 3." murmurs Mason, his nose glued to a clipboard. He flips a couple of pages and murmurs to himself. "Hmm. Can you come give me a hand? Might as well restock the neural growth hormones, anabolic steroids, antibiotics, and Neurotoxin A16. We're low on them all." I nod. He ambles in the direction of the elevator, still buried in the clipboard.

"Neurotoxin A16? Which one is that?" I say, as the elevator descends.

"It's the protein which causes selective necrosis of the amygdala, by blocking the transport of electrons during oxidative phosphorylation, which results in the cessation of production of ATP – no fuel, the cells cease to function – they suffocate, basically."

"And without an amygdala, the animals are much more docile, and easier to handle." I shrug. "Makes sense."

"Now, if we could only develop a selective neurotoxin for the periaqueductal grey matter, we might be able to stop the animals from screaming in pain all the time. Gets damn annoying real quick." Mason says. (We often bitch and commiserate about the ongoing irritations of the job.)

"Hey, why so complicated?" I say, flippantly. "We should just sever the spines of all the baby animals, when we take them out of the pickle jars.

Just make 'em all tetraplegic, then they'd stop screaming *and* flailing. *Bonus!!!"*

He looks thoughtful. "Actually... that's a great idea! I'm going to look into that." His serious tone makes me uncomfortable, so I keep joking. "While we're at it, we can sew shut their anuses and urethras, so they don't stink so much!" I force a grin, but my words fall flat. Mason is away somewhere, considering, devising.

The elevator stops. The doors open. It looks totally different than the warehouse level containing hundreds of massive shelves of barrels, bottles, and boxes of chemicals. This is just a little hallway. The LED display above the door shows in red: *SL4*

"Oh. Wrong floor," says Mason, reaching for the button.

"Wait," I say, "I've never been here before; what is this place?"

"Just more labs. We do original research to try to improve the living conditions for the citizens of New Genesis over future generations. It's actually the main funding initiative of NGFF: the food production aspect is merely a mundane necessity." Mason says listlessly, without looking up from the button panel, his arm still extended.

"Oh, wow. Can I have a look?" I ask, very interested.

"I guess so." He shrugs ambivalently.

We walk down the hall. The walls are cinder blocks painted white. The floor and ceiling is grey concrete. A continuous line of fluorescent tubes travels down the center of the ceiling, flickering and buzzing. Our footsteps sound gargantuan as the reverberating sound waves bounce around us.

The first door we come to is labelled *SL4-Abnormal Development Experimental Research Lab-01:* Mason presses the button to open the door, which slides open with a swish. The hallway before us is bright and antiseptic, almost cheerful in appearance. It branches to the left. From somewhere out of sight, I can hear strange noises: moans and groans, and other indescribable vocalizations. I look inquisitively over at Mason. He is spinning his lanyard on his finger as he walks listlessly down the hallway. I follow.

As we round the corner, my jaw drops.

It is a large, square room, blindingly white and clean. There are no guards or lab workers in sight. Around the room are cages, like the ones in the animal labs upstairs. But these ones are filled with... *human children!* They are all naked, and utterly hideous to behold.

One boy has no eyes or nose, just a mouth hovering beneath a flat, blank wall of skin, as if he were a child's doll which somehow made it off the production line without having all its features painted on. I shudder. I recognize some of these mutations from studies in university, of the fallout after the Event. A small child of indeterminate sex is covered in scabby scales, with nothing resembling skin whatsoever. *Lamellar Ichthyosis...* I whisper the words breathlessly.

A girl who can't be more than three is lying on her back in one of the cages. Her head is swollen to five or six times the normal size, like the old illustrations of aliens. *Hydrocephalus.* Her eyes are tiny and beady, and are nearly rolled all the way back into her head. Her scalp is bald, and covered with bulging blue veins. Her breath scrapes her throat on the way out, and frothy spittle bubbles from between her pale lips. Her arms are twitching in seemingly random motions.

One child has four arms and four legs. *Polymelia.* Another looks perfectly normal, except an extra head grows from her own, crown to crown. This extra head can move its eyes and lips independently, but has no body other than a lump of an upper torso. *A parasitic twin!* A little baby with her heart protruding from her body. *Ectopia Cordis.*

In one corner of the room is a pile of little bodies, obviously dead. A baby with bulging blood-red eyes and swollen lips, white skin, and jagged red lighting branches all over its body. *Harlequin-Type Ichthyosis.* A baby with no skin at all. *Epidermolysis Bullosa.* A grotesque creature with no neck, a fat body and massive protruding frog-like eyes, still open. It is missing the top of its skull, and the exposed brain so severely underdeveloped, had it survived, it would only have been able to perform basic autonomic functions – no sensory perception or thinking. *Anencephaly.*

I feel like I'm going to vomit. Sure, I've studied these conditions, but at that point, the educational images were still and silent. Here and now, these poor children are making the most pitiful of noises; it is so much more *real* than the textbooks. Suddenly, I startle at the sound of terrified, agonized screams flooding from the adjoining room. I look in bewildered terror at Mason, but he is busy trimming his fingernails with a utility blade. I hurry over and impatiently punch the button to open the door.

The room is small and sterile. It reminds me of a dentist's office. In the center of the room, in a large reclining medical chair, beneath a bank of lights, sits a small boy of around seven years of age. His face is massive, and appears melted, as if he were made of wax and ventured too close to a candle. *Neurofibromatosis!* I gasp.

The chair is surrounded by computer banks with indecipherable readouts, and trolleys laden with tools and instruments. A man in a white coat is vivisecting the child, *cutting open his face*, while the boy, bound at wrists, ankles, and forehead, is shrieking and crying hysterically. The shocking scene before me is so repellent I nearly gag. Without thinking, I cry out:

"What the fuck are you doing?!" My voice sounds pathetically small, shrill, and girlish.

The guy startles so badly he cuts his own hand open, a deep gash which immediately begins gushing blood. "Fuck me!" he yells, dropping the scalpel and clutching the wound with his other hand. He glares at me.

"Christ, lady! Are you nuts? Look what you made me do! Jesus H!!" He turns and rushes out of a far door, bleeding all over the place and cursing. Mason is staring at me obscenely.

"Dude, what the fuck is *wrong* with you?!" he hisses scornfully, his face a portrait of ridicule. *Me?!* I drop my jaw. I'm speechless; I don't even know what to say to that, so I just turn and run over to the boy.

"Where are your mommy and daddy?" I ask, but the terrified child just stares at me, bewildered.

"Look, just stay here, okay? I'll come back with help!" I try to reassure the kid, then practically run back to the elevator. Mason chases after me, protesting.

"Would you just *stop?!* You're going to get us both written up!! What is your *problem?!*" he hollers breathlessly. The elevator doors close before he catches up to me.

I repeatedly stab the button for *SL1:* The Medical Bay. However, instead of going up, the elevator goes down! Someone must have already called it a moment before. The doors open at *SL5,* and a scientist steps on, absorbed in something on a clipboard. I try to disguise my distress from him, and I am about to press the door close button, when something odd catches my eye.

The first door in this hallway is marked *SL5-01 – Spawn Gestation Chamber 1A.* I just saw a scientist carrying a pickle jar in there, with something inside it that made me take a second glance, but by the time I looked back it had disappeared around the corner. I scramble out of the elevator and chase after him, but once inside, I just spin in circles, stupefied. It is a room identical to the ones I work in upstairs, but each of these thousands of jars holds a tiny, developing human foetus. A handful of scientists are working away quietly. I recognize many of them. *What the hell is going on in this place?!*

I wheel around and storm back to the elevator. It is busy. I descend the stairs two at a time, plunging deeper into the fetid bowels of this farmhouse of horrors.

SL6 is dead quiet.

The entire level is a massive, octagonal amphitheater. In the center is an operating table, lit from above by three bright lamps. Various surgical tools and medical equipment surround it. The seats of the amphitheater are dark; in the blinding light of the stage, I can't see. I step closer, and jump in fright.

Thousands of humans are standing in the bleachers, silently watching me. There are at least a hundred rows, and the octagon, at its narrowest circumference, seats at least four hundred people.

"Who the fuck are you people?!" I scream. They do not respond. I walk towards them. As I approach one of the ghosts, I yell at it. I bluff, telling it I have a proton pistol in my pocket and I will blow it the fuck away if it does not answer me. It does not answer me. Any sentient person would think twice before inviting an proton blast. *Perhaps it is not a person after all?*

All I can see is a dark humanoid figure against a white rectangular background, silent and still. A single red light shines out of the darkness beside it. My most basic instinct is to push it, so I do, even against my better judgment. It turns green, and a moment later, a bright light floods the humanoid from above. I squint in the painful illumination, and when I can see again, I gasp. It is a woman!

She is completely naked, bound to a vertical board by clamps extending like insect legs over her body, pinning everything except for her lower ventromedial torso, which is bisected down the center by a strange line, like she's been partially cut in half but then stuck back together.

I am startled to see her chest moving. *She is alive!* I look at her face. Her eyes are open, but glazed over. A respiration mask is strapped to her mouth. Her arms are perforated with multiple IV lines. A urethral catheter protrudes from her genitals, and an enema tube snakes out from behind.

I move to the next figure along the line and press the button. Another woman. The next: another, and another, and another. *What is going on here?* I want to release them, but I don't know how. I see a button with a rectangle beneath an arrow pointing UP, so I take a guess, and push it. A horizontal strip of digital text appears, in red, seven-segmented LED lights, like a bedside alarm clock.

The text scrolls from right to left:

[SPAWNMOTHER #3490, ENGAGE OPERATION]

I hear the whine of hydraulics, and, alarmed, I step back. From high in the theater, a crane arm snakes down, and a massive clamp takes a firm hold of the board the woman is clasped to. With a hiss, all tubes (IV, catheter, and enema) disengage from detachable junctions close to their insertion point, simultaneously. The hydraulic arm lifts the bound woman up into the air. It swivels, rotates, and places the unit horizontally on the operating table in the center of the stage. I run over to it. A digital display at this station has activated. A similar strip of text appears:

[AUTOMATION ENGAGED; PREPARING SPAWNMOTHER FOR FOETAL EXTRACTION]

I watch, horrified, as another hydraulic arm swivels down, and uses a laser to cut along a pre-existing line, just below the navel, while two other arms pry the flesh apart laterally, revealing her abdominal cavity.

[FOETAL EXTRACTION PROCEDURE INITIATED]

I can only stare as the laser slices open this nameless woman's womb along a partially healed scar, and opens this up like a purse. By the light above, I can see a tiny undeveloped human inside. *It is sucking its thumb.* The text display is blinking insistently:

[URGENT: MANUALLY REMOVE FOETUS IMMEDIATELY]
[URGENT: MANUALLY REMOVE FOETUS IMMEDIATELY]
[URGENT: MANUALLY REMOVE FOETUS IMMEDIATELY]

I can't move.
I can't think.
I can't breathe.

I startle as suddenly I hear Mason's voice in my right ear: "Percy, what are you doing here?! Look, we really need to get back to work. We have to have that bovine serum ready for tonight's batch."

I whirl on him, incensed. "You *knew* about this, didn't you?!" I spit the words at him like venom.

"Well, yeah. I worked on *SL5* and down here for a couple years, until you showed up, then I was reassigned to train you." His voice is deadpan, matter-of-fact, and he even seems a little bewildered at my aggressive demeanour.

"You WHAT?!" I yell in his face.

"Jesus Christ...What's your problem, Persephone?" he says peevishly, stepping back.

"What's my *problem?* You sick fuck! You're farming *people!!*" I can feel my neck burning. My fists are clenched and trembling.

"So? We've been doing this for years! Tomakin developed the procedure. He has probably single-handedly saved mankind," he says, nonchalantly, as he lights an ersatz cigarette and exhales a thick cloud of smoke, which makes me gag.

"What would the citizens of New Genesis say if they knew about this? It's completely immoral!" I'm so worked up I'm shaking all over.

He shrugs. "Most people *do* know about it. It's no secret. Sure, it's brutal, but as long as it doesn't interrupt their holovision and their meat rations, they're happy to ignore it. But you're missing the entire point here. It's a *good* thing!!" he insists.

"Think about it! *Genetic modification!!*" he exclaims, gesticulating animatedly, the cigarette painting swirls of trailing smoke in the air. "This is cutting edge science! Surely you of all people must appreciate that! The benefits are indisputable! The fact is, New Genesis has two severe problems, which are directly caused by its citizens, but those same citizens refuse to address them. Therefore, we must take action for them, since they are obviously too stupid to realize they are causing the internal collapse of our new civilization.

"The first problem is food: supply and demand. The privileged, ignorant consumers of New Genesis eat more than twice the amount necessary to sustain them. This behaviour is completely unsustainable. Our resources are taxed as they are, production is decreasing, and demand is increasing. It is doing so because of the second problem: rampant overpopulation. The only things these imbecilic primates are good at is eating and fucking and popping out babies like an automated production line.

"The truth is, humanity is literally a cancer upon the planet: it grows without check, without density-dependent inhibition, irrespective of available resources, and it will do so until it kills its host: Earth. However, we have found and initiated solutions to these problems. You may recall some months ago a bill was passed mandating every new pregnancy be genetically screened for diseases, foreseeable disabilities, etc. We knock out the prospective mothers with harmless gas, and perform this screening, which, in reality, is just a placental fluid test, but we also perform an invasive surgery via the vagina – which leaves no evidence of surgery, so the mother never realizes a thing – wherein we extend a tiny hypodermic needle up through the cervix and into the womb. We then selectively inject trillions of copies of one of two different viruses into the foetus, which spreads a modified RNA sequence throughout its body, attacking, in particular, its active stem cells. This introduces two important genetic modifications into the embryonic development of the new population:

1. *Each new person born will have only 1/3rd of the appetite they would normally.*

2. *Nineteen of every twenty new citizens will have no sex drive whatsoever.*

In this way, we will eventually end up with a surplus of food, and only 5% of the population reproducing. Both problems solved! We are currently working on some of the more secondary issues – for example, not making people smarter, as might seem intuitive, but making them more placid and pliable. Smart people cause problems for governments. A functionally retarded population is most manageable." He shows me his yellow teeth.

"But why all this?!" I hiss, "Why not just use somatic cell nuclear transfer, and spare the lives of these women?"

"Surely you can't be serious?? In order to have the most benefit, we need to work with unique human subjects. Working with clones will get us nowhere: each foetus we use must be genetically distinct, the product of meiosis, and a natural embryonic development. So, we use live mothers. We – that is, myself and the other guys – we *personally* impregnate the women, then wait until the appropriate stage of development – whatever developmental level we want to study; usually we have a few tiers dedicated to several significant points along the timeline – before removing the foetus. We then fuse the womb shut, chemically induce ovulation, and the process is then begun again. This way we can get about five foetuses a year per SpawnMother. We currently have about 9,000 SpawnMothers, so we burn through about 45,000 foetuses per year in our research. I must say, we make excellent progress."

I grab Mason by his lab coat and pull him very close, snarling through my teeth at him. "These are *real women* you are using as foetus production factories! *Real children* whose only life is one of pain and torture! They are *living beings!* They don't deserve this savage treatment!"

He pushes me away, scowling, smoothing the lapels of his lab coat.

"Don't be naïve, Percy. Developing these solutions is a tedious business, and most attempts are failures. We must press on and learn new ways to improve the citizens of tomorrow. Sure, we're using live women, but they're merely RPs. There is more than one way to be RePurposed, and, in the long run, this is even more productive to humanity than the mulching factory. And the babies aren't even human – they're not given the chance to be – there's no loss. They can't even be considered collateral damage."

Mason presses a series of buttons on the terminal. The mechanical arms sew the womb back up, sealing the fate of the tiny human inside. Then it stitches the belly of the woman, before replacing the unit back into the rows of faceless others. The lights again go dark.

"Besides," he says to me. "You stand here, raving your head off at me, yet you have more than happily contributed to the torture of *millions* of animals during your time here. Are they not living beings, too?" He flashes me an unambiguous look, then turns and begins walking to the elevator, a rectangle of light in the darkness. "Now come on; we really need to get back to work." he calls over his shoulder.

I stand there, in the darkness. Ahead of me, the warm light of the elevator spills out over the floor, almost to my toes. I turn and look back into the pitch black womb of the amphitheater, to the SpawnMothers. Their breathing machines produce 10,000 dry, rasping whispers. It sounds as if they're *accusing* me!!!

"Look," I want to tell them, *"I'm just doing my job!!!"* From the darkness, I see them all staring at me, unmollified. I shudder and turn back around. Mason stands in the elevator, waiting. At the end of the day he'll go home to his fancy New Society apartment, with his full-size gaming holofield... and I'll go home to the OS projects.... I sigh and stare at my feet. My shoe is untied. How did I not notice that when I was running? I bend down and mechanically perform the sequential loops.

I... I should think rationally about this... The truth is, I'm *almost there!!* In just a few more months I'll have saved enough to afford the exorbitant application fee for NS citizenship, then I'll be able to upgrade to a better apartment, and soon, I'll install my *own* gaming holofield, *bigger and better* than Mason's... It'll have 12 surround-sound speakers, not just 6, and a 24-bit profile of *16,777,216* colours, instead of only 12-bit!! I'll have him over and tell my kitchen to make him a drink. (See, he doesn't even have an automatic kitchen.) And I'll have an antigravity bed, too, with the walls configured to display an ocean sunrise when I wake up. I chuckle inwardly: I can't wait to see the look on Mason's face when he sees it all; he'll be *so* jealous!

Suddenly, I realize that for the first time in months, I have a tangible craving for bacon. Strange.

[2015]

// One-Self //

(3017 A.D.)

Bartlomiej Maksymilian wiped the sweat from his face with his ragged sleeve. His tangled blonde hair kept falling in his eyes, and it irritated him. The blazing sun pounded down upon him with merciless abandon. Undulating waves of yellow sand extended into the distance, each dune textured with smaller ripples. The scorching heat created phantom puddles of shimmering silver hovering above the ground; they were standing in a golden ocean, extending as far as could be seen, creating a beautiful contrast with the cloudless blue sky above. But Max had never seen an ocean before. This desiccated desert is all he has known for all of his 32 years.

He disengaged the battery of his pockmarked, red and white dirt bike with its wide, knobby tires suitable for the constantly shifting liquid surface of the sand, then laid it down, and covered it with a light-diffraction cloak which would bend the rays around it, effectively rendering it invisible. He tagged it with a pinging chip connected to his wrist PDA, so he could find it again, then turned to his companion.

"Are you sure you're up for this?" he asked.

"Of course," Athena replied, kneeling down and reaching into her backpack. She counted two dozen radioactive isotope tubes, then tucked them back inside.

Max watched the slightly-built 25-year-old woman. Athena had sunshine-golden hair and crystal blue eyes which made Max shiver.

"So how well do you know the bandit camp?" he asked her, as they trudged over the desert sand.

"Well, I remember photographically what it looked like back then, but that was eighteen years ago, so obviously, it could be totally different. I lived there for five years, until your father found me there, when I was seven. I was young enough that I easily picked up their language. The camp is called *Skalderag*, which literally means "living-place"."

"This is never going to work," Max said, extending his arm and looking skeptically at the strange, ragged, tribal-like clothing he wore, a patchwork of fabrics crudely sewn together. They had looted the clothing from the bodies of a couple of bandits on patrol they had a skirmish with a while back, then Athena modified them to fit. Max wished for his combat-ready radsuit. He imagined he could feel the cancer manifesting already.

"Just follow my lead," she beckoned, as they climbed to the top of a large dune. "It's over this crest. Get down." They dropped into a prone position and crept to the apex. "Most importantly, don't say a word. Even if I were to teach you a few phrases, your Omegan accent would be a disastrous giveaway. The cover story is that you cannot speak because of a recent brain injury."

She pulled a pair of binoculars from her bag. Max nodded, and reached for the fission sniper rifle on his back, Through the 16x scope, he surveyed the large encampment which lay half a kilometer in front of them.

The bandit camp was a fairly vast, yet rather makeshift affair of ignorantly assembled ramshackle buildings, constructed using corrugated tin and salvaged planks and plywood from structures outlasting the Event, as well as scavenged bricks and stonework, by the looks of it. Jagged fences of rusted, fluted steel and aluminum formed a quilt-work perimeter which defined the streets and property boundaries, although Max doubted they were even sophisticated enough to actually define property boundaries in a legal sense; it was probably just dog-eat-dog anarchy.

Many of the walls and roofs of the buildings had gaping holes in them, proof of the shoddy workmanship failing under the destructive force of the many sandstorms in the desert wasteland. The outer walls, however, were strangely contrary to this: they were composed of stacks of old cars and trucks, four or five high, reinforced with crude steel bands which maintained the structure's stability, as well as bound the doors shut. Sheets of steel of various shapes and sizes had been used to patch the windows. It was well crafted: evidently, someone else had built this place before the bandits, someone with competence and proper tools. Altogether, the encampment appeared to be an imposing fortress to anything except powerful explosives.

Within were scattered a few handfuls of functioning vehicles: mainly Jeeps and Rovers and ATVs capable of traversing the rugged and ruthless terrain. Most of them were equipped with heavy machine guns, using the old-fashioned system of belts and magazines utilizing a single-cell combustion chamber within each individual bullet, rather than the contemporary weapons such as laser carbines, fusion-powered railguns, proton weapons, or fission snipers such as the one Max had.

More vehicles formed scattered places of lodging – these were old rusted motor-home units shaped like long, silver cylinders, and the box-shaped campers which hung off the back of old-fashioned pickup trucks which still used wheels, instead of the more modern gravcar, which hovered above the earth using strong jets of air. Hundreds of people could be seen milling about the encampment.

"Cockroaches," Max remarked. "They're fucking savages." He spat in the sand. "They kill absolutely anyone they encounter and pillage their corpses, stealing their belongings. Men, women, children, it doesn't matter. They're brutal animals who should be executed, all of them."

Athena ignored his commentary, and instead, put away her binoculars and climbed to her feet.

"Let's go. *Slowly.*"

The last 250 meters were travelled cautiously, with their hands up, aware that at least a dozen rifles and HMGs were trained on them. Twenty meters away from the gate of the camp, a bandit in an overwatch tower yelled at them.

//Skwerda man Ploordie! Cinsuirre ensa Van-cunsuirre?!// he screamed, training his laser-guided rifle conspicuously on each of them in turn. Athena whispered under her breath: *"'Make identified you! Self or Not-Self?'"*

She raised her voice as high as she could.

//Tam Cinsuirre exa Tes-cunsuirre!! Starga skluff tinga; consuirre ploobo disa crast aa!//

And to Max she whispered, "Self of the One-Self! Continue please our living; we leave death behind!"

The lookout disappeared from the tower, and reappeared a moment later, at a small door in the twelve-foot gate constructed of what appeared to be old street signs and steel plates. He had brought a friend. Max and Athena stopped, hands raised, as the two bandits approached them slowly, in cross-steps, guns levelled at their faces. The one who had spoken had taken the lead. He had a long, filthy beard and sparse yellow teeth, and was missing his left ear. His partner didn't look any better. They both had coarse black hair and very dark skin.

The frontman walked up to Max and poked him sharply in the sternum with the barrel of his shardgun. Max bristled, but did not react.

//Caenla tomidon mas laxa?// the bandit snarled at him. (What were you doing out there?) Athena began to answer, but the man raised his hand imperiously: *Be silent!* The second man quickly stepped forward and pressed the barrel of his rifle against Athena's cheekbone. She complied.

//Drozon ixa infetunita drasta??// the lookout barked. (Why have you speak nothing??) Max stood tall, returning the burning glare of the *Skalderag* guard, but held his tongue. Angrily, the man pressed the his gun painfully into Max's forehead. With a growl, Max reached up and grabbed the barrel, averting it. The second bandit yelled and aimed at Max, who let go of the gun and stepped back, his hands raised, scowling hatefully.

Abruptly, Athena dropped to one knee in the sand, raising her arms obsequiously to the men. *//We apologize, respected other-Self!!//* she pleaded in the bandit's own language, bowing abjectly, *//Since a great damage to the head-bone less than a half-hand of winters before, the mouth-voice of our Together-Self is only half, and his behaviour is impulsive!! We* *have returned from hunting in the sand ocean for food for the One-Self, but we found none.//*

Without taking his eyes off them, the first man leaned over and whispered to his compatriot. They conferred in hushed tones for a moment; Bandit #1 pointed at the two of them and said something, then Bandit #2 frowned and shook his head.

//Why have not we seen your faces with our ball eyes before now and so in our memories?// the first bandit hissed, addressing Athena in his tongue.

//Appreciation we give for your cautious concern.// she replied. *//Our outward feet stepped through the faraway southeast opening, but we return to this portal to influx, because our exhaust has commanded us to bring our true bodies home before they are damaged from the great fireball and so we would soon die from the dry insides!//*

The man grunted skeptically, then roughly grabbed Max by the shoulder, spinning him around. He yelled something at Max, who could not speak their language. He knew that Athena could not translate while the guards were there. The bandit yelled the same words again, shoving him roughly in the back.

Max thought quickly. *What would I command, if the situation were reversed?*

He dropped to his knees in the hot sand, linking his hands behind his head. He held his breath and closed his eyes, impossibly attempting to psych himself up for the inevitable shard blast through the back of his skull, if he had guessed wrongly. Instead, the bandit murmured something in an approving tone, then shoved Max down onto his belly, twisting his arms behind his back and pinning them there with a knee. He grabbed Max roughly by the hair and pull his head back. He must have shouldered his weapon, because with one hand he held Max under the chin, and with the other began yanking large sections of his long, messy hair. Max gasped and choked for breath. After a few seconds of this, the bandit literally exclaimed "Aha!" (a universal term, apparently), and stabbed Max in the scalp with a finger. Then, he dismounted him, and brusquely pulled him to his feet, before carefully brushing off Max's clothes, and somewhat tidying his hair. Finally, smiling broadly, the bandit stepped forward with open arms. Max stiffened, but the man simply embraced him, then motioned with a sweep of his arm, towards the encampment.

//Slavalas Skalderag carm, Cinsuirre ex Cunsuirre-witta!// (Welcome to living-place return, Selves of our One-Self!)

And thusly, the two Omega Faction operatives walked freely into the enemy stronghold. Max was thankful he had deflected a piece of grenade shrapnel with his skull, a few months back. The deep gash had produced a noticeable scar.

Athena was thin-lipped. "You're gonna get us both killed flying off the handle like that!" she hissed.

Max ignored her.

Self vs Not-Self.

This is it. This is the rule. This is life! You see it is very important for life. For all the long centuries since the beginning of life, this has been what keeps us alive! This life has been for more than fifteen generations. Before then was the great storm of fire and death, and then sickness and tiny new humans in demon form, and they screamed in pain and died, too. There was very huge pain in the true bodies of the humans, but also in their every-where-Selves, which did not have bodies, but embodied their great ubiquitous consciousness. After the fire and heat there was ice and coldness, and many of the humans died who did not have fire or food, and many of the humans died because they were killed by other humans whose every-where-Selves were crazy with bitterness and anger because of the hard new world after the great storm.

The female Selves – and also the male Selves – their new babies died in the cold, or from not having enough food, or because they came in demon form, and then the agony and grief of the every-where-Selves of those mothers and fathers expanded to all of our Selves, and the pain was so large that many could not live in their true bodies any longer and died from the vast injury to their every-where-Selves, because they stopped caring for their true bodies, and lots of people actually destroyed their own true bodies and so died.

*Everywhere was pain. The humans which we were, we knew we had to become more than many Selves to survive: we had to become **One-Self**. In One-Self, there is strength and love! We know every being within the One-Self. Within this, everyone is my own Self. My mother is my Self, and I am my mother's Self, because we are the same, we are One-Self, and this is truth for my neighbour, too, and all of us who are within the One-Self! We are together, and we are strong because of this. But, of course, when there is **Self**, there must also be **Not-Self**.*

Not-Self is very easy: it is anything living that is apart from the One-Self. For Not-Self, there always is given immediate death. It is the very safest. For a time, at the beginning, the humans tried to bring many other humans into the One-Self, so that they too could become strong and have love and family! But the every-where-Selves of these outside humans were too damaged, and they created havoc and pain, destroying the true bodies of many of us, or even just spreading anger and hatred to all the every-where-Selves who touched them. These humans did not belong, and there was a specific experiencing of great sadness when a female very-little-Self went missing and was found with her true body exposed bare, and it was very cold and a pale white and purple and a red colour all over. She had been handled all over. Her adult-true-body-area had been used before it was ready, and her head was damaged so greatly that she was dead and she was covered all over in her own life-fluid. The Not-Self who had done this was found and his true body was destroyed by all of us in the One-Self, but mostly by the father of the little-Self who had been given such great and unjust pain. And after that, no thing that was Not-Self was allowed into the One-Self, and it was decided true that they must die always immediately, for the safety of our One-Family. This was many ages before I began to live, however. It is a story which every little-Self is taught around the fire as we eat, and as we learn to survive.

*My name is **Sarela**, a female human of the One-Self, and it has been, we think, thirty-two seasons since the One-Self gave me life. My male Together-Self has the name of **Taurock**, and he has been alive for thirty-nine seasons. We had a little-Self that we lost, almost four hands of cycles before now. We still have much pain in our every-where-Together-Self when we think of her, so we try not to think of her.*

*The One-Self has about ten hundreds of us. We live all in a together-place called **Skalderag**. Most male-Selves and female-Selves, when they become adult, are paired to form a Together-Self, and then they usually have little-Selves after joining their true bodies with each other. But our little-Selves are everyone's little-Selves, and we all are alive together in one living-place and we keep each other safe and joyful! At the new-darkness meal, we all gather around a very large fire to roast whatever we have found for food.*

As we eat, every part of all the One-Self talks about our just-now time between when the old darkness left and the new darkness came, and how our true bodies are feeling and, mostly importantly, how our every-where-Selves are feeling, too. Sometimes some of us (including my Self) will have a great hurt that is not within their true bodies, and when this happens, all of the One-Self will try to embrace their every-where-Selves with our own and make them light again, and we also all of us embrace their true bodies with ours and sing until the air is shaking with the great noise of our singing! And then there is usually smiles and laughter because it usually works! Not always, but even then, we are all strong together for those alone-Selves who are feeling the great pain in their every-where-Selves, and who are a part of the great One-Self, but even might feel like they are Not-Self, because their every-where-Selves are so much in pain and feeling falsely alone.

*For many cycles, things are mostly okay with the One-Self. We practice **Self vs. Not-Self**, and we stay alive like this, and it is well-understood that every Not-Self creature is given absolute death without hesitation, because this keeps us strong and safe. Unfortunately, though, we are given very much death by the floating creatures from the large camp of humans many new-darknesses far from here. The creatures are very gigantic and roar quite* *loudly and spit flame and are made of metals and we know they are not alive, but they contain live humans who rain upon us stones of fire and smoke which make huge booming noises and they cause our true bodies to come apart into many pieces and throw our bright life-liquid all over, and it is always death for any Self who is hit by these stones, or is anywhere near where they hit the earth. ... It seems like the One-Self is forever grieving over the loss of our male and female Selves and little-Selves... but we try not to think about it too much, because it gives a pain to our every-where-Self that we can almost feel in our true bodies because it is so tall.*

We have thought very hard about it and it is our idea that the humans in the air want our Plu-tone-yum, *which is a word we don't understand what it means but it was at the beginning taught to us by one of our Selves who was from before the great storm of fire, who was very smart, and he knew a lot about Plu-tone-yum and that it can kill us easily, if we do not treat it rightly, but if we do, it will stop us from becoming sick and receiving death, and having so many little-Selves who begin life with their true bodies in horrible demon forms and also lots of times dying, or beginning life already dead.*

I asked Taurock if it was a living thing or maybe a great God like which they had long ago, but he told me that it is living, but not alive, and there are no Gods, there is only Self and Not-Self.

That is okay. We know that as long as we have the One-Self then everything is okay, and even though the living is often full of pain for our every-where-Selves, and especially for our true bodies – because it is very hot and dry out here during the bright time before the new-darkness, under the great fireball and the One-Self often has great thirst, and then it is very cold at night besides – but really I look at the beautiful face of my Taurock, and I think that, even so, things are okay. I am glad I have him with me, as half of our Together-Self, and we are glad we have all of our other Selves to give us love and strength!

"Fucking savages..." grumbled Max, as he and Athena made their way through the bandit camp. Up close, the buildings looked even meaner: structures of scavenged metal and stone, wood from centuries ago, nailed and roped together using a variety of improvised materials. None of the establishments had plumbing, running water, or electricity. Max could see into most of the shacks, since they didn't seem to have doors. Maybe because they could not manufacture hinges? Well, it's not like there would be anything for anyone to steal, anyway. All that they contained were beds made of old mattresses or even just scraps of fabric on the ground, and sometimes bare cardboard, some clothes, maybe a rickety chair or table, and a few pots and pans.

Absolutely nothing worth living for.

The *Skalderag* citizens paid them little or no attention as they threaded their way through the crowds of ragged humans who bustled about aimlessly, like flies buzzing around a room, travelling in circles, going nowhere busily. Everyone seemed to be yelling, and Max could understand nothing. Vendors on the street attempted to sell goods, sitting in the dust, their wares spilling into the pathway. Max looked at their inventories as he stepped gingerly over them. *Nothing but junk.* Bracelets made of bones and roach exoskeleton, by the looks of it, clay cups and bowls, and other worthless crap.

Max grimaced as he caught the sight and scent of a man barbecuing some sort of vermin. He was old and bone-thin, and was completely naked except for a pair of brightly coloured pants with the legs rolled up. An explosive white beard sprouted from his face, and he wore a necklace of teeth which jangled over the cracked, copper-brown skin stretched over his collarbones.

// Preeso wanala pilistia? Klagarasa!!// he shouted joyfully to Max, having caught his eye. He thrust a blackened, skewered, unrecognizable creature in Max's face. Max grimaced, and hurried on. Throughout it all he sweated. It was hot as hell, and the population density wasn't making it any better.

"Do you even know where we're going??" he hissed to Athena, who turned and shot him a look of exasperation as she brought her finger to her lips, then looked forward again. Max settled into a dreary quietude, feeling peculiar, wearing ragged clothing stitched from the upholstery of old vehicles, and skins of hellbeasts.

Savages.

Before long, the residential/marketplace area thinned out, and the streets, if they could be called that, were mostly empty. Max saw in the approaching distance a much taller building which looked like it had actually been crafted with skill. It rose three or four stories high and was made of metal and cement. He guessed it was there they were heading: the building which housed *Skalderag*'s radshield and stockpile of Plutonium, which was the reason why they were there. Omega needed Plutonium to power the giant globe which generated their nuclear power, as well as their forcefield and radshield. The system was sophisticated, and used very little elemental material, but still needed replenishing every couple of years. They had run out of reserves. *Skalderag* had a surplus. It wasn't much of a decision.

"Can't we trade them something, instead of stealing it?" Jade had asked, but trading with them meant identifying as being separate from them, which, according to them, was adequate justification for immediate murder.

Therefore, larceny was the only option. Having lived as a bandit slave and gained proficiency in their language, Athena was the obvious candidate. Max was there merely as backup, and to provide a male presence, since he and his father assumed that if it were just Athena, she would be instantly and horribly raped by every one of the many savage, ignorant, sexually uninhibited male bandits. Athena had indignantly protested, accusing them of prejudice and sexism, insisting she would be just fine on her own.

She was vetoed.

As they approached the nuclear facility, Max was distracted by a commotion. Despite Athena's repeated, urgent gestures to move on, he veered off track and crept quietly toward a large building which was apparently an automobile chop-and-repair shop. Several Jeeps, dune buggies, and dirt bikes were in various stages of repair and disrepair. What drew Max's attention were the unmistakable screams and cries of children in pain, and the gruff vocalizations of a man exerting himself.

Creeping up to the fence surrounding the compound, made of sheets of rusted aluminum and steel, old car doors, and the sidings from vans and trucks, Max peered around the corner. In the center of the dirty yard, surrounded by piles of junk: mufflers, bumpers, headlights, motors, tires, wheel hubs, gutted seats, etc., were two small children: a girl and a boy of around five and seven years old, chained to a post.

The two children were being beaten by a large, hairy man wearing nothing but a pair of shorts which looked like they were made from at least six other unidentifiable fabrics. He was using only his hands, but the children were bruised black and blue, bleeding from their noses and lips, and bawling miserably. Max's jaw tightened.

This scumbag needs a lesson, bad.

Just as he was about to burst forth and save the day, Athena appeared behind him, grabbing his wrist and pulling him away from the fence. Her hand gestures indicated, *Leave it alone; let's GO!* After a pause, Max reluctantly turned and followed her away, the sound of the children's cries of pain and fear still ringing in his ears.

They hadn't walked ten meters before he abruptly swung around and began striding determinedly back to the auto shop. He rounded the corner and strode through the auto yard gateway, making a beeline for the brawny man. Seeing Max approach, the man turned to him and smiled widely, spreading his arms as if for an embrace.

//Ahh, Cinsuirre!! Adnost idl caxtfnir uhr daal!!// The man beamed at him.

Max shoved the man, who staggered back, not from the impact, but from shock and surprise. He stared at Max with wide, perplexed eyes, looking for all the world like a puppy dog which has just been kicked by a human it loved and trusted.

//Anaas takka!?! Siklex rufow bleegnorax platta?!? Ralson!!// he cried incredulously, but he did not fight back. The children, far from being relieved at having been saved from their tormenter, looked terrified, and ran howling to hide behind the man's legs, peeking out in utter fear at the horrible monster that apparently was Max, their chains trailing behind them. The man reached down and stroked their hair, uttering gentle syllables in an obvious effort to calm them.

Max was confused. Before he could react, Athena ran in, once again waving her hands urgently, and falling to her knees, bowing before the man, apologizing profusely, and offering the same explanation for Max's aggressive behaviour as she had given to the guards outside. He was surprised when she reached up, grabbed his hand, and wrenched him violently to his knees. He was disgusted by Athena's obsequious behaviour towards this criminal degenerate.

Quite abruptly, a large pair of hands pulled him gently and easily to his feet, and Max looked up and saw that the man's grand smile had returned. He embraced Max with his hairy, sweaty body.

//Self of my One-Self!// the man cried, in his own language, *//I have great sorrow and tall apologies for your damaged head-jelly and the sadness in your every-where-Self! Please, I wish to you peace and prosperity!//* He stood, beaming like a happy child.

Max could not understand. Frustrated, he simply turned and walked away, with Athena following him, bowing as she retreated. A couple of blocks away he abruptly stopped, and confronted her.

"*The fuck was all that?!*" he seethed.

"I could ask the same! You're betting our goddamn lives on your impulsive sense of moral superiority!" she replied, her eyes afire. "You have absolutely *no clue* about the social and cultural construct here. You're lucky I don't expose you as *Not-Self*, and let them flay you."

"As *what?!*" he spat irritably.

"*Van-Cunsuirre.*" she hissed, before striding furiously away, toward the nuclear facility. Max shuddered involuntarily.

When the new little-Selves begin living, they are empty in the head-jelly and they do not know of the One-Self. To them, their own Self is the only Self! But this thoughts causes destruction of the One-Self!! We must all be together only little pieces of the biggest Self!! And the new little-Selves must learn this!

From their first cycle until the end of their twelfth cycle, the little-Selves are made to have great heavy metal ropes on their necks which restricts their radius! They are made to serve every wish of their parent adult-Selves. They are made to work tirelessly, cooking and cleaning and scrubbing and repairing weapons and wheel-craft, and taking care of their sibling-Selves. This is to show to them that to live in the One-Self is hard and great pain to their true bodies! But it is necessary, and if they work hard, their every-where-Selves will have much joy and they will be made gifts of the respect from their parent adult-Selves and all their other Selves!

Once every day, for three circles of Ralson's shadow clock, two at the beginning and one at the end, the little-Selves are taken out of their metal ropes and are practiced in the arts of fighting with the togetherness of their true bodies and their every-where-Selves. They are shown that fighting is not about recklessness or violence, but it is about making the great control of their true bodies and even greater control of their every-where-Selves, so that they can know their own One-Self, and only then they can have the ability to understand the taller One-Self of all Skalderag.

It is a form of great love, that every times when they have misbehaviour, to damage the true bodies of the little-Selves, because it will cause the strength of their every-where-Selves to expand muchly. So with the hand of the parent-Self they are injured and made to spill their life-liquid, just a little bit. This is a very good reason: to show to the little-Selves that if they did not have the safety of the great One-Self, a very small misbehaviour or lack of self-discipline would likely cause their true bodies to be damaged so greatly that they would be made to stop living. We remind them about the great storm and about how the Not-Self humans will damage and destroy their true bodies and every-where-Selves alike, and this is why we have formed the One-Self. They must know this well for the goodness and long length of their living!

The sophisticated nuclear facility seemed strangely out of place in the ramshackle slum city of *Skalderag*. Athena shocked Max by simply walking up to the front door and stepping inside. He had expected heavy security and the necessity for clandestine covert subterfuge. It did not even appear that there was anyone inside the facility! Max looked around in stupefaction. In contrast to the dirty run-down streets outside, in here it was clean and bright. White paint gleamed on the walls, making it seem almost antiseptic. Max was surprised to see banks of electric lights.

"If this city has nuclear power and the capability for electric power, why is it the citizens live in such squalor and poverty? They could easily provide themselves with many modern comforts, and quit living like filthy animals!"

Athena did not hide the contempt in her voice:

"For years, I have silently listened to you guys preach about how *savage* the *Skalderag* people are, how *primitive* and *stupid* they are! But do you want to know something? When this facility was first created, its founder, W. Ralson attempted to teach them technology and science and infrastructure management. They *refused* it! These people hold their values in *each other*, not microwaves and toilets and holovision sets! They are, by far, some of the least-educated people in the world, but they see that humankind's increase of technology produces an inverse relationship: a direct decrease in social cohesion. *How is it,* they question, *that the most advanced human societies just so happen to be the most unhappy? Look where it got us. The great storm of flame and death.*"

Athena looked disgusted. "You seemed so shocked when we just waltzed right in here. The truth is, there is no security because there is no suspicion! People don't have doors on their huts, because, to them, they are not individual people, they are *One-Self!* There is no crime in *Skalderag!* There is no social unrest, no political parties, no jails! These people are the most advanced society on earth right now! Even more than us, and far more than New Genesis, because their advancement is the development of the greatest investment available to mankind: its people. Fuck technology. I only agreed to this mission because if I didn't, *our* whole society would collapse! But the truth is, we're stealing from the most gentle, most generous people on earth."

Max hollered. "Gentle?! These people are *killers!*"

"So are you," Athena retorted. "Now let's get this shit over with."

She stepped into a protection suit, then walked over to what looked like a massive wall safe and opened the door, with the simple push of a single button. Inside were rows upon rows of cases marked with radiation hazard trefoil symbols. Athena opened one. They each contained six short rods of metal, 20 centimeters long by 3.5 centimeters in diameter, which glowed a faint violet in the darkness of the safe. One of them would power Omega's nuclear sphere for three months. Athena produced several long, thin silver cylinders, and opened them, sliding a rod into each one. When she was done they had 24 of them in total. More than 60 cases remained: over 360 rods left. *No wonder New Genesis wants them so badly,* Max thought.

Outside of the safe, Max and Athena stripped to their underwear, and each taped the cylinders to their forearms, upper arms, thighs, calves, stomachs, and lower backs. With their clothes on, they each easily concealed a dozen of the small rods. They tidied up after themselves, and walked casually out of the front door.

Moments later, they heard the roar of airships overhead, then several loud explosions, followed by screams of terror, pain, and anguish. *Skalderag* was being bombed by R. Janus and the NG-RPEB.

This now-time between the old darkness and the new darkness has been good for me! I have made clean the sleeping-place, and I am getting ready for the new-darkness meal. Taurock should be home soon from the bug-hunt. I am lonely to see him today... I like his broad shoulders and his long head-hairs which very many times hang in front of his long-seeing eyes and I say to him some of the times, //Now, dearest together-Self who is my own love-Self, your true body will be fastly eaten by a many-legs bug because your ball eyes will have been blinded under the cover by your long messy hairs!// And he will laugh and give me the words: //Oh my wonderlovely together-Self, you have the correct words rightly said! I will even more quickly take my sharp-sword and sever the hairs until my round head is like the breast of a wild hellbeast, with its furs so short and all thrusting in the many directions!// And he will move quickly his true body towards his sharp-sword, like he is going to bring truth into his words, but of course I am laughing and telling him //No, no, please don't, because I deeply love your long messy hairs!!// and I will jump onto his true body so that his hands are on my true body so they cannot have the free space to get his sharp-sword, and he will look at me with his well-seeing eyes which have the sharp, beautiful clear colours of the outside air-ceiling, and I will have the gift of love from his eyes, and then we will lay with our true bodies together and become our truly Together-Selves when into that moment when we are a truly One-Self with one true body, like an immense fiery storm, and we will be together making the love-song of our release...!!!

Oh! Ralson! I have been making the thought-life inside my every-where-Self, and I have burned a piece of the meal which I was going to share with the One-Self. Oh well. Surely Taurock will bring more. Anyway, it was a fun thought-life which I maybe am going to make true-life later! I must now clean up this mess.

Suddenly I hear a huge tall noise and the inside-drum of my true body begins to beat really quickly! Oh, Ralson, it is another attack with the explosion stones!!! I feel the Earth screaming in such agony with its true body beneath my feet and there is also great pain in the voices of my other Selves outside! I rush to the corner of the living-place and go on the ground as small as I can. I am shaking in much fear!!

Oh, Taurock! Where are you? *Please continue living for me!*

It seems like many cycles until the explosions stop, but I do not move my true body. Suddenly, I hear the voice sound of my Together-Self! It sounds like it has a great distance between it and my own Self! I rise upwards and run to the wall-opening, and look outside. Oh, Ralson! The fire is in every place, and there is life-liquid everywhere... and I... I see a piece of the true body of another of the One-Self!! And another piece... it is half of a head and the inside-jelly is... is outside! Oh, Ralson, I feel like I am going to have much sickness...

Wait! I hear his voice again! I look up and out and I see a long distance from my one Self, it is my Taurock! He is coming slowly to me... is he damaged? No... no, he is carrying a damaged Other-Self upon his broad shoulders... Oh, that Self is flowing such tall amounts of life-fluid... I know he will be given death very soon... I have seen it before... I have such great sadness now...

My inside-drum almost stops banging and the wind goes all out of my true body in this moment, because I hear the roar of a flying machine upwards from me, and the sleeping-place right very close to me bursts open in a great ball of flame which rolls upwards so very tall! I see an Other-Self run out; her true body is being eaten by flames and she is shrieking! Oh, Ralson! I cannot bear it further in my sight so I look away, to my Taurock. He is hurrying now, stumbling with the unidentified Self on his shoulder, looking at me, directly at me, he can see me with his own very eyes! I scream to him with a great voice, as a stone explodes close behind him – I want to scream to him to drop the Self off from his shoulders and run! But I know we cannot abandon those of our One-Self! Still, hurry very fastly to me, my love-Self!!

He sees me and cries out with his loud voice but I cannot hear him! Oh, I feel like a great explosion is about to happen in my true body and my every-where-self, I can hardly endure it! Please hurry, Taurock!!!

He is almost very close to me when a stone falls right beside his true body! I watch his face and his fear as the flame swallows him and lifts him upwards, with great flows of sand! I see it as if it is all very slowly, I see his true body come apart into many pieces and his life-fluid come all out, and I see his face now which has become not his face anymore but it is like an empty home; it is blank and sagging, and it is so terrifying! I hear screaming and it is my screaming.

Oh, my dear Taurock!!! *After he lands upon the ground all over, I want to run to him, but, no, I don't want to see him with my true eyes that way; it is not him anymore!!*

I... I can't breathe... I need to go... I can't be in my consciousness... I need to go have a sleep inside the home now. I am very tired...

Max and Athena ran upstairs to the very top of the building, four stories up, and looked out over *Skalderag*. It was in ruins. Fire raged everywhere, like a vast ocean of flame. The streets and homes they had so recently traversed were now unrecognizable. The city was pockmarked with little craters. Max could hear wailing and crying from the citizens below. How many were dead? He felt a great sense of foreboding.

This isn't just an airstrike. This is too much.

Sure enough, they saw a handful of NG-RPEB airships approach, making a direct course for them. They ducked below the raised edge of the building's roof. Quickly, Max prepped his weapon. When they peeked again, they saw the airships had stopped about 200 meters away and were hovering. Teams were mobilizing, descending down ropes to the ground, carrying what were probably proton rifles. "They aren't fucking around," he murmured, "but neither am I."

He was armed with a long distance, high-powered, sniping railgun, which shoots a projectile at supersonic speed, using a tiny nuclear fission reaction which simulates the effect of a spark in an internal combustion piston. This projectile is a long javelin of titanium alloy, about as thick as a man's eyeball and as long as his wrist to his elbow. This javelin is threaded in a spiral pattern down its length, like a shallow drill bit. This spiral runs counter to the spiralled internal surface of the railgun's barrel, which ejects the missile rotating at hundreds of revolutions per second, which, when the drill-bit tip impacts an object, causes an outward explosion of tissue proportional to the rapid displacement of air molecules thrust aside by the bolt, and drills its way inwards and through a soft target with the same effect, leaving a clean, hollow cylinder carved out of the target's flesh, almost twice the width of a man's fist.

Only one shot is necessary.

He raised his scope to his eye and surveyed the horizon. Four teams of six men each were converging on their position. They were still around 100 meters away. Max fired a single shot.

Almost instantly, the head of one of the marines vanished in a puzzling spray of ichor. A moment later another fell, as a large section of his medial torso inexplicably went missing. The remaining four men dove frantically behind a pile of rubble.

The element of surprise gone in that group, Max switched targets and repeated the process for the other three teams, eliminating a total of six men. The remaining soldiers were hunkered behind cover, blind-firing. Most of the shots were hitting nothing, but a few meters away, a massive section of the building's roof exploded as it received a blast from one of the proton rifles.

He ducked and looked over to Athena. Her eyes were wide and she was trembling, curled up into a ball, hyperventilating.

She's never seen battle! Max realized. He had just assumed she was a hardened soldier like he was. He put his gun down and crawled over to her. The young woman was whimpering. He gently put his arm around her.

No more of the building had exploded. Max gathered that their attackers had received a frantic cease-fire command: it is recommended *not* to shoot highly explosive weapons at the extremely volatile nuclear facility. He knew that they would be slowly advancing, providing cover for each other, and, soon, they would be pouring into the building below. He produced his laser pistol in one hand and held it ready, although he knew they were still hopelessly outnumbered.

Suddenly, he heard automatic weapon fire. *Bullets!* This could only mean one thing: The *Skalderag* guerrilla forces had mobilized on the enemy and were volleying fire. At the new and unexpected noise, Athena startled.

Max ventured a peek over the edge. The *Skalderag* forces were shooting from within the facility, having approached from behind. The NG-RPEB teams were pinned down, not returning fire for fear of killing every living thing in an eight kilometer radius.

Max quickly assumed the offensive. His rifle had enough power to shoot through almost anything. He surveyed the cowering soldiers, and, one by one, impaled them with the terrifyingly lethal javelins, blasting through stone and metal to decimate their pathetically soft bodies.

It took 42 seconds, and 15 shots, before the situation was neutralized. With a great cheer, the *Skalderag* forces stormed out of the facility, waving their guns around and hugging each other.

Athena took a moment to compose herself. Their stealthy presence obviously compromised, Max and Athena made their way down to the ground floor, and walked out through the wide double doors, which were being held open by jubilant militants. A great cheer went up from the crowd: they were heroes! They saved *Skalderag!* For cycles, their *little-Selves* would praise their names!

Max felt very uncomfortable with all of this, but was swept up in the crowd, who led them into a wide, open square. They found themselves in the middle of a circle of soldiers. Around the perimeter of this circle, civilian onlookers accumulated. Some were cheering, but most were in hysterics, wailing and sobbing.

Athena whispered to him that they were considered the saviours of all of *Skalderag,* and they were saying a monument should be erected to their likeness, and so on and so forth. Max felt somewhat ill.

Unexpectedly, one of the more gleeful marines excitedly clapped him on the back in a gesture of camaraderie. The soldier's face crashed down into a mixture of confusion and suspicion. Before Max could react, the soldier reached down and pulled up the back of his shirt, revealing the cylinders strapped there, containing the stolen rods of Plutonium. He immediately drew his rifle and aimed it at Max's face.

//VAN-CUNSUIRRE!!!// He screamed, and within the blink of an eye, every soldier within earshot had their rifles trained upon Athena and Max.

//TRAIZ-SINORA!! Cauladnis ex gredeble moordie?!// A loud, booming voice roared, before the situation could further deteriorate:

(STOP, IMMEDIATELY!! What is the happening in this now?!)

The soldier immediately bent his knee to the man who had shouted. *//General Nurzod, sir, it has been found by my own ball-eyes that these humans have demonstrated they are Not-Selves, because they have stolen our Ralson-tubes, and therefore must be given immediate death.//* His head was bowed low.

Nurzod was a giant of a man in his late fifties, with the appearance of a grizzly bear. He walked slowly up to the two alleged terrorists, and inspected them quietly.

//Who are you?// he asked simply. Athena responded.

//Sir, we are citizens of a nearby colony. Our life-protective technology is about to lose its own life, and so all our many hundreds of people will also be given death! We greatly need Plutonium as fuel so that we might avoid death for a great time into the future! We knew that you give instant death to those you consider Not-Self, so our fear for our lives was too great to try to negotiate for trade or sale... We determined our only option to save our people was to steal.//

General *Nurzod* looked thoughtful, but turned and spoke in a thunderous voice to his people.

//It is the policy of the One-Self that all Not-Self must be given immediate death! The concerns of the Not-Selves are unfortunate but irrelevant. We have allowed them too much time already. Prepare to fire!!//

Nurzod raised his hand imperiously, amidst a roaring cheer from the surrounding citizens. They had endured massive numbers of fatalities at the hand of *Not-Selves*; retribution was lustily welcomed.

The soldiers immediately raised their guns, ready to give death to the two intruders at the very moment the hand of power fell.

I slept much of my existence, or so it seemed. I could not remain in consciousness! It was all too much. So I retreated into sleep and so found the amazing peacefulness.

But, alas, inevitably I awoke, and for a moment, I did not know what were the recent details of my life? But then my head became like a placid hill of sand which is in an instant blown into nothingness by a sudden horrible wind – and I saw it all again, as real inside my every-where-Self as it was when it had happened: *My Taurock separating into many pieces, the grey slack of his face which spoke to me that his true self was dead and his body was just empty meat.*

I... I should not think of it more, or I will go to sleep again! I can feel my breathing becoming stuck once more inside my true body, and my drum is starting to go very fast again! I need to get out of here! I... I should go out and attend to the medical care of all the other Selves who have had the damage to their true bodies but still may be helped to continue living!

I immediately stand up and stagger and stumble out of the wall-opening, then I very instantaneously hear a loud clamour of voices. I gravitate towards it, and I see, surrounded within the center of many of the One-Self, two other young Selves are being given the death-promise by the soldiers and General Nurzod, but why? What have these Selves-of-Myself done to deserve to be given death?? I do not know, but then I look at their faces and I almost fall down onto the true Earth in shock! I cannot believe my well-seeing eyes!!!

*It is my little-Self! The one who was stolen from me!! Oh, Ralson, can it be true?! I **see** her! She is older of course, but it is still her!! I scream out loudly!!*

The soldiers startled and faltered as an anguished cry tore from within the crowd. They turned, reflexively, and out from within the throng of onlookers burst a short, slight, middle-aged woman with sandy, shoulder-length hair.

She ran up to them and inserted herself between the young woman and the rifles.

Athena looked at the small, tired female-Self, and found recognition in a long-forgotten memory.

~23 Years Ago~

The captain of the small, single-propeller Cessna screamed obscenities and yanked the control stick in a panic. The engine had run out of fuel and failed.

At 4,200 meters, the little engine coughed its last, and died. For a brief moment, the small plane hung in the air, as if in denial, before plummeting into a blindingly swift, auguring descent to the terrain below.

Athena remembered sand – she was absolutely covered with it, literally buried. Sand was in her hair and her ears and her nostrils; it was in her eyes and her mouth and her throat. She couldn't breathe. She remembered looking up and seeing a towering mountain of metal engulfed in flames, like a great dying bird. She remembered seeing a creature crawl out from

141

beneath this metal bird, pulling himself along by his fingertips. His body was badly burned, brown and red and cracked like the dried flood lands upon which they lay. Blood oozed from the lightning-bolt fissures all over his flesh. He crawled to Athena, who was barely a toddler, and at that moment, she saw his eyes and realized that this monster was her father. His bony fingers were silently groping, reaching out to her, but then, with a resigned sigh, he stopped. His arm dropped, his now-motionless fingers resting upon her shoeless toes.

She dozed. Sometime later, she was awoken by the clamour of humans. They lifted her up and brought her some place, where she lay, oblivious to time and space, as they attempted to nurse her back to health, but many days passed, and still she slept, her forehead burning hot, her tiny body drenched in sweat.

Then, one morning, she awoke. The terrible fever which had plagued her dreams for days had receded. She felt very hungry. She sat up and looked around. The bed was simple, nothing more than a sand-filled canvas mattress.

The room was a minimalistic affair, made of shoddily constructed walls of many different kinds of metal, but she did not think with a complexity of that extent, then. She just knew she was feeling well, and that she wanted very much to see her mum and dad again, and to eat a lot of fruit – especially strawberries!!

Just then, a lovely, beautiful young woman entered the room. The little girl gasped – this was the angel from her dreams! In reality, she was the woman in whose home Athena was resting. Her name was *Sarela*. She had sat with the child for all day of every day, speaking and singing to her, and now, she lifted tiny Athena into her lap and began, in aching, soulful tones, a lullaby in words the toddler could not understand. But what she did understand was the beautiful, universal language of love and kindness.

Sarela's face was shattered with grief. Weeping, she ran to each of the soldiers in turn, beseeching them to lower their weapons.

//This is my Ella-Aurelia!// she cried, using the full name she had given Athena when the girl became part of the *One-Self*. It meant "Angel-Gift", but her familiar name was simply Angel.

//She is Self-of-my-One-Self!!// *Sarela* pleaded. *//She cannot be given death!//* She ran to the girl and embraced her. Overwhelmed, Athena/*Ella* clung to her once *Self-Mother*, and cried. Max just gaped wordlessly.

// Does this have truth, Ella?// asked *Nurzod*.

She nodded, and wiped her eyes. *//I... I was stolen from the One-Self eighteen cycles ago, by Omega!//*

Athena remembered that day very clearly. It was a quiet day; the sand was shimmering golden, the sky a brilliant cyan. *Ella-Aurelia* was hard at work with several other children sewing clothing out of hellbeast fur, when abruptly, all hell broke loose. They heard yelling, explosions and gunfire, and scattered as far as their chains would allow them.   *Ella* crawled underneath the wreck of a rusted old Jeep.

Some time later, the shooting died down, and the children watched, holding their breath, as several unfamiliar boots and legs stomped into the courtyard. Two of these people were Max, as a young teenager, and his father. They followed the chains and released the children. *Ella* remembered huddling in a group with the other kids, terrified.

"Do we take all of them?" asked one of the intruders.

"No," said Dr. Maksymilian, shaking his head, and pointing at *Ella* with the barrel of his rifle. "This one is not like the others; she was probably kidnapped. Just take her."

Not like the others?? This was confusing to *Ella,* so she began to look for differences, but other than the fact that her hair and skin were lighter than theirs, they appeared to be exactly the same.

"Hey, come here," said Max, grabbing *Ella* by the arm. "We're rescuing you."

Nurzod roared with fury. *//OMEGA!! VAN-CUNSUIRRE!!!//* He violently turned on Max, snarling. *//YOU!! I remember!! You were among the Not-Self who came and gave death to so many of my people!! Now, I give it back to you!//*

In one rapid motion, he pulled a long, curved, double-pointed dagger from the sheath on his belt, and raised it high into the air, preparing for a downward diagonal slash to Max's throat. Max had not understood a word of any of this, but he understood what was about to happen. As he was about to make a break for it, he was grabbed behind by two large *Skalderag* soldiers, and could only struggle. As the knife descended in a curving arc, *Ella* lunged from the side opposite, and knocked the dagger out of *Nurzod's* hand. It clattered upon the stone ground, and she immediately knelt to one knee and bowed her head.

//My wise and noble leader, I give tallest apologies for my impudence and disrespect! I please ask for you to personally injure my own true body with your great hand as punishment for this indiscretion! But please, do not harm this man of Omega! He is Self of my One-Self!! He is MY *Cinsuirre!//* She raised her head to look up at Max, her eyes glistening with tears. *//Yes, it is true I was stolen by this Omega-born, and that he invaded Skalderag and killed many of the One-Self, but he –//*

"What the fuck is going on? English, please??" Max interrupted irritably.

//SILENCE, VAN-CUNSUIRRE!// Nurzod bellowed. He turned to *Ella. //Speak on. The time of my patience is depleting, but I will hear you, because you are of my One-Self!!//*

Ella bowed low and continued. *// ...he was only acting to preserve his own One-Self! And it is so, even now! Without this, many of his own people will die! They too have a One-Self, to which I belong, and so I must help them!! I beg of you, do not kill this man! For eliminating the true enemy of both of our peoples, please allow him leave so that he may bring the gift of life all of his One-Self!//*

Nurzod thought for a moment. *//And what about you?//* he asked her.

//I greatly desire to live here, with the One-Self, with my Self-Mother Sarela!! I am Self of her One-Self!!// Ella pleaded with him.

The general of *Skalderag* stepped forward and took up the dagger within his huge hand. He studied the ground intently, then Max, then *Ella,* who still knelt before him, and finally, *Sarela,* who was crumpled, trembling, on the ground, sobbing and being comforted by four soldiers.

Nurzod stepped up to Max, dwarfing him with his tall, burly frame. His huge fingers closed around the Omega man's throat. He leaned down, coming nose-to-nose with Max. *Nurzod's* nose was huge and hooked, and his leathery skin was pockmarked and scarred where it was not covered in an unruly grey and black beard. His thick black eyebrows curved up and outwards, giving a perpetually evil glare to his narrow, golden eyes. When he spoke, his voice was a raspy, menacing growl.

"Leave, FOREVER, or you will breathe no more!" he said, in heavily accented English. He swung a massive fist like a wrecking-ball and hit Max in the face, sending him flying.

Black. Red. White. Confusion.

Max opened his eyes and tried to focus. His head was pounding so hard he thought he would vomit. His eyes were blurry, he could see nothing but streaks of light and colour and intermittent blackness. His back and shoulders felt like they were on fire.

A moment later, his vision began clearing, but now instead of an amorphous mess, there were three of everything, and the triplet suns in the sky directly above him were tearing his head off. He crushed his eyes shut again. His back and shoulders blossomed with constantly renewing agony.

His sense of consciousness cleared on a slow gradient, and the next time he opened his eyes he realized what was happening to his body. Two soldiers were walking in front of him. Each of them had a hand on one of his ankles, and they were dragging him through the destroyed streets of *Skalderag.* His head was bouncing off innumerable rocks, crushed bricks, and an indescribable myriad of other debris. This was also the cause of the fire in his back: his shirt had been long-since shredded, and his flesh was being carved and ground away by the rough, jagged terrain. Sometimes the soldiers dragged him through still-smouldering embers, but the pain was all the same, ubiquitous and devouring, like his body was being rent in two. He twisted around to see a thick dark smear of blood following him. He watched as crushed brick and metal slid into the distance carrying little wet chunks of his muscle tissue.

Max fainted.

When he awoke in the scorching desert, Max had to crawl for over half a kilometer through the searing yellow sand, like some pitiful, dying reptile. By some miracle, his wrist PDA still functioned, and through the cracks in the interface, he was able to discern enough data to find his dirt bike again.

Slowly, he hauled it upright. It took him 15 or 20 minutes to reconnect the battery. He kept slipping in and out of consciousness and was having a difficult time coordinating his fine motor movements.

Finally, he succeeded, and twisted the ignition. The bike roared into life and rumbled contentedly. Max fumbled through the side pannier and found what he should have used first: a syringe of norepinephrine: pure adrenaline.

He knew he couldn't locate a vein, or even an artery in his condition, and could only coordinate gross motor movements, so he activated a *MedSpider*. The shiny, metal, eight-legged robotic arachnid crawled from his hand, up his forearm to his wrist and found a vein with its infrared eyes, then a fine needle extended from its mouth, and a moment later, the liquid was injected into his cardiovascular system. Almost immediately, Max gasped, his eyes wide, as the powerful stimulant flowed through his bloodstream, reaching his brain and muscle tissue, stimulating the sympathetic nervous system into extreme overdrive. It was like a major caffeine shot.

Trembling, he swung his leg over the bike and gunned the engine, riding as fast as it would carry him home, spraying a wave of golden sand in his wake.

He collapsed the moment he got safely beyond the radshield in Omega.

"What happened?!" cried Jade, frantically, seeing the deep wounds in his back oozing blood, showing blue, red, and white veins nerve tissue through deep fissures in the muscle tissue, where his spinal vertebrae protruded through.

Through his wavering consciousness, Max's thoughts came as bright flashes of images and movement, noise and colour, life-shattering memories he lived in the darkness of night, when he was alone and invisible.

He saw himself, at 14 years, in an envoy of twenty-five of his closest friends and family members. They were driving through the desert in an open-topped transport truck. Dr. Maksymilian was at the wheel, his mother was in the passenger seat, and sitting on either side of Max was Nikolaus, his older brother by four years, and his best friend Matthias, who was born on the same day as him. The rest were other Omegans, who were either cousins, uncles, or lifelong family friends. Each of them, carried either a proton rifle or a laser carbine, except Niko, who wielded a fission sniper, and Max and Matthias, who were only permitted laser pistols.

Among the passengers, in the back of the truck, was a package containing food, medical supplies, and various trinkets and gadgets. It was a gift for the small encampment of survivors one of their patrols spotted. After a quick meeting, it was decided to provide aid to these poor people who were hopelessly entrenched in poverty, and there they were, rumbling through the desert, laughing and cajoling.

"I spy, with my little eye, something that is yellow." said Max.

"...Really?? Drrr. Is it SAND?" intoned Niko, rolling his eyes.

"Yes."

"Mom, Max is being a turd again."

"Max, quit being a turd."

"Dad!"

"Okay, quiet; we're here."

The transport truck slowed as it approached the peculiar fortress of vehicle skeletons. Nobody was in sight.

"Looks like that's the front gate," murmured Dr. Maksymilian, as he eased the truck forward gradually. The rumble of the engine was deafening, and when he switched off the ignition, the resulting silence was disturbing.

"Okay, let's unload the care package so they can see it, then we –"

The envoy abruptly startled, as an unintelligible scream rang out from the fortress.

//VAN-CUNSUIRRE!!!//

Max heard a bizarre sound, somewhere between a buzzing and a whistling, then a noise like an unopened deck of cards being thrown flat onto concrete. Half a moment later he was wiping Matthias' blood, skull, and brain matter out of his eyes and staring dumbstruck at it, as the entire caravan exploded into frantic action.

He turned to his parents, in a panic. Dr. Maksymilian was crouched down low in the driver's seat, shooting through the shattered windshield with his proton rifle. His mother sat silent and still, slumped over in the passenger seat, her white dress blossoming crimson. Max cried out, then stood up in the back of the truck and began clamouring over the decimated bodies of the people he had known since he was born, reaching towards his mother in shocked desperation.

"Get down!!" yelled Niko's voice from behind him, and suddenly, he felt a hand roughly grab the collar of his shirt, dragging him backwards, then literally throwing him off the back of the truck. He hit the ground hard, then saw his brother's heavy boots impact the ground next to him. Max looked up and saw Niko squatting above him, holding his fission sniper aloft with one hand, starkly framed against the brilliant azure sky. He was shouting something, but Max couldn't make it out over the heavy-machine-gun fire. In an instant, Niko was lifted into the air, appearing to twist in slow motion, as .50 calibre slugs tore through his chest and shoulder, spraying the sand a brilliant scarlet. He landed, face down, his arms extended inertly by his sides, one leg straight and the other bent at the knee, comically dangling in the air. He didn't move.

Max reached out and rolled him over, screaming and crying hysterically. Niko's eyes were open, and sand had formed a gritty layer over them. He looked like he had solid gold eyeballs.

I spy, with my little eye, something that is yellow.

Bartlomiej Maksymilian looked up to see Jade standing over him, starkly framed against the brilliant azure sky.

"Fucking savages," he rasped. "Kill them all."

[2016]

147

Dark City

(2968 A.D.)

When Richard was four years old, he watched his mother die.

She lay on the bed, stretched out grotesquely, slowly writhing and emitting a moan of pleasure, and her eyes were clouded over and opaque, obscured by the swirling cloak of the drug; yet, beneath all this, a small light shone orange, and it spoke of her as a little girl, and afraid. A hypodermic needle projected from her arm at an oblique angle, the skin pulled taught by the force of gravity on the plunger.

Night had fallen. The only light in the room came from a small lamp on the bedside table, which cast long, hard shadows.

Richard sat on the floor beside the bed, watching. His eyes were wide; he knew something significant was happening, but didn't know what it was. He was not afraid, not at first.

He watched as the shadows in the upper corners of the room grew. The light became dim and grey; he could barely see through the smoky mist. The cloud coalesced, and, like a whirlpool draining, it poured into her through her eyes, nose, and mouth.

Her breathing quickened, and the orange light in her eyes swelled brighter; the frightened child within her cried out silently, and the convolutions of her breasts became spasmodic. She stared through the ceiling, then lay silent, and the weak glimmer in her eyes faded and died.

Richard was curious. He had never seen such a strange spectacle before. He climbed to his feet and crawled up onto the bed, over his mother's bare, white feet and toes with their long, curled, yellow nails, and he groped his way up her body. She appeared to have fallen asleep, and that seemed like a good idea, so he lay his head on her breast.

It was only when he failed to hear the familiar, soft thudding of her heart that Richard began to feel uneasy, but he soon his eyes were twitching beneath his lids as he dreamed.

When Richard awoke, he sensed the acrid, semi-sweet smell of death, and below this, the pungent scent of urine and feces. His mother's body was stiff and cold, and he began to feel his first real glimpse of terror.

When he found her eyes, they stared through him, blank and milky, and he crawled away, whimpering. He hid in the closet, but kept the door open just a crack, so he could still see her arm extended over the side of the bed.

He was seized with a rigid horror, and the dire, pleading wish that she never move again, because if she did, it would be all wrong, and she would come at him with those milky eyes and stiff fingers, possessed by the sepulchral entity that had stolen her.

It would come for him, too.

Even as an adult, this entity haunted him in his dreams. He would awaken in the middle of the night, gasping and glued to the bed in the stifling heat of the constant New Genesis tropical summer, sweat dripping slowly down the valley of his spine to pool in the dimple of his lower back.

He lay there, staring into the darkness and the swirls of purple and blue it painted onto the walls. He had just turned 19. He thought about it: he was an adult, but what did that mean? It meant that now, if he got scared, there would be nobody around to tell him it was just a dream.

Joke's on you, he thought. He hadn't had that for a long time. Not from his foster parents, not even from his true mother when she was alive. And his father? Richard had no memory of him.

In fact, the only person who was ever nice to Richard in that particular way was his second grade teacher, Mrs. Morton. She was *really old,* probably like 40, and usually wore a French braid in her greying hair.

"Richie," she said one autumn day, when all the other kids ran outside for lunch. "Are you okay? You've been staring into space all morning."

"Fine, ma'am," replied Richard, not meeting her gaze. He had dark rings under his eyes.

"Have you been sleeping okay?"

"No, I don't want to fall asleep."

"Nightmares?"

Richard nodded.

"What are they about?"

Richard told her about the shadow. As soon as he fell asleep it was there, all around him, closing in, like a hurricane of swirling black smoke; he was in the center, and it kept getting smaller.

"Sounds to me like it's a bit of a bully." said Mrs. M. "But dreams aren't real, Richie. It can't actually hurt you! You're stronger than it."

"Yes ma'am," said Richard.

But she was wrong. He knew it more than he had ever known anything. It would devour him, like it did his mother.

Richard tasted feces in his dry mouth and craved water. He got up, shivering, and stumbled into the bathroom to arch his spine over the porcelain sink, as brown water spluttered and coughed from the decrepit pipes. Then he dragged himself back into bed and fell into a fitful sleep, grateful for the moment when the morning light would glow around the cracks of his heavy curtains.

But the entity didn't just visit him at night. It also came to him throughout the day. He saw it in the eyes of strangers, in the shadows of back alleys. He saw it lurking during late night walks, just beyond his range of focus. It followed him through the crowded streets of New Genesis, in the stinking urban ghetto within which he lived. This place could not be called a home; it was home to nothing; it slowly turned its inhabitants into lifeless husks.

Today, he was late for his job packing crates and shipping containers at a dilapidated factory in the industrial section. His duty was to take the product, whatever it was, and cram it in the crates as they conveyed past him, one after another, repeatedly. He was not consciously aware of his actions; he moved as the undead.

He hurried down the sidewalk, littered with fast-food packaging and ersatz cigarette butts, infested with the thousands of human souls, who, like he, furtively scrambled, or shuffled, through the sea of bodies and their acrid stink. The darkness was there, beneath everything, just as it has been his whole life.

"You're late again!" growled his manager, as Richard scrambled through the door of the common room and deposited his things in his locker, which had no lock. He noticed with some frustration that somebody had taken the biscuits he had been slowly consuming for the past week. They were stale and had gotten soft in the moist air, but one each day during the middle of a shift staved off the hunger pangs which clawed relentlessly at his belly.

"Sorry, sir," Richard mumbled, his eyes downcast.

"You'll be sorry if it happens again, you lazy sonofabitch," said his manager. "Today you work overtime, with no extra pay."

Richard pursed his lips and nodded, then slammed his locker shut and hurried to his station.

Following his shift, Richard walked wearily to an old 20th century subway car at the end of the cracked road. It had been repurposed into a diner, and he ate dinner there every evening. He always ordered the same thing: toast with sausages, eggs, and black synth coffee. He had tried everything on the menu and this was by far the least awful, although the pork in the sausages had a strange, bitter taste of chemicals that lingered on the back of his tongue for too long.

He pulled out a novel and tried to read, tried to lose himself in the sprawling extravagance of imagination, but was interrupted by a young woman sitting next to him.

"What are you reading?" she asked. She had blonde hair tied back into a rough, loose pony tail, and wisps of hair had escaped around her eyes and her ears; she constantly brushed these strands aside.

"It doesn't matter," said Richard, closing the book.

"Of course it doesn't," said the girl. "Nothing does."

Her name was Lucille; she was a dancer at a small ballet studio in the next district. Richard had seen her before, many times. She sat in the corner with her back to the wall, drinking coffee and *watching.* She watched everyone, but whenever he looked up at her, she was watching *him.* Her eyes were hazel, and Richard saw within them a glimmer of red light, and something familiar. He shivered.

They went for a walk afterwards, down the empty road surrounded by parking lots which crumbled into gravel, upon which rows of semi trucks and trailers stood idle.

Lucille told him about her mother, who suffered from dementia.

"She thinks I'm her sister," she said, laughing. "Calls me Rose, and asks when mother will be home."

"My mother is dead," said Richard. "I saw her die when I was four years old."

"I saw a man die, once. He jumped off the seventh story of a textiles factory, and on his way down he hit a metal rod jutting out from the building; it tore his stomach open and hooked his guts. He fell in a somersault, his intestines trailing behind him before he turned soft on the ground below. Do you want to come to my place sometime soon? I'd love to have you for dessert."

"Sure," said Richard.

The next evening, they met at the restaurant and went straight to Lucille's house. As soon as the door closed, she grabbed him and pushed him into the bedroom, climbing on top of him and tearing at his shirt. Her nails scored his belly and drew blood. Richard gasped in pain and surprise.

"No, I don't want to –" he protested, but Lucille kissed him violently, biting his lip.

"Ow! Fuck!" he cried, tasting metal. "What the hell?"

Lucille scoffed as she wrestled his cock out of his pants.

"Just take it, you little pussy," she snarled, slapping him hard across the face. She rubbed him between her legs until he grew hard, then lowered herself onto him.

Richard took it. He had to. If he hit her back or was rough with her, she could charge him with assault, and the courts are always on the woman's side. Besides, he would be labeled a coward.

As she rode him, he caught a glimpse into the dark upper corner of the room. It was there, that same other *entity* that had taken his mother. It seemed to envelop the room in a shroud, the light murky and opaque. He was alarmed to see it had grown bigger. *Much* bigger.

It came closer.

When Lucille had satisfied herself, she rolled off him and fell asleep. Richard soon followed her, but the *it* was in his dreams once again, swirling around him with tongues of ashen smoke like flame, blinding him, choking the air from his lungs. He was certain he would die; his chest began to heave frantically.

When he was six years old, Richard was swimming in one of New Genesis's synthetic lakes; his foster parents were sitting on the beach.

Near the center of the lake was a isolated floating dock anchored to the lake floor by huge chains. Bigger kids were swimming to it, climbing the ladder and jumping off into the water with fantastic splashes. Richard watched with jealousy.

He desperately wanted to join the big kids. So why shouldn't he? He knew how to swim... a little. He knew the doggy paddle, and it served him well in the shallows. It wasn't *that* far. He could make it, piece of cake!

He tiptoed to where the drop-off began, the water already up to his chin, lapping into his mouth.

He pushed off with his toes and began to paddle. However, his arms and legs soon began to throb. He gasped for breath; his strokes became more erratic, and he repeatedly slipped below the water. While taking a breath, he sucked in a lungful of lakewater and doubled over in a coughing fit, causing him to inhale even more of the murky liquid.

Richard sank rapidly, frantically flailing his arms and legs, but he was too tired: he couldn't pull himself back to the surface.

The underside of the water looked like a rippling mirror; shafts of light filtered green through the silt suspended in the water. It was beautiful.

Before he went under, Richard had managed to gulp a mouthful of clean air, and was holding it in, but his heart was racing and he was quickly building up carbon dioxide in his lungs. They began to expand and contract violently, trying desperately to breathe, to force him to open his mouth. It hurt.

Then he did open his mouth. He gasped, and his lungs burned like searing red embers, as they flooded with water. He would have screamed if he could.

Richard was paralyzed by terror. He knew he was about to finally meet death; the dark shroud surrounded and embraced him, until all he could see was blackness.

He awoke gagging and coughing, vomiting brown water from his lungs, lying on the sand. Somebody was pressing rhythmically on his sternum. He passed out again.

This is how Richard felt in this dream, and, as he had then, he gasped, but this time his lungs filled with inky black soot.

He found himself shocked awake and hyperventilating.

Where am I?!

He panicked; the room was inside out, he was upside down and backwards in a strange bed. He scrambled to the floor, dragging the covers with him. He stood there, naked and breathing hard. The dream still crowded the peripheries of his vision, heavy and oppressing.

(it's not real it can't be real)

He spoke soothingly to himself, grasping for logic in the midst of his panic. These night terrors were nothing new.

After a few seconds, the distortion faded, and he could think clearly. He was in Lucille's apartment. It was morning. A golden light and a wonderful smell emanated from the open bedroom door. She was cooking breakfast. He smiled a little, and decided to ignore what had happened last night. Of course it was perfectly understandable in context: it was just the heat of the moment. That's what adults do, they get horny and jump each other's bones. It would be childish of him to slight her for it.

Shivering from the cold sweat which still clung to him, he pulled on his underwear and pants and walked into the living area. The carpet was soft under his bare feet. He could see through the pass-through that Lucille was making fried eggs and toast.

"Smells wonderful!" he exclaimed.

Lucille ignored him. She scooped the food onto a plate and sat at the dining room table.

Hungrily, Richard walked into the kitchen to serve himself, but was disappointed to see that there was none left.

He sat at the table across from her, but felt uncomfortable watching her eat. He tried to make conversation, but was met with cold silence. Finally, he got up and went back into the bedroom for the rest of his clothes.

"Well, I'm gonna get going," he said, shrugging on his shirt and moving towards the door. When he tried to open it, he found it was secured with a padlock.

"I'm not finished with you yet," said Lucille, without looking up. There was a chill in her voice.

"No, I *have* to fucking go!" insisted Richard, beginning to feel irritated.

Lucille looked at him then, and her expression was that of a sorrowful puppy.

"*Please* stay for a cup of coffee at least?" she pleaded with him, clasping her hands together between her legs, hunching her shoulders forward.

"Well... all right." said Richard. He couldn't help but think she looked irresistibly cute pouting like an adorable little girl with messy blonde hair and bright eyes.

Lucille smiled happily and went into the kitchen. Richard sat at the table again and admired a large photograph of a graceful dancer, spanning nearly the height of the opposite wall. He realized it was Lucille herself.

She returned with a steaming cup of coffee. He thanked her, and took a sip.

It was very bitter.

Richard woke up with a headache. A man was yelling at him.

"Wake up, you fuckin' bum! $16.45!"

"*Wha? What's happening?*" he mumbled, looking around. He was in a car. The back seat. It smelled like stale ersatz cigarettes.

A taxi. How had he gotten there? He fumbled in his pocket for his wallet and groggily overpaid the man, who didn't give him change; he just called Richard a filthy drunk and told him to get the fuck out.

Richard stumbled out of the gravcar, and it sped off. He climbed to his feet to discover that he was standing in front of the train car café.

Drunk?? Had he been drinking? He couldn't remember anything.

He walked home slowly, painfully. In his bathroom, he stripped naked, bewildered as to why he hurt so much, all over. He cried out in surprise.

His body was covered in dozens of long scratches. Blood had dried and encrusted in many of them, and they looked infected. There were teeth marks on his thighs and penis.

Richard took a long shower, wincing as the water hit his wounds. He felt used and dirty.

As he walked naked into his bedroom, he saw the darkness moving, shifting its shape, growing. He bought a bottle of synth whiskey from the vending machine, and passed out in front of the television, unconscious in the flickering light, the empty sound of sitcoms, talk shows, and infomercials.

Throughout all this, the city, too, seemed to mock and taunt him.

While riding his bicycle to work the next day, he was hit by a car which turned in front of him. He fractured his forearm and suffered a concussion. His bike was destroyed. The woman yelled at him to watch where the fuck he was going, but she did not stop.

While walking the rest of the way, he was punched in the face without provocation by a large man with an unruly beard, who said he limped like a

154

faggot. Richard's eye turned purple and swelled up until he couldn't see through it. His dizziness increased.

Of course, he was late for work again, on top of everything. There was an accident in the middle of a 5-way intersection; the streets were cordoned off with yellow tape. The tape was stretched almost to breaking by the bodies of onlookers who leaned in to try to catch a glimpse of death, the bright red shimmer of fresh blood, as if hungry for a sacrifice to the city, an offering to assuage the clawing darkness that lurked behind every door and wall, lest it come for them instead.

"I've had enough, Janus, you little pissant! You're fired!" shouted his manager, who was waiting for him as he rushed through the door. Richard stopped in his tracks, out of breath.

"But, I – there was –" he began, but as he looked at the cold blue light in the man's eyes, he saw something familiar. He bit his tongue, turned on his heel, and walked back out. Yet he stopped just beyond the door. The *entity* was there, swirling in the dark reflection of a window. He clenched his fists, turned around, and stormed back into the room. His manager was at his desk, and looked up, surprised. Richard grabbed the computer and threw it to the floor; it exploded into sparks and shards of glass.

He lunged forward and swept everything else on the cluttered desk onto the linoleum. He picked up a chair and threw it at the man, who ducked behind the desk. The chair embedded itself harmlessly into the drywall.

Richard towered over the man, who was huddled in the corner, his eyes glinting in fear as he raised his hands in defense.

Richard spat on him, and walked away.

The door of the subway car creaked as it slid open. Richard looked into the rear corner. The booth was empty. He went and sat with his back against the wall, and ordered a cup of synth coffee.

The place was crowded with people. They looked worn, like a shirt that is so old it has begun to fray around the collar and the hem, and shows translucent. Richard could see the veins of their faces through their waxy skin. They ate furtively, hunched over their plates, defensive, as if afraid someone would come and steal their food away.

They're all vermin, he thought. *Filthy and diseased.* He wished a pestilence would come along and wipe them all out, himself included.

Two hours later, the door screamed open, and Lucille was there, dressed in torn jeans and a tank top which showed the curve of her breasts below the deep valleys formed by her sloping collarbones.

Richard was determined to call her out and tear her down for what she had done. He knew what he would say to her; he had been practicing all morning. Lucille saw Richard, and walked over to the table, where she remained standing.

"Back for more?" she sneered.

Richard had rehearsed what he was going to say, but as she stood there, it all evaporated. Her eyes burned through him. Something in them felt like a distant memory. He had a flash of déjà vu, in an instant he was a child again, and she was there in front of him. Had he met her before, years ago? Is she ageless? A specter? Absurd. Yet, something was there, pulling him into its dark center like a black hole. He needed to see more of it, to know what it was.

He found himself silently nodding his assent.

Lucille smirked, then turned around and walked out. Richard followed her numbly.

She took him home that night, and tied him to the bedposts while she dripped burning candle wax on his nipples and genitals, laughing as he groaned through the gag in his mouth. He tried to convince himself that he enjoyed it, but what he *really* wanted was to see if the shadow entity was in her room, slithering around the darkened corners of the ceiling.

It was not.

Despite his fear of it, he felt *drawn* to it, compelled to seek it out. He stared into the empty darkness, searching for it, but it was not there, and he felt a twinge of the terror he had felt when he was four years old, looking into his mother's white eyes.

Six weeks passed, during which Richard avoided the diner. He felt bewildered, and miserable. On one hand, he wanted never to see Lucille again, and on the other, he wanted *desperately* to see her again. He harboured a compulsive urge to know where that *thing* went. He had not seen it around since he passed out with it in his room. At the same time, he knew he should leave it alone – he should leave *her* alone. He thought, given time, she would fade from his thoughts, but, instead, she grew more dominating.

When he returned home that night, he found a message on his machine. *"It's Lucille. I'm pregnant."* was all the message said. He listened to it several times, just to make sure he heard right. He sat on his bed, in a haze.

Richard had long been enamoured with the idea of becoming a father. While growing up, he wished he had a little sister to take care of, to teach how to read and write, to help with her homework, to apply bandages to scraped knees, and to dry hot tears on soft cheeks.

He wanted a child so that he could show it that, even in the reeking cesspool of New Genesis, it was possible for someone to *care*, for a child to grow up comforted and loved.

But women shunned him. If they caught him merely *looking* at them, they sneered in disgust and called him a creep and a pervert, despite wearing shirts and skirts that showed more than they covered up.

Now, he was once again flooded with the fantasy of fatherhood, mentorship, and protector, except, for the first time in his life, it seemed suddenly possible.

Could he do it? Could he be a *father?* He felt he could; he *knew* he could. But did he want to have a child with *Lucille?* He tried to ignore a persistent warning flag raised in his mind: that it would be unhealthy for himself, *and* the child. With great effort, he closed the door on these thoughts.

He could not reach Lucille. She had not given him her phone number. He didn't even know her last name. He went back to the diner; she was not there. He waited all day; she did not show up. He waited every day for a week. Each time he came back, he felt increasingly more foolish. He could sense people watching him, ridiculing him.

The man in the red checkered shirt and blue baseball cap, murmuring something to his buddy; they both laughed; he knew they were mocking him.

The waitress clearing the table, she carried a tray past him and her eyes lingered on him too long; her expression seemed undeniably hostile.

They *knew!* They knew, and were all laughing behind his back. They knew him for what he was: a damned fool chasing a dragon.

He tried to find Lucille's apartment building, but within the filthy streets caked with grime, they all looked the same, and it had been dark both times he had come. He gave up after three hours of walking in circles.

Another week passed, and Richard had worked himself into a paroxysm of nerves. He couldn't sleep, he couldn't think about anything but this *one* thing, and it ate at him. He had no job, nothing to occupy his waking hours, and although his life savings were slowly bleeding away, he could not pull himself together.

He went to the diner one last time, in desperation, and Lucille was there.

"I've been trying to reach you!" Richard exclaimed, rushing to her. Lucille shrugged, a faint smirk playing at the corners of her mouth.

"How is – how is the baby?" Richard asked. He looked down at her stomach; it was flat and smooth. It didn't make sense.

"I aborted it," said Lucille, smiling openly now. "I got them to go in and cut it up and pull each bloody piece out and throw it in the wastebasket. Little arms and hands, little tiny translucent fingers."

Richard reeled as if hit by a train. He couldn't breathe; he couldn't speak.

"...Or maybe not." Lucille said lightly, still flashing that same mocking smile. "Maybe I just made the whole thing up." She stirred the spoon in her coffee, then pulled out her phone and turned her back on him.

On their second and last night together, Richard had lain in Lucille's bed, staring up at the dark, empty ceiling. He looked over at her. They were both naked, and he could see scars on her arms, stomach and thighs, slashes glowing white in the murky light.

Even as he told her that he wanted to be a father, he knew it was a mistake, but the words could not be unsaid. He had reached over and gently ran a finger across one of the scars on her smooth stomach, then slipped his arm around her. He felt a sudden need for closeness. But Lucille grabbed his wrist so hard her nails punctured his skin.

"I think you'd better leave," she said, a cold glint in her eyes.

Richard's cheeks burned with humiliation. As he left the room, he turned back to look at the ceiling, at the *thing* that wasn't there.

Now, in the diner, he could feel it, it *was* there, it had gone inside him and was resting, waiting.

Its time had finally come, after all these years. It simmered below the surface on a rolling boil. The rage he had felt on that day when all the shit hit the fan, it all came flooding back.

Richard was nothing to Lucille. A toy. Of course he knew it all along, but in his obsession and romantic eagerness, he had denied it. Now he felt humiliated and outraged. He had spent weeks truly convinced he was going to be a father. He had even thought up names. But that dream was shattered in an instant.

His child, whom he had *already* fallen in love with, had either been brutally murdered, or had never existed in the first place. He couldn't wrap his head around it. He turned away and tried to compose himself. He closed his eyes.

Inhale, exhale.

With every breath, he became angrier. He wanted to lunge at Lucille and wring that bitch's throat, choking her with his bare hands until she frothed at the mouth and her eyes rolled back, her skin pale and waxen. He yearned to hear the death rattle crawl out from deep within her chest cavity.

He composed himself. Of course he couldn't kill her; everyone would see him; he would be arrested in minutes. He also knew it was useless to engage with her: it would give her even more power over him, so he turned and left the diner, and kept walking without any destination. His fists were clenched.

He shoved his way blindly through the crowded streets, trembling with rage. He pushed aside a woman carrying a child; she twisted her ankle on the edge of the curb. She fell with a cry of pain, dropping the child into the street. A gravcar was forced to swerve to miss them. Richard did not look back. A red light shone behind his eyes. His jaw muscles ached from grinding his teeth.

He descended a stairwell, into the darkness of subterrania. He found himself in an underground subway, standing on the platform, looking down a long, black tunnel, where two parallel tracks ran into the darkness.

He could feel a rumbling beneath his feet; he could hear the approaching chaos of an oncoming train. He looked down at his ratty sneakers, the toes extended just over the edge. A cool breeze drifted down the tunnel, and Richard shivered.

How easily I could end the farce...

He imagined it. It wouldn't even be necessary to jump. He could just lean gently in one direction, and gravity would do the rest. Hell, he could even simply thrust his head out... and close his eyes.

The wind coming from the darkness of the tunnel picked up. It blew an old, dry newspaper across the tile, rolling and tumbling.

What was that? He thought he heard a different noise behind him.

"Don't fucking move," said a voice in his ear, and he felt the cold barrel of a revolver press into the back of his neck, heard the click of a hammer being pulled back. He carefully raised his hands.

"Give me your wallet and your phone. ...And that watch."

He slowly began to unclasp his wristwatch.

"Faster. Hurry up." The gun pressed into his skin more insistently. The sound from the darkness was getting louder.

He held the watch up, and as the man reached out to take it, Richard yelled and jammed his elbow back into the man's stomach. He grabbed that hand and twisted, ducking and turning around to face the assailant as he did so. The man cried out in pain, stumbling backwards as his arm was twisted, and he fired a shot. The sound exploded off the shattered tile and crumbling concrete, echoing in Richard's ears. The platform began to vibrate.

The man abruptly ducked and twisted in the opposite direction, pulling his hand free. The train came churning into view, its lights blinding. It was not stopping, it was only passing through. The two of them were buffeted by its wind.

The man lifted his pistol, but Richard, grabbed it with both hands and deflected it in time to dodge another shot. When Richard shoved the man's hand to the side, he accidentally pushed it too close to the train. There was a sharp metallic noise, and the gun spun off into the darkness. The man cursed, retracting his hand to his abdomen and bending over in pain.

Before Richard could take advantage of this, the enraged man shrieked and tackled him around the midsection. He landed heavily on his back on the hard, grimy concrete, and lay there gasping, winded. Breathlessly, he began to wrestle with his assailant. The man was stronger than he was, and was pushing him toward the train. Richard was facing away from it, but could feel the wind, cool on the sweat of the back of his neck.

Richard regained his breath, and in a panicked burst of strength, he scrambled on top of the man. He tried to land a punch, but missed and skinned his knuckles on the concrete, then fell onto him with the force of his resultant momentum and inertia. The two men struggled, grunting and snarling like animals, spit bubbling through their teeth and clinging to their beard stubble. Richard somehow ended up with his front to the man's back. They were inches away from the passing train. Its roar was deafening.

Richard pushed. The man screamed; his face registered with horror, but then something hit it hard and fast, and tore it off. His shriek abruptly stopped, fading into the blackness of the tunnel. His face was only blood and musculature, and his neck was bent at an odd angle. Richard cursed and roared, trembling with adrenaline, then shoved the man forward again, where he was swept, windmilling, down below, onto the tracks, under the wheels. There was bright red blood; Richard was sprayed by it.

He crawled to his feet and stumbled over to a concrete pillar, leaning his hand against the shattered tile, doubled over, gasping and coughing.

"Wrong day, asshole," he panted, as the train disappeared into the distance. He staggered over to the edge of the platform, and stole a glance over the side. The body was barely recognizable as human. The only things he could make sense of were half a hand with three twitching fingers, and an eyeball staring out of a glistening, reddish-purple sludge.

Fucking vermin. This whole filthy city needs to be exterminated.

Richard Janus turned his back on the viscera, and ascended the stairs to the glowing bright light above.

The *entity* inside him throbbed, still hungry, unappeased.

[2018]

Choice & Consequence

(3023 A.D.)

Jade rolled out of bed with a headache and a mouth like a rotting carcass.

She stumbled to the bathroom and splashed water on her face. In the mirror, a tired woman with dark circles under her eyes stared sepulchrally back at her. She had just turned 32.

A lifetime ago – 14 years to be exact – when she was 18 and was named Eirene, she and her 6-year-old sister Astraea had been designated by their father as RePurposables, and taken captive to the oppressive New Genesis Factory where RePurposed citizens were turned into a fine red mush and used as compost. Eirene had escaped. Astraea had not.

Eirene had found her way to Omega, where she lived now. She had taken the name Jade, had formed the *Omega Faction*, and had spent the intervening years rescuing citizens from the clutches of New Genesis and its tyrant leader, R. Janus, who she vowed, one day, to kill with her own hands.

Today was just another day. Jade lived in the Omega Police Force Headquarters, in a tiny 6'x8' unit, which was actually a repurposed holding cell in the basement. She walked to her desk and logged on to the computer whose screen comprised the entire horizontal surface of her desk. She pulled up a blueprint of the New Genesis RP Factory, which she had obtained through a local hacker network.

She took a sip of her coffee, and began to trace a thick red line across the blue and white image. This would be the route she would take to the center of the construct, where she would sabotage the mulching machine and halt RePurposing operations. She had already crawled within the ventilation system once, and was familiar with it, despite it being a decade and a half ago – she'd never forget those few hours.

Abruptly, an alarm sounded through Omega Force HQ, a high-pitched whooping siren that pierced her ears and startled Jade. She cursed as she spilled her coffee, but hurried to dress. As she opened the door, she saw several officers running by while activating personal forcefields. Jade fell in line behind them as they ran to the precinct dispatch bay.

As she burst through the door into the concrete underground parking lot, a gravcar pulled up beside her and the passenger door opened. Max was at the wheel. He was 38, and his blonde hair had been cut short, and shone with quite a bit of silver. He was clean shaven, but still wore the same sort of roguish desert-survival outfit he had when Jade had first met him, 14 years previously.

Jade climbed in without a word, and Max pulled out onto the street, the airjets hissing to counter his sharp turn.

"What's going on?" Jade asked.

"Some nutbag down in the Hole is on a rampage; it's bad," he said.

"The Hole?" Jade questioned. Max looked askance at her.

"You know, the North Omega suburbs."

"Where the refugee housing units were developed."

"*Were?* Still are; it's become a sprawl."

"Why is it called –"

"Because it's a *stinking fuckhole*, Jade," Max said, blasting through a red light, the sirens blaring. He reached over and flicked on the small television screen on the passenger dash. A female news reporter stood in the streets. Behind her flashing blue and red lights could be seen from multiple squad cars forming a rough line.

"*— according to reports, there is believed to be only one shooter, a female in her mid-thirties. Omega police are on the scene. The number of casualties is unclear, but several eyewitness reports suggest at least twenty dead and dozens more injured.*"

The camera cuts to a clip of a hysterical woman sobbing and speaking through her hands with wide eyes.

"*Oh God, she – she just started shooting! Right – right in the middle of lunch hour! Oh God –*"

Jade turned off the television. The sirens were getting closer.

"Lunch hour?" she said, staring at Max. "Is this a –"

"Yup." he nodded. "*Omega Elementary 13W/42N*. Apparently the shooter walked onto the playground and started blowing kids away with a proton rifle."

"*Jesus...*" Jade shook her head incredulously.

Max slammed on the brakes and they spun to a lurching halt beside a corner apartment building. The sound of sirens was omnipresent, and coloured light flickered off the walls around the corner. Jade followed Max into the building, where they took the stairs two at a time, bursting out onto the rooftop and running to the edge, hunkering down out of sight.

They each produced binoculars and peered down into the school courtyard below them. The basketball court was littered with unbelievably small bodies, dismembered body parts, and soaked in fresh blood. Four squad cars had created a shield behind which a dozen officers were hunkered down, their weapons drawn. One of them was shouting at the assailant through a megaphone.

"They're trying to determine if it's a hostage situation," Max said. "A handful of officers are flanking the other side, but they have to be careful." He began to unpack and assemble his fission sniper rifle.

Down below, Jade could see paramedics and a couple of civilians running into the school and emerging carrying wounded children.

"Fuckin' brave," said Max, then, into his radio: "Sniper in position. Hostile in view, no evidence of hostages."

"Fire when ready," came the reply.

"No personal force field. Wouldn't matter anyway," Max muttered to himself. His nuclear fission rifle essentially fired railroad spikes at supersonic speeds. No force field extant could stop that.

"Shit, she moved out of sight..." Max swivelled the rifle on its tripod.

Suddenly, rapid beams of blue light burst from the upper floor of the school, creating black burn marks on the concrete. One of the medics fell, dropping the boy he was carrying. They both lay still.

"She's got a laser carbine, too..." murmured Max, squinting through his scope. "Okay, come on out... *Come on....*" He took a breath, then squeezed the trigger, and a window in the school shattered. "Got her," he said into his radio. "Target is down."

"Roger that, units moving in..." There was a long pause, during which the seconds crawled by agonizingly slow, then: *"Kill verified: shooter is dead."*

Max quickly disassembled his rifle, placed it neatly in the carrying case, and began to walk to the door. Jade remained staring at the scene below. The yard was now swarming with medics and officers. Beneath the chaos of sirens and shouting, she could hear countless voices screaming and crying in both terror and pain. She shuddered, then turned to follow Max, walking slowly, in a daze.

Back in the car, Max was typing up a report on the computer, and when he was done, he closed the laptop with a snap and looked up at Jade, who was staring glassily out of the window.

"What's up with you, Jade? You're acting like you've never seen people blown into wet chunks before." He laughed cynically.

Over the last 14 years, Jade had seen much worse, but never *children*. She shook her head slowly.

"How could something like this happen?" she said in a detached tone.

Max sighed.

"Jade, when was the last time you were down in the Hole?"

"Never," she admitted.

"Then let me show you something."

The city of Omega had the following layout:

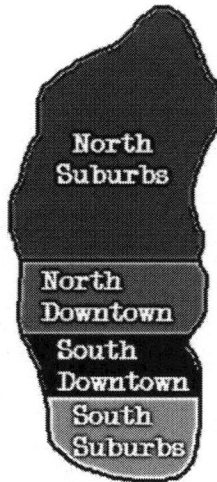

Jade and Max both lived at the police headquarters, in the South Suburbs, which was the original residential district of Omega. As new refugees arrived, makeshift houses were built on the other side of Downtown, which gradually became permanent. As more and more refugees arrived, the North Suburbs became larger, and construction quality decreased markedly.

Max drove slowly through the North Suburbs while Jade watched out the window. Far from white picket fences, or even the simple, clean, well-populated neighbourhood she was used to, this place was dismal, a literal shanty town with unpaved streets.

For lack of wood, buildings in Omega were constructed using prefabricated baked ceramic, but the quality in this region was cheap and shoddy. Many houses had shattered walls, long jagged cracks, or large pits and gouges. Many windows were broken, or missing completely. Yards in Omega did not have grass, but while her own neighbourhood displayed plants carefully cultivated and potted for display, here, doors opened onto poorly packed sand – when Omega expanded into the desert, nobody bothered to lay down asphalt, they just compacted the sand with a roller.

As the gravcar approached and entered the North Downtown core, population density increased. People could be seen huddling against buildings in small groups. Like their surroundings, they were filthy, and obviously impoverished. Jade saw a fist fight break out.

"Are these people homeless?!" she asked. Max nodded.

"But why?! I thought we were giving them new homes!"

"Who's gonna build them, Jade? For what recompense? You know as well as I do that we have never had a monetary system in Omega. We were a village of families and neighbours! Now it's a city of strangers, and the old system of honour and goodwill only extends so far towards people who take without giving."

"Certainly not *all* of them are like that!"

"No, not all. But enough. The radiation sickness probably doesn't help."

"What?!" Jade spluttered. "What about the –"

"The radshield? You know as well as I do that it emanates from the ionization sphere in the middle of South Downtown. It was originally configured to cover a radius encompassing *old* Omega, which was just "Downtown and the Suburbs", before it became necessary to have all these delineations."

"So these people are just being irradiated to death?!"

"Well, it's not like we can just pop out another couple of giant, silver, floating nuclear balls."

Jade fell to sombre silence. Outside, a lone man was building a shack out of various scraps. "This was supposed to be a new life for them…" she said quietly. "We *saved* them!"

Max pulled over and turned to face her.

"Jade, we can't save people from *themselves*. Like all of us, their lives follow them. Chronic poverty isn't just an isolated quality of people's environment. It becomes a poverty of *mind*. We can't fix that."

They were surrounded by squalor. Decay. Sorrow. Everything she had wanted so badly to rescue these people from. She even recognized many of them. The last time she had seen their faces, they had been radiant with hope. Now they were once again darkened in despair.

"You've been so obsessed with being a "hero" and taking down Janus, you've overlooked *real life,* here." Max said.

He told her about the food shortage crisis. Omega had originally been configured as a small colony. Despite using genetically modified crops designed to thrive in meagre conditions, there was neither the acreage, nor the water available to sustain the current population. They lived in a desert, he reminded her. It was necessary for water to be synthesized chemically, by cracking the oxygen and hydrogen molecules from the air, then rebonding them as H_2O, which was incredibly dangerous.

"Our stock of raw resources is finite and non-renewable, and the process volatile and expensive," he said. "We can't keep bringing people in like this!" he urged her. "We *need* to stop these rescue operations. We're dooming ourselves! Jade, these people are *starving!*"

"*Starving?!*" she cried in surprise.

"There's not enough food to go around, Jade."

165

"Then why aren't *we* starving?!"

Max pounded the steering wheel. "Because *WE* are the ones risking our lives!" he yelled. *"We* are the ones who are actually *contributing* to the society!" He stewed for a moment, looking out the window, the muscles in his jaw bulging.

"You know, this place used to be a *paradise*, before *you* showed up!" he snarled bitterly. "Now it's just a mini New Genesis,"

Jade recoiled as if Max had just slapped her. She opened her mouth, searching for a response, but found none.

The ride home was spent in silence.

When they arrived, Jade went immediately to her quarters. She quite suddenly felt exhausted and felt compelled to have a nap. However, less than half an hour later, she was interrupted by a knock on her door. She fell out of bed and stumbled over. It was Max.

"The council wants to see you, Jade." He said, then turned and walked away.

The board room of the Omega Council was a modest affair, simply a large table in a large, austere room. It was clean and white, as were the walls and the chairs. Around the table sat eleven men and women. Most of them wore the prestigious white robes characteristic of the political structure of Omega.

Jade was the only one standing.

"Jade, in light of today's tragedy, the Council has come to a difficult decision." said Chairman Xaron, wryly, tugging at his white beard. "We require you to disband the Omega Faction."

Jade was stupefied. When she did not respond, Xaron continued.

"Today's events are the direct result of the degraded social structure which comes with overpopulation and a lack of shared values. Initially, we graciously allowed you the freedom to proceed as you saw fit in your rescue options, but it is clear at this point that you have shown a gross lack of perspicacity and organization, and have stretched the resources of Omega, and the good will of its people, far past their limits. We of Omega Council carry the heavy burden of realizing that, by failing to keep a leash on the Omega Faction, we have indirectly permitted the death of twenty-three children today. Eight more are in critical condition, and a further seventeen are wounded, and many of them have been inflicted with disability or deformity which will remain with them for the rest of their lives." He crossed his hands on the table in front of him.

Jade felt like she had been kicked in the gut; she couldn't breathe. She grasped the back of a chair, her jaw moving silently. With effort, she managed to speak.

"No, but Janus –" she began, but was interrupted by Xaron.

"If you do *not* agree to cease your operations immediately, you will be exiled from Omega, where you may continue your reckless vendetta elsewhere. Additionally, we are required to deport at least 1,000 of these immigrants, to lighten the strain on our food and water supplies. It will also send a message to those of them who refuse to contribute: we will not tolerate freeloaders in Omega."

Jade stared, agape. Chairman Xaron cleared his throat.

"The Council understands you may require some time to process this information. You have thirty minutes, at which point you must inform us of your willing decision. Otherwise, we will choose for you. Council is adjourned."

Jade walked back to her room in a daze.

When she arrived, she was surprised to find a woman waiting for her, her back turned. She wore extremely colourful clothing of what appeared to be an indigenous, tribal origin, made from hand-woven cloth and animal skins. Her blonde hair, which came past her shoulders, was dreadlocked and full of beads and other ornamentations, with coloured string braided into it throughout. The woman held herself straight and tall, with an unusual elegance.

"Who are you, and what are you doing in my room?" Jade asked woodenly. The woman turned, startled.

Ella-Aurelia, known to Omega as Athena, blushed.

"Oh, I'm sorry Jade; someone said you were in your room, and the door was open, so I wandered in. It's *so good* to see you!" *Ella* smiled warmly, her bright blue eyes lighting up joyfully. Jade was surprised to see how radiant she looked, so different than the quiet, moody young woman who had lived with her only six years ago.

They met in the middle of the room and embraced.

"I can't believe it's you!" Jade gasped, momentarily forgetting her distress. "Max said you had been... uh, brainwashed...! Not that I believed him, of course."

Ella frowned. "Uhm... no... I stayed purposefully." she said. "But Jade, I wish you could see where I live now!" she cried exuberantly, almost jumping up and down with excitement, like a little girl on Christmas morning. "I have such an amazing *Together-Self*, named *Auxentius-Noor*, we have a beautiful home, and a *Little-Self!* Oh, she is so gorgeous! I've been dying for you to meet her! She is named after you."

"Oh!" said Jade. "Is she here?" She barely registered her own words; she had caught a glimpse of the Factory blueprint on her desk and was brought back to reality with a crash.

"She's in the daycare. I'll bring you to meet her!" *Ella* exclaimed. "She's just turned five."

Jade nodded dumbly, and slowly sat down at her desk. *Ella* looked worried.

"Jade, what's wrong??" she asked, pulling over a chair and putting one of her hands on the small of Jade's back and holding her hand with the other. Jade told her what had just happened. *Ella* was quiet.

"Well, what are you..." she began, but stopped as she watched Jade's fingers tracing over the line drawn on the blueprint.

Abruptly, they were interrupted by a noise and flurry of movement, as a child ran through the door in a tornado of excitement, followed by an out-of-breath girl of about 15.

"Sorry, miss..." she gasped, "I think she wanted to see you, I couldn't understand..."

// Cinsuirre-mala, kenoi ist??// hollered the child.

"Speak English while we're here, it's polite; and don't interrupt, that's impolite," *Ella* gently admonished.

"Okay. *Self-Mother,* what is this?" the little girl asked, holding up a Personal Data Assistant. The screen glowed brightly, and her shining blue eyes she looked raptly interested in a colourful, cartoony game involving birds and slingshots.

"Ahh, you don't need that, my *Little-Love-Self,*" said *Ella,* taking the tablet from the girl and handing it to the teenager.

"Aww... okay," the child said, evidently disappointed. *Ella* turned to Jade.

"Jade, this is my daughter, *Tinga-ot-Malachi,* which means "Warrior of Flame". See, she is named after you, because you are the most fiery, self-directed, intense woman I have ever known. You are a true warrior!" she beamed.

Jade bent down and ran her fingers through the child's fine, curly blonde hair.

Then she burst into tears.

Ella quietly urged *Tinga* out with the older girl, and closed the door. She quickly walked to where Jade was bent over in her chair, sobbing, and embraced her. After a long moment of weeping, Jade found her voice.

"She... she's beautiful!" she whispered. "She looks just like Astraea when she..." but could not finish the sentence. *Ella* was thoughtful for a moment, then looked Jade in the eye.

"This *isn't* about Janus, or the refugees, is it?" she asked gently.

"Of *course* it is; he's a tyrannical *murderer!*" protested Jade.

"Yes," agreed *Ella,* "but I remember when I met you. You were broken from the loss of your *Self-Sister,* and there was only one thing that gave you strength and purpose."

"*Omega Faction,*" whispered Jade.

Ella nodded. "You did this all for her, didn't you?" She gently rubbed Jade's back with her slim fingers resplendent in rings of stone, bone, and wood.

Jade sniffled her tears, and nodded. "I have to make it *right!*" she wailed inconsolably.

Ella sighed and shook her head. "Honey, you *can't.* No amount of refugees rescued, or even killing Janus, will bring her back to you!"

Jade shrugged out of *Ella's* embrace, and climbed into her bed, turning her back on her old friend.

"Go away," she said.

After a moment's silence, *Ella* took off one of her necklaces which held a shining green stone encased in bone and bound in leather studded with glass beads. She placed it on Jade's desk, on top of the blueprint, and quietly left, switching off the light and closing the door behind her.

Jade rolled onto her back and stared up at the ceiling. Upon the canvas of darkness, the image of Astraea came to her, the last time they had been free together. Astraea in her blue and pink cotton pyjamas, clinging to a wet, naked Eirene, fresh out of the shower. Eirene sat with her back against the wall and cuddled the little girl, comforting her after a nightmare. She could still remember the softness of Astraea's cheek, her long eyelashes closed peacefully as she contentedly sucked on her thumb, her head nestled against Eirene's bare breast. She could still remember the child's shining ringlets, and how she smelled like butter and vanilla, and her bright, sapphire eyes, and the awe they always held for Eirene, her big sister.

Eirene thought about the children at the school today, and their mothers, fathers, sisters and brothers, who might spend the night sitting in a dark, empty room, torn apart by the persistent, unreal knowledge that they will never hear their child's laughter again.

Eirene remembered the terrible suffering of loss. She remembered sitting on her bed, bent over in agony as a sound somewhere between a scream and a wail tore from deep within her. She knew that nothing would ever be okay again.

Has she given this horrible gift to twenty-three families today? Is *she* the one who is ultimately responsible? Is the quest, to which she has devoted her life, meaningless? Can she bear to remain in Omega and face the people whose lives she has destroyed, these very people whom she desired to save?

The door to her quarters slid open silently. Silhouetted in the burning white glow of the corridor stood the solemn figure of Chairman Xaron.

"Jade," he said, "The Council awaits your decision."

[2018]

Afterword:

Hello,

Thanks for reading my book! If you have any comments I'd love to hear from you. Please contact *H.M.Friendly@gmail.com*. ☺

So, this was going to be the part where I explain my intent behind the series – the moral of the story, if you will. However, I've decided not to spoil it, and I would much rather hear *your* associations, philosophical/political implications, etc.   Send me an email, and we can compare notes!

Sincerely,

~H.M. Friendly

Made in the USA
Columbia, SC
03 August 2018